Jihad on
34ᵗʰ Street

PHIL NOVA

ISBN-13: 978-0692366318
ISBN-10: 0692366318
Five Borough Publishing
New York

Cover design by Mark Lagana
laganamark@sbcglobal.net

CHAPTER 1—THURSDAY 3:28PM

Just as Mohammed stepped off the metal extension ladder and onto the noisy street, he realized he forgot his thermos and lunch container in a plastic bag tied to his scaffold.

Making sure to stay within the orange cones as cars whipped by next to him, Mohammed turned and saw Kenny, a tall black laborer with a stars and stripes hard hat, walking under the sidewalk enclosure among the crowd of pedestrians.

Preparing to take the ladder down, Kenny untied the rope that secured it to one of the blue metal pipes holding up the sidewalk bridge.

Mohammed spoke with a Pakistani accent, but his English was clear. "Kenny. Please, wait. I forgot something on my scaffold."

"Everyone's down already," responded Kenny. "Can't it wait 'til tomorrow?"

"I will be only one minute. Please, my friend."

Kenny sighed then said, "Okay, but hurry up." He re-tied the rope to the pole.

Mohammed climbed the ladder to the top, then stepped over the blue plywood parapet wall and quickly crossed the wood-planked bridge that protected the people on the sidewalk below from falling construction debris.

He approached his scaffold, a metal platform with waist-high guardrails and safety netting enclosing it on three sides. Cables hanging from the roof stayed firmly locked into electric motors at each end of the platform while ropes secured the scaffold to the building.

Tied to the top guardrail, Mohammed's plastic bag flapped around in the cool November wind. He untied it, then, just as he turned around to go back down, he heard voices. Someone speaking Pashto, a language he knew from Pakistan.

He stepped closer to the twenty-story beige office building and heard male voices talking about explosives and blowing something up. The voices became louder as he approached a window. They were talking about Jihad—Holy War—on American soil.

Kenny yelled from the sidewalk, "Hurry up, Mohammed!"

From the side, Mohammed peeked into the second floor through a partially open window. It was an empty office with three young men wearing building maintenance uniforms, blue shirts and blue pants. One man held a bulky black backpack. They appeared to be from either Afghanistan or Pakistan. They all had brown skin, thick black hair, and bushy black beards.

They looked like Mohammed.

The smallest man had a name patch on his shirt, but Mohammed couldn't make out the name. They continued their conversation, and they used the word explosives more than once.

Kenny shook the ladder hard, rattling the whole bridge. "Mohammed! If you don't come down, I'm gonna leave your ass up there!"

Mohammed hurried to the ladder and climbed down to the street with his plastic bag in hand. Traffic slowed and then stopped as the yellow light on the corner turned red.

"What took you, man?"

"I am sorry, my friend."

Kenny shook his head then untied and pulled the ladder down before carrying it toward the building's loading docks. The orange cones were already gone.

Mohammed headed the opposite way, toward the corner. The temperature plummeted as the sun disappeared behind a glass skyscraper across the street.

He usually used the bathroom in the basement to wash up before heading to the subway, but after what he had just heard, he forgot about the bathroom and just started walking.

About a block and a half away from the rolling newsflashes

and giant LED screens of Times Square, Mohammed crossed Seventh Avenue with a herd of pedestrians. To his right, a wall of yellow taxis waited for the red light to turn green.

Car horns echoed throughout the valley of skyscrapers as Mohammed maneuvered his way through tourists and shoppers while going west toward Eighth Avenue.

He thought about what those three men said. Pashto was not his primary language, so there was always room for error. He also considered the fact that words can sound garbled from the other side of a window, not to mention traffic noise from the street below. He wondered if he just misunderstood what they said. They could have been talking about anything, maybe a terrorist attack that had already happened, or maybe even a movie they'd seen.

But what if they really were planning something? Mohammed had witnessed a terror attack in Pakistan and the horror he experienced haunted his dreams almost every night.

He decided to wait until tomorrow and look for the three men so he could confront them himself. If he still suspected them after talking to them, he would report them, but not yet, just in case he was wrong. He didn't want to jeopardize his resident status or his job. He had received his green card last year after living in the United States for the past eight years and working in construction for the past five years.

After turning the corner on Eighth Avenue, Mohammed glanced at an assortment of paper turkeys hanging in the window of a Duane Reade drug store. The smell of roasted nuts from a cart on the street followed him as he descended the staircase to the subway station below.

Mohammed's mind raced as he stood on the busy platform waiting for his train. He moved out of the way for a woman pushing a baby carriage and then stood against a yellow steel column and looked around at all the people as they went about their business. He wondered how many of them had family and friends who loved them, people who would miss them if they died in a terror attack. That baby would never get to grow up.

He did not want to believe that any human being could be capable of such a terrible act, but he knew the opposite to be true.

The tracks rumbled before the train's headlights reflected off the tile walls, then it roared into the station and slowed to a stop.

The doors opened and Mohammed followed a group of

people onto the train.

The doors closed and the train accelerated and made its way through the tunnel, toward Brooklyn.

There were a few empty seats near a homeless man with two big black garbage bags full of who knows what. Mohammed knew the man must have smelled bad or some of the people standing would be sitting.

Standing near the door, holding a pole, Mohammed unzipped his gray hooded sweatshirt and used the back of his hand to wipe the sweat from his forehead as the heat pumped. He felt like a coward. He considered getting off the subway and going straight to the cops.

The train pulled into the next stop and the doors opened. Mohammed almost got out, but then stopped, his feet cemented to the floor. People passed him as they left the train, then other people passed him as they boarded.

The chime sounded and the doors closed. The train began toward the next stop while Mohammed's fear conquered his guilt.

As the steady rumble of the subway numbed his physical senses, his mind drifted back to when he was fourteen-years-old in Islamabad, the day he'd witnessed a terror attack first hand.

It was a dark cloudy morning and Mohammed's father decided to take his two sons fishing at Rawal Lake. Mohammed and his older brother hated fishing, but Mohammed knew how much his father enjoyed it so he kept quiet. His older brother, however, had no dilemmas about telling his father how much he hated it.

On that particular day, Mohammed sat in the back seat of his father's car while his older brother sat up front. Their father had just picked up his paycheck at the hotel where he worked in the Blue Zone. He usually took the Kashmir Highway straight to the lake, but because of traffic that day, he took the streets, which made Mohammed's older brother complain more than usual.

At Constitution Avenue, they turned and headed toward the lake.

Something exploded in the distance.

People in suits scattered out of office buildings and banks. Security guards and cops yelled and blew whistles while racing down the streets.

Mohammed pleaded with his father to get out of there.

Mohammed's older brother was excited, telling his father to get closer so they could see what was going on. As other cars tried to flee the chaos, curiosity drove Mohammed's father to continue toward it.

Just as a cop stopped them and told them to turn around, another explosion, many times more powerful than the first explosion, shook the earth.

Huge chunks of concrete flew away from the Egyptian Embassy leaving an exposed staircase. Mohammed froze when a charred corpse landed on the ground just a few feet from the car.

A small chunk of concrete smashed the windshield. Mohammed, his brother, and father, all ducked covering their faces then jumped out of the car. They suffered minor scratches and dust covered their entire bodies, but they were fine.

People everywhere screamed, but Mohammed knew they were no longer screaming in panic, they were now screaming in pain. He covered his ears.

As the dust settled, Mohammed saw men and women limping and hobbling, some missing limbs or big chunks of flesh. Some had too much blood to see their wounds. Their faces looked like zombies. Emergency service vehicles tried in vain to get through cluttered streets. Some paramedics raced to the scene on foot.

In the distance, Mohammed saw the burning remains of a pick-up truck and a crater in the ground next to the Egyptian Embassy. Mohammed's father told his boys to get back in the car. There was no room to turn around so he backed up, easing his way through building debris and frantic people.

The subway chime brought Mohammed out of his trance and back to the present.

The train doors closed.

He just missed his stop. He looked around at the other commuters as if they knew he had made a stupid mistake.

After shaking the terrible memory from his head, Mohammed got out of the train at the next stop, went up the stairs, and crossed over to the platform on the opposite side.

Within a few minutes, the next train arrived and Mohammed got on.

While staring at the ads on the wall, he noticed one he'd seen hundreds of times before but had never meant anything to him, a poster that showed a backpack left under a subway bench. The headline read, if you see something, say something.

CHAPTER 2—FRIDAY 1:09AM

On a cold quiet Bronx street, on the third floor of a red brick apartment building, thirty-nine-year-old Diane Lasalvo sat on a metal foldout chair in a dark empty room. Wearing black slacks, a tight blue shirt, and a black blazer, she sipped coffee from a paper cup while occasionally peeking out the front window through a filthy set of vertical blinds.

She checked the viewfinder of a video camera pointed outside and saw a young man wearing baggy black sweatpants and an oversized black sweatshirt with the hood covering his head and most of his face. The young man stood next to the front door of an apartment building across the street. He was a lookout for the crack dealers who had recently set up shop there. Every time a patrol car passed, he called someone on his cell phone and started strolling along the sidewalk.

Diane glanced over at her partner on the chair next to her, Detective Garcia: short, fat, and bald, with glasses and a goatee. His white dress shirt and beige slacks looked two sizes too small. He sipped on a super-large coffee and watched out the window as crackhead after crackhead went inside the building and came out a few minutes later.

Diane put down her coffee, tightened her ponytail, then took a cigarette out of her pack and reached into her pocket for her lighter.

Outside, an undercover officer, a short young man wearing blue jeans and a Yankees cap, approached the building and went for the door.

Diane and Garcia got closer to the window and held their breath as they watched what was going on outside.

The man on lookout picked up his phone and made a call. He spoke to someone while heading up the sidewalk, just as he did when the patrol cars passed.

Diane said, "He made him. I knew this would happen. I told you that rookie has cop written all over him."

"Damn it." Garcia stood and made a call on his radio. "They made him."

Diane took her gun out of the holster.

Garcia said, "You won't be needing that."

"I hope you're right." She didn't put it away, she just checked the safety and held it down at her side.

They watched out the window as the lookout, still on his phone, crossed the street and stayed out of view.

A few minutes later, the undercover cop exited the building across the street and proceeded back the way he came. After a few blocks, he turned a corner and disappeared from sight.

Diane put her gun away and kept her eye out the window.

Garcia waited a few minutes then picked up his radio after it beeped. "What happened?"

The undercover answered, "Nothing. He wouldn't sell to me."

Garcia asked, "How many were there?"

"I only saw one, but I heard feet shuffling upstairs. Couldn't tell how many."

Outside, another crackhead approached and entered the building. The lookout went back across the street and stood in front of the building, but not too close to the door.

Garcia picked up his radio and said, "McCarthy, I want you and the rookie to grab that crackhead who just went in. He just came from your direction, probably going back the same way. Wait for my instructions."

Garcia turned to Diane and asked, "What do you think?"

Diane said, "It's your call."

"Thanks, that helps."

Diane said, "I guess it's worth a shot."

They watched out the window for a few minutes. The crackhead left the building and hurried down the block in the same direction the undercover had gone.

Garcia picked up his radio and said, "McCarthy, he's coming your way. He's wearing a red down jacket. Pick him up."

Diane picked up her radio and said, "We're going back to the house."

A few minutes later, a gray Lincoln pulled up to the building. The license plates read TLC, but the car wasn't really a car service. It belonged to the NYPD.

Diane and Garcia put the camera in a gym bag, locked up the empty apartment, and headed down the stairs.

Just as they stepped out of the building, a patrol car cruised down the street as a decoy. The lookout picked up his phone and began walking. Diane and Garcia got into the Lincoln unnoticed. They drove off as the lookout made his way back to his post.

On the second floor of the 46th Precinct, Diane and Garcia approached a large holding cell and stood in front of the black steel bars. Three men sat on concrete benches, and two others sat on the dirty concrete floor.

The crackhead they had arrested was one of the two men on the floor, Terek Johnson, a short skinny thirty-one-year-old light-skinned black man with bad teeth. Terek had been smoking crack since he was nineteen, and his big buggy eyes were proof.

Garcia said, "This is your third possession this year, Terek."

Terek said, "It wasn't mine, man. I told you. I found it."

"That's original." Diane unlocked the cell door. "Let's go. Time to get that statement."

Garcia showed Terek a pair of handcuffs and asked, "Will you be needing these?"

Terek responded, "Where am I gonna go?"

Garcia snapped the cuffs back onto his belt and followed Terek who was following Diane down the white tile hallway to a gray door.

Diane unlocked the door and they all entered a small musty room with two plastic chairs, one on each side of a small metal table. Terek sat on one side and Garcia sat on the other.

Diane tightened her ponytail, stood against the wall, and lit a cigarette. She saw Terek eyeing her cigarette and knew he wanted one. "You want one of these?"

Terek nodded.

Diane lit a cigarette and gave it to him.

Garcia waved the smoke out of his face and said, "Okay, Terek. Time to make a deal."

Terek steamed the cigarette and said, "Hold up. A deal? I didn't say nothin' about no deal. I ain't makin' no deals with no cops."

Diane said, "What if we tell everyone around the way you're a rat?"

"You cops tried that bullshit with that kid Mike from Morris Avenue, and no one believed it. Everyone knows you cops lie." Terek sucked in another drag of the cigarette.

Garcia shrugged and said, "Okay, but do you know how much time you could get for possession of a kilo?"

"A kilo? Someone must have mixed up my files, man. I only had two nicks."

Garcia said, "Who do you think the DA will believe? You . . . or us?"

Diane said, "I didn't have a scale with me, but that package did look a lot like a kilo."

"This is bullshit, man! I never even seen a kilo before. This is bullshit." Terek quickly steamed the cigarette down to the filter.

Garcia asked, "So, you ready to talk about that deal now?"

"No way, man. No deals. I didn't have a kilo, and you don't have a kilo, so you got no case. You really think I'm that stupid?"

Diane finished her cigarette and stomped it out on the hard gray floor. "I checked a kilo out of the evidence room today, said it was for a drug bust. I'll have it back in evidence by the time you're getting your asshole reamed open on Riker's, then it's upstate from there. And don't think I can't get it back for your trial if I need to. The evidence room clerk is my cousin."

"Fuck! What do you want from me?"

Garcia put two small plastic vials with red tops on the table. Inside each vial were two small white rocks, crack. The same crack the undercover officer confiscated from Terek when he arrested him.

Terek stared at the vials on the table. His jaw started to move, beads of sweat formed on his forehead.

Garcia said, "All you have to do is buy some of this stuff for us, with our money."

Terek said, "Marked money."

Garcia said, "That's right."

"No way, man." Terek tried keeping his eyes off the crack, but they kept going back.

Diane said, "We won't go in until you're long gone. No one will ever know it was you."

"Bullshit. They'll know."

Garcia said, "No one will know. You just do what you did tonight. How hard is that?"

Diane said, "You can take those with you when you go home tonight, and we'll drop the possession charges. And, you can keep some of what you buy tomorrow."

Garcia put his hand on the vials, covering them for a moment, then he slid the vials closer to Terek and removed his hand. "Go home now with these two jumbos or go through the system and get a mayo sandwich for breakfast. It's your choice."

Terek covered the two vials with his hand and said, "Okay. You got a deal."

Before Terek could pull his hand away, Garcia clamped his chubby hand down over Terek's bony wrist and held it there while staring into Terek's eyes. Garcia said, "And don't even think about trying to fuck with us."

CHAPTER 3—FRIDAY 6:30AM

The modern steel and glass skyscrapers on Seventh Avenue towered over smaller brick and stone buildings that were almost a hundred years old. Many of the older buildings were covered with pipe frame scaffolds or hanging scaffolds for repairs or restoration.

The city was quiet at that time. Only a few taxis roamed the streets while trucks made their deliveries to stores before the morning rush.

On his way into the building's loading dock, Mohammed showed his ID to the security guard and signed in. Even though he'd been working on the building for a few months, he knew the security guards still looked at him with suspicion. It didn't make sense. They knew he was a working man. Why would they still suspect him of being anything else?

A few of Mohammed's co-workers came in after him and signed in with building security.

They all headed to the freight elevator and took it down to the basement. Most of the men were joking and laughing, but Mohammed was quiet. He was always quiet, so no one noticed anything different about him.

Once downstairs, most of the workers changed into their working clothes and drank coffee. Mohammed never changed. He wore his work clothes to and from his job. He just didn't feel comfortable putting on clean clothes after sweating and eating dust all day. He only came down to the basement to sign in with his foreman, use the bathroom, and drink a cup of tea before beginning his day.

When he began work on this building a few months ago, there were two other Pakistani men on the job. The three of them always ate lunch together until a few weeks ago when the company transferred them to another jobsite. Mohammed's scaffold partner had told Mohammed to eat with him and the other guys, which he did, but he never involved himself in their conversations, even when he was interested.

Although most of the men on the job were friendly with him, he still felt that they looked at him with suspicion, as did most Americans. There was a time he considered shaving his beard, but he could never go through with it. He didn't believe he should have to give up his religious beliefs and his roots just to fit in, even if he did love this country.

After signing the foreman's list, Mohammed realized he forgot his tea and his lunch at home. He couldn't believe it. How could he forget? He prepared his lunch and his thermos early this morning, just as he always did, but then placed it on the kitchen counter and forgot to take it with him on his way out. He was distracted. His mind was still on those three men, wondering if he would find them today, wondering how they would react if he approached them.

He had a little cash with him, so he decided he would order a cup of tea from the apprentice at break time and buy a Sandwich from the Halal cart on the sidewalk at lunchtime.

Mohammed followed everyone into the freight elevator, outside the building, onto the sidewalk, then up the ladder to the sidewalk bridge.

After retrieving his tool bag and safety equipment from a big metal gang box, Mohammed approached his scaffold.

While putting his harness and hardhat on, he turned and saw his partner, forty-two-year-old Tony Lasalvo, climbing the ladder. With his hand on his chest, Mohammed bowed slightly and said, "Good morning, Tony."

Already out of breath, Tony climbed onto the bridge and said, "What's up, Mo?"

Tony walked over and grabbed his tools from the gang box then returned to the scaffold. Wearing a faded green New York Jets sweatshirt and a shiny new Jets hardhat, Tony put on his harness, which wrapped tightly around his big upper body and enormous belly. The leg straps hung loose around his skinny thighs.

A young apprentice came by with a sheet of paper and a pen, taking orders for break time. Mohammed ordered a tea with milk and gave the kid two dollars. The kid continued to the next man and took his order.

Without trying to draw attention to himself, Mohammed kept peering into the window of the second floor, at the empty office. No one was there. He kept his eye on the window while continuing to prepare his scaffold. He untied two ropes and a black electric cable hanging from the roof while two laborers brought them their material. Mohammed and Tony loaded their scaffold with white canvas blankets and big power tools.

With a metal locking device, they connected their harnesses to the ropes hanging from the roof. In case the scaffold ever fell, the locks would grab onto the ropes and the worker would hang in the air by their harness. Mohammed had never witnessed that, and hoped he never would.

They got on the scaffold platform, and at the same time, both men pressed the UP button on their motors. The humming motors gripped and rode up the steel cables hanging from an outrigger and counter-weight system on the roof.

Hanging like a marionette puppet, the twenty-four foot aluminum scaffold ascended along the side of the building. A pair of rubber wheels kept them far enough away to avoid scraping the wall on the way up. At times, they had to use their feet against the wall to kick the scaffold away from the building to avoid the occasional light fixture or air conditioner sticking out.

The air was cool, but the sky was clear. The rising sun began to bring life to the city as traffic on the streets and the sidewalks below began to increase. Mohammed usually admired the vast skyline as the scaffold went up, but today he was looking in windows. Even though he saw those men on the second floor, he still checked every window on the way up.

Tony yelled from his side of the scaffold. "Hey, Mo! Where's that lintel, on nineteen?"

Mohammed also had to yell for Tony to hear him on the other side of the windy scaffold. "Eighteen!"

Tony nodded. They kept their fingers on their UP buttons

while the scaffold continued its ascent at the slow pace of thirty-five feet per minute. They stopped at the eighteenth floor and examined the window in question while Tony stuffed the last of his bear claw into his mouth and washed it down with some coffee.

Using a hammer-drill, they anchored the scaffold into the wall to keep it from moving. When the scaffold was stable, they nailed the white canvas blanket to the wall and stretched it out on the scaffold floor to protect against broken bricks going down and landing in the busy street below. The sidewalk bridge was there to protect against that, but things have been known to bounce off the bridge and into the street.

Although Mohammed's mind was elsewhere, he performed his work as he always did. He and Tony took turns using the heavy power tools. First, they used a big saw with a twelve-inch diamond blade to cut through the top cement joint, then they used an electric demolition gun to remove the old bricks. They replaced the bent, rusted, steel angle iron with a brand new one that had already been painted at the shop with oil-based enamel.

While applying the rubber waterproof membrane to the new lintel, Mohammed's hand slipped and he sliced his own finger with his razor knife. Blood shot out of his finger as he pulled it back and squeezed it with his other hand.

"Holy shit! You Okay?" Tony looked at Mohammed's finger. "How deep is it?"

Mohammed cringed while opening his hand and removing his glove. The cut was bleeding heavily, but it wasn't deep.

"It's not bad." Mohammed bent down and retrieved a roll of duct tape from his tool bag.

"Are you kidding? You're in the union now. You cut yourself, you go downstairs and take care of it."

Mohammed said, "It is almost break, only fifteen more minutes, then I will fix it the right way. It is not deep."

Tony checked the time on his cell phone and said, "Okay, but don't come crying to me if it gets infected."

Mohammed wrapped a piece of duct tape around his cut finger and went back to work. They finished the waterproofing then placed wood supports in the hole before taking the scaffold back down.

On the bridge, the Shop Steward gave Mohammed some hydrogen peroxide and Band-Aids. Mohammed cleaned his finger and covered the cut while Tony helped two laborers clean the debris from the scaffold and load it with new bricks and fresh cement.

Just as Mohammed turned around to give the open bottle back to his Shop Steward, he saw someone in the second floor window. He jerked his head to get a better look and dropped the bottle. The bottle hit the wood planks and rolled across the bridge, peroxide pouring out.

Inside the empty office, Mohammed saw a man in a suit with a few other men and women, all dressed in business attire. He recognized the first man, the building manager.

Tony approached and asked, "You Okay, Mo?"

"Yes. I'm okay."

The Shop Steward came back with the almost empty bottle of hydrogen peroxide in his hand and told Mohammed, "Better not do that with any bricks while you're up there."

Mohammed lowered his head and said, "I am very sorry, Shoppy."

The shop steward replied, "Don't be sorry. Be careful."

Before they had a chance to return to their scaffold, the apprentice came up the ladder with their break orders. Since Tony and Mohammed were already down, they got theirs first.

They sat on overturned five-gallon buckets and drank their tea and coffee while the other scaffolds on the building descended.

Tony and the Shop Steward talked about sports while Mohammed stared at the building.

The second floor office was empty again.

Mohammed wondered if those three men even worked in the building. Maybe they snuck in. It was a longshot, though. He knew how the security guards looked at him, and there was no way all three of them got through security unnoticed. Unless, they had another way in. But, how?

CHAPTER 4—FRIDAY 9:45AM

Andrew Miller, a thirty-three-year old white man in a charcoal gray suit and black leather gloves, took a small wood crate out of the trunk of a black Chevy sedan. He closed the trunk and the sedan sped away, down the ramp of the almost empty parking garage.

Behind him, a fifteen-year-old faded gray Maxima sat next to a brand new black Chevy SUV. He opened the trunk of the Maxima and placed the crate inside. Using a mini-crowbar that was already there, he opened the crate and removed eight cylindrical metal containers about the size of coffee cans. He carefully placed the canisters into a black gym bag that was also already there.

He opened the last container and checked its contents: a bomb, four canisters tied together with a plastic zip-tie and wired to a small circuit board. He inserted the bomb back into the canister, placed it with the others, and zipped the bag closed.

Andrew slammed the trunk lid closed and scanned the quiet parking garage to be sure no one was around before getting into the driver's seat of the Maxima. He placed the black gym bag on the floor behind his seat and took off down the ramp. He drove down to the first floor and paid the parking attendant in cash while keeping his face out of view of the camera.

He cruised out onto the main street of a quiet New Jersey town. Small stores and office buildings lined both sides of the street, but only for a few blocks until spacious two and three story houses occupied large lots with manicured green grass. The neighborhood kids were already in school, and the rush hour commuters were already in New York. The sidewalks were devoid of people, and only the occasional car passed through these streets.

Andrew entered an onramp and took the highway east toward New York, which was about thirty minutes away without traffic.

Throughout the ride, he kept his eye on the rearview mirror, making sure no one followed him.

Andrew Miller had the face of a model. His teeth were perfectly straight and white, and his facial features were defined and pleasantly hard. His perfectly combed short brown hair was the same dark shade of brown as his eyes.

Traffic slowed ahead as he approached the entrance to the Lincoln Tunnel.

A Port Authority cop sipping coffee in his parked car glanced at Andrew as he entered the tunnel.

CHAPTER 5—FRIDAY 11:30AM

Mohammed and Tony finished laying the last few bricks on the new lintel and began scraping up the spilled cement from the canvas drop cloth on their scaffold.

Tony said, "Hey, Mo. What's going on there?"

"Where?" Mohammed looked up to see what Tony was talking about. One brick on Mohammed's side was different from the other bricks. It was dull, and the manufacturer's name stamp showed. Mohammed had put the brick in backwards and didn't notice it, not even while striking the joint. "I am very sorry."

"Don't tell me sorry. Tell the architect."

"I will fix it." Mohammed used his trowel to scrape the cement out from between the joints and separate it from the other bricks. The cement had started to dry, but it was far from cured. He then removed the cement-stained brick and cleaned out the opening.

Tony said, "What's going on with you today? First you forget your lunch, and then you cut your finger, and now a backward brick?"

"I am sorry, my friend. I did not sleep well last night." Mohammed liked Tony, but didn't know him well enough to tell him what was on his mind. He threw a trowelful of fresh cement into the hole and inserted a new brick. It only took a few minutes for Mohammed to point it up then they were on their way down for lunch.

After landing the scaffold on the bridge, and still wearing his harness and hardhat, Mohammed followed a few other men down the ladder to the street and then into the building.

They took the freight elevator to the basement. Everyone got off to use the bathroom, but Mohammed stayed on.

His palms began to sweat. The doors closed. He pressed two. He also pressed the twentieth floor, just in case someone got in at the first floor and asked why he was going to the second floor. He could always say he was on his way up to the roof, but pressed the wrong button.

The elevator door opened at the first floor and a janitor got in with a mop and a bucket. Just what Mohammed didn't want.

The janitor pressed eight and the door closed.

The elevator went up to the second floor and the door opened. Mohammed just stood there, staring empty offices, not knowing what to say.

The janitor asked, "Are you going to two?"

"No. I pressed it by mistake. I am going to the roof."

The janitor looked irritated as he pressed the 'close doors' button.

The elevator went up to the eighth floor and the janitor got out.

The doors closed and the elevator continued up to twenty. Mohammed got out and went up a flight of stairs to the roof.

He approached the outriggers, I-beams lying across metal pipe frames with steel counterweights holding it down in the back. The cables that held up their scaffolds hung from the front of the beams with an extra tieback cable secured to a brick bulkhead on the roof in case of emergency.

Mohammed pretended he was inspecting the system while really checking if anyone else was there. He knew his lunch break would go by quickly, so he headed back down the stairs to the freight elevator. He pressed one and two and hoped no one else would get on this time.

The doors closed and the elevator descended. He watched the digital numbers as they counted down on the screen above. He held his breath while passing each floor.

The elevator stopped at the fifth floor. The doors opened into a small lobby with a logo on the wall, but no one was there. Mohammed pressed the 'close doors' button, twice. The doors closed and the elevator continued on its way down.

He passed the third floor, and he was still alone. Relieved, he exhaled and his heart rate began to return to normal.

The doors opened on the second floor and Mohammed stepped out of the elevator. Startled, he stepped back. A group of people in business attire stood right in front of him, the same people he saw from outside. He thought they were gone. He was happy now that he didn't get out before.

They got on the elevator while all of them except the building manager, who had seen him many times before, stared at Mohammed. On their way down to the first floor, the building manager described the building's delivery policies. Mohammed knew these people were potential renters.

The elevator doors opened. The building manager led his group down a long hallway to a locked door that led to the main lobby. Mohammed headed the opposite way down the hall, out through the loading docks and onto the street.

He ordered a sandwich from the Halal food cart on the corner and ate it while standing on the crowded sidewalk under the bridge, watching the loading dock for any of the three men.

It wasn't long before lunch break ended and it was time to go back to work.

Mohammed and Tony took their scaffold up to an area between the ninth and tenth floors where they repointed mortar joints between bricks. With a long skinny metal tool in one hand, they pushed fresh cement off a flat piece of metal in their other hand. After filling the joints, they used a round metal tool to smooth the cement and give it a concave look.

They enjoyed working in the warm sun for a couple of hours before it took refuge behind a skyscraper on the next block.

Mohammed knew he was running out of time. The workday was almost over and he wouldn't have another chance to find any of those men until Monday. By that time, they could have blown something up already, if they really did have access to explosives. He knew that if he could not find them after work, he would have to call the authorities and tell them what he'd heard. His hands kept working as his mind kept thinking.

At three o'clock, Tony finished pointing his side and threw his tools into his bag without cleaning them. He turned to Mohammed and said, "Come on, Mo. Time to go down."

"I am almost finished, partner." Mohammed finished the small area that he'd already started. He wiped the cement off his tools before putting them away, adjusted his safety harness, and headed over to the motor on his end of the scaffold. He turned to Tony and said, "Okay. I am ready, partner."

On their way down, a gust of wind blew the scaffold away from the building. Tony and Mohammed kicked their feet out behind them and waited for the scaffold to come back in while continuing their descent. The wind passed and the scaffold came back in. They used their feet against the wall to prevent the scaffold slamming into the building.

A few years ago, when he first started working on high buildings, these gusts of wind scared Mohammed. Now, he was used to it, and sometimes it was even fun. He just let nature have its way and rode the wind like a surfer on a wave.

Mohammed looked up. The other scaffolds were all descending. He remembered a conversation a few of his co-workers had in the freight elevator. They spoke about what they were going to do during their four-day weekend next week. When the wind calmed down enough for his partner to hear him, Mohammed yelled across to Tony and asked, "Tony. We are we not working next Friday?"

Tony shouted back, "We never work the Friday after Thanksgiving. That's how it's always been. It goes all the way back to the pilgrims and the Indians. We stay home, eat turkey, drink beer, and watch football. Who the hell wants to wake up and go to work after that?"

"I see," said Mohammed while kicking his side of the scaffold away from the building to avoid hitting a metal light fixture on the wall.

Within a few minutes, they landed on the bridge.

A skinny Irish laborer approached. He lifted two empty buckets and a half-full bucket of mortar off the scaffold and scolded Mohammed with a heavy Irish brogue. "What'd I tell you about ordering too much mud, you Taliban bastard?"

Mohammed continued tying down the scaffold, ignoring the laborer and his rude racial comments. Tony removed the power tools from the platform, carried them over to the gang box, then returned to the scaffold to unplug the motors.

Two small Mexican laborers passed with heavy bags of

garbage in their hands. The Irish laborer barked at them on their way by. "Andale, Andale, you little Chihuahuas! That garbage better not cut into my drinking time today!"

Mohammed pulled down as hard as he could on the electric cable and tied it tight to the scaffold's back rail to avoid the cable swinging and banging against the building at night.

Before walking away with the empty buckets, the Irish laborer glanced at Mohammed and said, "Come on, Taliban! Hurry up with those lines! You're not tying down the Titanic!"

After everyone finished cleaning their scaffolds and packing up their tools, one by one, they climbed down the ladder to the street.

The mood on Friday was always cheerful among the men, but Monday would not bring such cheer. Some of them left right away and others went into the building to use the bathroom in the basement.

On the sidewalk, Kenny looked at Mohammed's empty hand and said, "Don't tell me you forgot it again."

Mohammed realized Kenny was talking about his thermos and lunch container. He answered, "Oh, no, I did not have it with me today."

"Good. I don't wanna be here late on a Friday, man."

Kenny took the ladder down and carried it into the loading dock while Mohammed followed him in. They got onto the freight elevator together and took it down to the basement.

Mohammed waited until everyone else was finished, then went to the bathroom and took his time washing up.

After everyone was gone, he made his way out of the bathroom and into the elevator. He pressed two, but the elevator stopped and the door opened on the first floor anyway. The building manager got in with one of the janitors. Mohammed had no choice but to exit the elevator and then the building.

He stood on the sidewalk for a few minutes watching the loading dock, which was empty except for one UPS truck making a delivery.

Mohammed knew he couldn't stay there all day, so he decided to go home and come back tomorrow. It was his day off, but he could hang around the building for a couple hours. Maybe those three men work Saturday.

Mohammed wondered if he should call the authorities, but he

was too scared, and he kept telling himself there was still the possibility that he had misunderstood what they were talking about.

He decided to wait a little longer before deciding what to do. He needed Allah to guide him.

CHAPTER 6—FRIDAY 3:43PM

Andrew Miller had been waiting in the faded gray Maxima for over two hours and was getting restless. He looked at the Citizen watch that his wife gave him for Christmas last year then continued waiting, watching.

The car sat in a crowded parking lot outside a shopping mall in a suburban Long Island neighborhood. The lot was less than half-full of cars. Only a few shoppers passed by now and then. The mall security guard passed by twice in his little green car, but Andrew was sure the security guard didn't notice him. The man was only paying attention to the giggling high school girls as they entered the mall in groups.

Finally, Andrew recognized an approaching man in his rearview mirror.

A young Arab man with a black mustache and eyebrows that resembled sleeping caterpillars approached the car wearing a blue Adidas jogging suit with white stripes on the side. He peered into the window at Andrew.

Andrew unlocked the door.

The man got in and sat in the passenger seat.

Andrew glanced at his watch. "You're late."

The man spoke perfect English without any hint of a foreign accent. He sounded like a typical New Yorker. "I was tied up. But I'm here now." He glanced at the black gym bag in the back seat and asked, "That it?"

25

Andrew reached for the bag, pulled it to the front seat, and unzipped it. He took one of the canisters out and opened it showing the man a phone number written with black marker on the inside of the thin metal lid.

Andrew said, "Each bomb has its own phone number written on the inside of the lid. It will ring twice, then, when it beeps, they have to enter the key code. The key code for each bomb is the same as its ten digit phone number."

The man clarified, "The phone number and the key code are the same?"

"Makes it easier to remember." Andrew closed the canister and placed it back in the bag, which he then zipped up and handed to the man.

The man took the bag, but his eyes stayed trained on Andrew's hands as Andrew reached under his seat.

"Relax," said Andrew. "If I wanted to kill you, don't you think I'd be a little better prepared?" Andrew pulled out a large yellow envelope, which he then handed him.

The man took the envelope, opened it, and looked inside to check the contents: stacks of old money, hundreds, fifties, and twenty-dollar bills. He stuffed the thick envelope into his jacket when he saw two women with shopping bags in their hands sashaying toward the little red BMW parked next to them.

They waited for the women to get into their car and pull out of their parking spot then they shook hands before the Arab man hurried out of the car and disappeared behind a van in the next row.

CHAPTER 7—FRIDAY 4:31PM

Mohammed exited the subway when it arrived at his stop in Brooklyn then headed up the stairs to the street. A cool breeze blew brown and orange leaves along the sidewalk. The sun was setting quickly, and Mohammed wanted to get home before dark so he picked up the pace.

Every night, he had to pass the housing projects before reaching his apartment building, and every night, without fail, someone had to harass him.

He stayed on the edge of the sidewalk, the same as always, as close to the line of parked cars as he could get while keeping his eye on the ground for piles of dog shit. He could have crossed the street, but there were more of the same red brick project buildings on the other side, and more hoodlums.

A few young punks with their pants hanging down below their boxer shorts and wearing big gawky earrings and fake gold pendants were leaning against a wall. Their baseball caps were huge and sideways. They passed around a blunt while joking and laughing. The smell of the weed was still noticeable despite the chocolate smell from the blunt wrap.

Mohammed kept moving forward. He didn't think they noticed him, but they did.

"Yo! Al-Qaeda!"

Mohammed stayed his course while looking down at the sidewalk. He didn't want any trouble.

27

A brand new white Mercedes with dark tinted windows cruised by nice and slow while playing Biggie Smalls so loud that Mohammed felt the sidewalk vibrating.

Another of the punks yelled. "Yo! You deaf, Al-Qaeda? My man is calling you!"

A young skinny kid followed Mohammed. The kid wore orange and white Jordans, baggy blue jeans, an oversized white hooded sweatshirt, and a huge orange baseball cap that covered the top of his ears.

Mohammed didn't want to appear scared, so he didn't speed up. He just kept moving forward at his normal pace, looking down, and keeping to himself.

The kid was getting closer. "Yo, Al-Qaeda! Lend me a dollar, yo!"

Mohammed knew he could take the kid if he had to. He was just a skinny young punk. But then what? Everyone in the projects would come after him, and he'd heard the gunshots and the blood curdling screams late at night.

Just as he stepped off the curb, the kid stood next to him and smiled. Mohammed was relieved when he saw a cop car parked on the corner, right across the street. He knew the kid saw it too, because he turned around and strutted back to his friends without saying another word.

Mohammed crossed the street and continued another block to the next corner where he unlocked the door of a four-story apartment building on the corner that was built in the 1920's and looked like it hadn't been repaired since.

Standing inside the foyer, he made sure to lock the outer door before unlocking the inner door. He crossed the ancient Terrazzo lobby and checked his mailbox on the wall. There was one item, the electric bill.

He hiked up the stairs to the third floor and unlocked the four heavy-duty locks to his almost empty one-bedroom apartment.

He had just moved to this neighborhood and he hated it. For the past eight years, until a few months ago, Mohammed had lived in a quiet neighborhood with his cousin. He had to move out when his cousin got married. He took this apartment because of the price. In this tough economy, he didn't want to take on a high rent, and he'd already sent a good portion of his earnings to his family back home in Pakistan. The landlord was also Pakistani and lived on the first floor, which made Mohammed feel a lot more comfortable about living there.

Just as he turned on the light, a tiny black kitten with a white face and white paws pounced on Mohammed's feet. He smiled and picked her up. She licked his face. Mohammed laughed while crossing the small living room, which was unfurnished except for two wooden chairs and a cheap TV tray that his cousin had given him. A portable DVD player sat on the floor in the corner for the rare occasion when he rented a movie.

In the kitchen, after placing his forgotten lunch into the refrigerator, he washed out two plastic bowls on the floor then filled one with milk and the other with canned cat food. The kitten drank a little milk then went for the food. Mohammed stroked its back a few times. He never gave the kitten a name. While the kitten ate its dinner, Mohammed headed into the bathroom.

Fresh out of the shower, Mohammed went back into the living room and dropped down onto his hands and knees. Facing Mecca in the east, he performed his prayers, just as he had done every morning and every night.

After finishing his prayers, he went back to the kitchen to warm up what should have been his lunch, leftover chicken with some flat Chapatti bread, all of which he quickly devoured.

Back in the living room, he sat on one of his two wooden chairs while his kitten slept in a small cardboard box with a throw pillow and a baby blanket. Mohammed opened his Quran.

After reading page after page, his eyes began to hurt, so he closed the book and rubbed his face with his hands. His body was tired from working all week, but his mind was wide-awake. Thoughts flooded his head from every direction. What would he say to those three men if he found them? What if they didn't work tomorrow? The possibilities continued to bombard him.

CHAPTER 8—SATURDAY 12:59AM

Looking out the window at the same red brick building as the night before, watching the same lookout as the night before, Diane Lasalvo checked her Guess watch and turned to her partner. "This guy better show."

Detective Garcia had half of a jelly donut in his mouth. "Relax. Crackheads aren't the most punctual people."

Diane watched Garcia stuff the rest of the donut in his mouth and wash it down with some coffee. "Didn't the doctor tell you to cut down on the sweets? I just finished breaking you in. I wouldn't want to have to get a new partner now."

"You sound like my wife." Without even glancing over, Garcia took a chocolate cream donut out of a paper bag and made a grunting sound as he admired it.

Diane shook her head. "Is the chocolate one for dessert?"

"Very funny." Garcia took a bite and wiped the cream from his lip with a paper napkin.

The way he enjoyed it made Diane feel like having one, but she didn't need the extra carbs. She lit a cigarette and watched out the window.

Garcia finished the donut, burped, then stood and waddled to the bathroom.

A few minutes later, Diane saw Terek approaching the building. "Garcia, hurry up!"

Garcia stumbled out of the bathroom pulling up his pants.

"I hope you washed your hands." Diane tightened her ponytail then took her gun out of its holster and racked it.

Garcia buttoned his pants and picked up his radio, "We're ready."

A man responded on the radio. "On their way. Be careful."

Diane and Garcia raced out of the apartment and down the stairs to the street. Two cop cars, one from each side, screeched toward the building. The lookout started walking, going for his phone.

Garcia pointed his gun at him. "Drop the phone and put your hands in the air."

The lookout dropped the phone and raised his hands. He turned and glared at Terek as he left the building untouched.

Two uniformed cops jumped out of each of the two patrol cars that just pulled up.

A young Asian cop helped Garcia arrest the lookout as Diane ran into the building with the other three cops.

There were two staircases, one on each side, and an elevator in the center of the run-down lobby. Two fluorescent lights flickered overhead.

With her gun drawn, Diane pointed at two of the cops, a tall black man, and a robust older black woman. She quietly directed them to guard one staircase each.

Diane pressed the elevator button and stood to the side as the third cop, a short Irish man with a sergeant rank on his shoulder, moved to the other side of the elevator door.

Everyone waited with their guns drawn. Diane heard her own heartbeat. She wondered if the others could hear it. This felt like the slowest elevator in history.

The elevator finally descended. The doors opened. She pointed her pistol while peeking inside. It was empty. She exhaled.

Diane and the short cop entered the elevator. The doors closed and Diane pressed six, the top floor. The elevator just passed the third floor when she heard two gunshots. Then a dog barking. Then more gunshots, rapid fire—too many shots to count—and from more than one gun.

Diane's body temperature increased as goose bumps covered her flesh. She pressed four, but it was too late. They were already passing the fourth floor.

The gunfire continued downstairs.

Wondering what was happening, Diane's mind involuntarily ran through every possible scenario, even though she was trying to concentrate on what she was doing.

She pressed five just in time. The button lit up. Then went out. The elevator stopped and the doors opened. Diane stayed to the side with her gun drawn. She stuck her foot out to hold the elevator door open. The short cop did the same on his side as the gunfire downstairs continued.

After one single shot, the barking dog was silent. Two more shots from another gun, and then everything was silent.

Diane snuck out of the elevator, pointing her pistol while looking both ways. She moved toward one staircase as the short cop moved toward the opposite staircase. The silence scared her as much as the gunshots did. She prepared herself mentally, or at least she tried. Thank God, she was wearing her vest. She just hoped it was enough.

Time to move. She motioned to the other cop to check his staircase then she hurried down the stairs on her side, slowing down and checking the next floor to make sure there was no one waiting to ambush her. The smell of gunpowder traveled up the stairs.

On her way down, she heard two gunshots in the opposite staircase. She crept into the hall with her gun ready to fire and moved forward. With two hands, she held her pistol out in front of her, waiting for someone to jump out.

She inched forward.

When she reached the opposite staircase, she peeked inside, only able to see the landing and a few steps above it. She turned around for a quick glance to make sure no one was coming up behind her. She tried to consider every angle, but everything was happening so fast.

Just as she was about to move forward, two gunshots shattered the eerie silence.

A tall, thin man dressed in all black bolted up the stairs in front of her, taking two steps at a time.

Diane stepped back and yelled, "Stop! Police!" She looked around one more time to be sure she was alone before going up after him.

At the top of the staircase, standing against the wall, she kicked the bulkhead door open and lunged outside onto the roof with her gun ready to fire, her trembling finger just a fraction of a millimeter away from the trigger.

On the other side of the roof, the thin man was running. He hopped up onto the parapet wall and leaped across an open space of about four feet. He landed on the roof of the building next door and rolled to safety.

Just as he stood, Diane started running toward him. The man continued moving, over another parapet wall to a connected building the same height.

She raced across the roof following all the moves of the man she was chasing. She climbed up onto the parapet and jumped across the alley. Her arms and legs were too short. It didn't happen the way she visualized it. Smacking into the wall of the building next door, Diane grabbed the parapet with both hands.

Hanging on with all her strength, her face scratched and bleeding and her body aching, she knew she had to pull herself up or die. She could do at least five pull-ups at the gym, but this was different. Holding onto a cold concrete stone was nothing like a comfortable bar that fits perfectly in her hands. No matter, she had to do it. She inhaled then began pulling herself up.

Almost at the top, just as she was ready to go over, her left hand slipped. She lost her grip. Dangling by just her right hand, she reached back up with her left and grabbed the concrete stone.

The cold made the throbbing pain in her hands worse. There was no time for pain, and no time for fear. She heaved herself up with both hands as hard as she could. Her face and chest scraped against the ragged old bricks as she finally made it to the top and threw herself over the wall. Her knee twisted as she landed on the roof.

While lying in pain, she tried to spot the thin man, but he was nowhere in sight. She couldn't help imagining her mother's voice telling her she almost died for nothing.

Diane struggled to her feet and saw two uniformed officers with flashlights checking the roof she had just jumped from. She yelled across to them, "He got away!"

One of the cops asked, "Are you okay?"

"I'm fine. I'll see you downstairs." She limped to the bulkhead and down the stairs to the street.

Diane arrived just in time to see a pair of paramedics wheeling a stretcher toward an ambulance. She got closer and saw the tall black cop who was guarding the stairs, dead. She saw the bullet hole clearly in the side of his neck. Her mind replayed her own voice telling him to watch the staircase.

The older female cop was wounded, blood dripping from a bullet hole in her forearm. She stayed at the young cop's side, holding his hand. The paramedics loaded the stretcher onto the ambulance and closed the doors.

The sound of sirens became louder, coming from all directions.

Diane limped into the lobby and saw a dead Pitbull with a spiked collar and blood dripping from multiple bullet holes in the body and one in the head. She stepped around the puddle of dog's blood and continued toward the stairs.

In the middle of the staircase, a young man lay face-down in his own blood.

At the top of the staircase, Diane saw the short cop lying on the floor with two bullets in his leg. She said, "Another ambulance is on the way."

He asked, "Is Armstrong dead?"

Diane nodded.

Neither spoke as two paramedics rushed in with a stretcher for the short cop.

The cop refused to get onto the stretcher, so the paramedics helped him walk. One paramedic went down the stairs and waited at the bottom while the other helped the cop down the stairs, avoiding the dead drug dealer and his dog.

Diane asked the short cop, "Did you see Detective Garcia?"

As the paramedics helped him toward the door, the cop told Diane, "Detective Garcia ran outside with his gun in his hand. Said he was gonna get that cop-killing bastard. I think he ran up the block."

Diane lit a cigarette and went outside where Garcia was standing bent over with his hands on his knees, gasping for air while trying to explain to two homicide detectives what had just happened.

Diane tried to keep her weight off her twisted ankle while approaching Garcia and the two homicide detectives. She told them everything that had happened after she entered the building.

People in the neighborhood watched out their windows, but no one came outside. Spotlights and sirens made it look like the middle of the afternoon.

Examining Diane's scratched and bloody face, Garcia asked, "What happened to you?"

CHAPTER 9—SATURDAY 5:12AM

Andrew Miller finished his first set of sit-ups on the polished hardwood floor of his dark living room, trying to be as quiet as possible not to wake his wife and kids who were still asleep in their bedrooms.

He did his workout in the small space between the coffee table and the TV. A brown sofa sat against the back wall and a matching loveseat occupied the side wall. Two large frames containing multiple family photographs hung on the walls on either side of the TV.

Wearing just a pair of cotton shorts and New Balance sneakers, Andrew stood and did a few stretches before going back down for another set of sit-ups. Perspiration began to form on his chiseled chest and abdominals. He cranked out his second set with ease then stood for more stretching.

Three months ago, Andrew and his family moved to New York from San Diego after Andrew accepted a job with the New York City branch of the DCTA, the Domestic Counter Terrorism Agency, a division of Homeland Security.

After six years in the Marines and five years at the San Diego Police Department, Andrew applied to the FBI, but they never contacted him. The DCTA recruited Andrew after he stopped a deranged man from detonating ten pounds of homemade explosives at the San Diego Naval Base. The man wasn't a career terrorist. He was an ex-veteran turned heroin addict who demanded more disability pay for the injuries he got while fighting in Iraq. The media however, sensationalized the story, taking advantage of the perpetual terrorist threat to America.

Andrew became a local hero and decided he wanted to help protect his country by fighting terrorism, foreign or domestic.

His wife supported him in his career, but she didn't want to live in any of the five boroughs of New York City, so they settled on a three-bedroom apartment in a quiet suburban neighborhood in Westchester County, about twenty miles north of the Bronx.

Just as Andrew began his third set of sit-ups, he heard raindrops against the windowsill. After completing his set, he approached the window where he saw gusts of rain and wind picking up outside.

Down the hall, the bathroom door squeaked closed.

Andrew checked his six-year-old daughter's bedroom. Stephanie was in her bed, asleep.

He checked his five-year-old son's room. Brian was also in bed, asleep.

Just as he turned toward his bedroom, the bathroom door opened behind him. He turned around and saw his wife, Amy, with her heavy pink flannel pajamas on. Her short blonde hair was a mess and her blue eyes were almost closed, but Andrew still found her beautiful. He smiled and said, "Good morning."

"Good morning?" She pointed at the window and said, "Did you see the rain out there? I thought Seattle was supposed to have all the rain, not New York."

Andrew said, "Well, it can't last all day."

"Yes, it can, and it is. The weatherman said it will rain all day. This sucks."

Andrew kissed her on the forehead and said, "I'm sorry, honey. I'll see what I can do about the rain. What time would you like it to stop?"

Amy smacked his hard stomach and gave him a quick peck on the lips before scurrying back to the bedroom.

Andrew went back to the living room for another set of sit-ups. He did five sets in all, then began to do his push-ups. Back in San Diego, Andrew lifted weights at the gym three times a week and went running three times a week. Since moving to New York and starting his new job, he hadn't had time to even join a gym, not to mention work out at one. For the time being, he had to be satisfied with some light calisthenics and an occasional run.

After his exercise, Andrew took a shower, combed his hair, and put on a dark brown suit and a beige tie. All of the men at the DCTA wore black suits all the time, but Andrew didn't want to look like a cliché federal agent from the movies, so he tried to wear different colors, nothing flamboyant, just different. He kept one black suit in his closet for funerals. The agency required everyone to wear a suit, but never specified the color.

Amy stayed in bed, watching Andrew get dressed in front of the mirrored closet doors.

After making the final adjustments on his wardrobe, Andrew approached the bed and kissed her.

Amy said, "I wish you didn't have to work today."

"I wish I didn't have to either, but terrorists don't take weekends off." He kissed her again and stood, adjusting his tie.

"Don't they have other people working today?"

"You know this is my first case, I have to be there every step of the way."

She got out of bed and continued out of the bedroom.

Andrew followed her into the kitchen. He loaded the coffee machine while she began to prepare an egg-white omelet and a bowl of oatmeal.

"After a while, I won't have to put in so much time, but right now I'm the new guy."

Amy gave him his oatmeal at the table and said, "I know your job is important. I just wish we could stay home together and snuggle today with all this rain. Maybe watch an old movie or something."

"That sure sounds nice. I wish I could."

She served him his egg-white omelet, washed the pan, then said, "I'm going back to bed." She leaned over and kissed him.

After finishing his breakfast and washing his dish and coffee cup, Andrew kissed both of his kids on the forehead while they slept and then he left the apartment.

He lived on the third floor, but never bothered to wait for the elevator when he was alone. He headed down the stairs and out the front door.

Outside, Andrew opened his umbrella and hurried along the concrete path that cut through the manicured lawns of the courtyard between the brick apartment building that he lived in and three other identical buildings.

The surrounding neighborhood consisted mostly of two-story houses with a few apartment complexes scattered around. Trees without leaves lined every sidewalk.

Outside the complex, two squirrels scurried past as Andrew entered an enclosed carport where he rented two spaces, one for his wife's light blue Toyota Camry and one for the black Chevy SUV with official government plates that the DCTA provided him.

He jumped into the SUV and drove down the wet street to the highway, which was almost empty. He turned on the radio and listened to 1010 wins, all news. His wife was right, rain all day.

The ride was smooth going through the Bronx then into upper Manhattan. Traffic began to build around midtown, but it kept moving. Headlights beamed as windshield wipers went back and forth in the rain.

Despite the weather, Andrew made it downtown with twenty minutes to spare. He parked his car in a four-story parking garage then walked two blocks with his umbrella overhead while passing a row of newly built beige and red brick buildings. Although the big New York buildings were a novelty when he first moved here, he was now beginning to feel overwhelmed and crowded. He remembered how far he could see when he lived in San Diego. Now he couldn't see past the next building.

He quickly closed his umbrella and entered an eight-story square glass building connected to a huge concrete skyscraper behind it. Both modern buildings seemed out of place surrounded by limestone-faced government buildings that boasted gigantic Greek columns and elaborate decorative stonework.

Once through security, Andrew took the elevator up to his department.

He passed a few people working at their cubicles. He didn't say hello to any of them, because he didn't know any of them. Since beginning work here, he'd only spoken with the few people whom he'd worked with directly. He wasn't trying to avoid conversation; it just always seemed like everyone here was always busy.

He said good morning to his receptionist, an older woman with glasses, black and white hair, and a face like a rock.

She forced out a good morning then went back to her typing.

Andrew closed the door behind him upon entering his office.

An L shaped desk sat against the wall and extended across the middle of the room. Two brand new chairs sat in front of the desk, and a computer chair sat behind it. The desk was clutter-free. The only things on it were a framed picture of himself with his wife and children, a computer monitor, and a phone. He kept all his files organized in a small file cabinet under the desk.

He sat behind the desk, powered on his computer, and picked up the phone. He dialed a number and waited as it rang and rang.

Finally, the Arab man he met in Long Island answered the phone, "Yeah." It sounded like he'd been sleeping.

Andrew said, "It's me. Is everything ready?"

The man answered, "Everything is ready. I gave them the package at 2AM."

"Okay. I'll contact you again this afternoon." Andrew hung up the phone and began typing on his computer.

CHAPTER 10—SATURDAY 9:15AM

Mohammed lay awake on his brand-new, full-sized bed, the only thing he bought for the apartment. He knew the value of a good mattress, especially with the lower back pains he frequently suffered.

He'd been up for an hour already, but stayed in bed while his kitten slept curled up next to him.

Mohammed usually woke up at four-thirty in the morning during the week to pray and drink tea before getting on the train to work. He enjoyed sleeping late on the weekends and always felt well rested after staying in bed for a while and doing nothing. But not this morning. After multiple nightmares that kept waking him, Mohammed's head hurt, and he felt just as tired as he did last night.

He glanced out the window and saw rain. All he could think about were those three men at his job and the bombing of the Egyptian embassy back in Pakistan. If he closed his eyes, he could still hear the chaos and the stench of burning flesh.

Could those three men really be terrorists? He kept telling himself it must be a mistake. He must have misunderstood what they were saying.

After lying there for a few more minutes watching the rain, he got up, stretched, and went to the bathroom in his boxer shorts. Thick black hair covered most of Mohammed's thin body. His shoulders and arms were defined and hard from work.

After the bathroom, he went to the kitchen and prepared his

morning tea.

While sitting on one of his two chairs in the living room, Mohammed sipped his tea and watched the rain outside as it came down heavier.

He thought about his going back to the building and wondered if it would be a waste of time. He knew if he didn't find those men quickly, he would have no choice but to report them. He considered an anonymous tip, but didn't have enough information for anyone to take him seriously.

He knew he had to go back to the building and find them, but he decided to wait until the afternoon, after finishing his weekly chores. Hopefully by that time, the rain would stop and God would give him the strength and courage he needed.

Just as he got up to pour another cup of tea, his kitten wandered out of the bedroom and stretched its legs and back before running toward Mohammed and crashing into his foot. Mohammed laughed and picked it up. The kitten licked Mohammed's face and beard.

He carried it into the kitchen and placed it on the floor while pouring some milk into its bowl. While the kitten drank, Mohammed poured another cup of tea and sipped it slowly.

The kitten finished her milk then curled up and fell asleep on the floor.

Mohammed picked her up and carried her into the living room where he gently placed her into her box.

Before doing his household chores, Mohammed prayed on his hands and knees.

He changed the sheets on his bed, cleaned the bathroom and kitchen, then mopped the faded wood floors in his bedroom and living room. He performed his work like a robot, thinking about what to say to those three men, if he finds them.

CHAPTER 11—SATURDAY 11:27AM

Andrew finished all the necessary paperwork that would allow him to set up an armed task force to take down The Second Revolution, a homegrown terrorist group. The DCTA suspected the group was involved with two murders and a failed bombing last year. There was no evidence, but the DCTA continued to investigate the terrorist group that started out as a drug running motorcycle gang from Long Island and later became political.

The bombs that Andrew gave the Arab man were fake. When detonated, they would let out a puff of harmless white smoke. The Arab was a collaborator. Even though various government agencies suspected him, they also used him when they needed to.

Although The Second Revolution was fundamentally a white supremacist group, they bought their bombs the same way they bought their drugs, from whomever or wherever they could get them. Andrew insisted on using an Arab, as he believed it would lend credibility to the operation.

Now that the terrorists had the fake bombs, undercover agents were tracking their every move. Andrew planned to lead his team and arrest everyone involved with the conspiracy after they planted and tried to detonate the fake bombs. Counter-terrorism 101.

He made backup copies of his files and transferred them to two separate flash drives. He always made two backups, in case something happened with the first. He placed one flash drive into his desk drawer and the other into his pocket before powering down his computer, leaving the office, and heading downstairs to the street.

Because of the rain, the downtown area was even quieter than it usually was on weekends. The concrete island with a tall cast-iron pylon standing in the center and the tree-lined benches in the small park next to it were both barren. Clouds covered the tops of the skyscrapers, making them look as if they continued endlessly up into the heavens.

A pair of cops in rain gear hid from the weather between two gigantic stone columns in front a government building on Centre Street.

With his umbrella overhead, Andrew hurried to the garage where he'd parked the SUV. He was excited about the case. He had assisted briefly on three similar cases during his first month at the DCTA, but this was his case, his first case, and he was anxious to make a name for himself.

CHAPTER 12—SATURDAY 11:55AM

Other than the old Chinese man who worked there, Mohammed was the only person in the laundromat. He wore a pair of black dress shoes, brown slacks, and a black dress shirt. Even though he had nowhere important to go, Mohammed liked to dress in nice clothes on the weekend. He liked the way he looked, and he got tired of wearing heavy work clothes all week.

Sitting on an orange plastic chair, he waited for his wash to finish, then took the wet clothes out of the machine, and put them into the dryer. After inserting his quarters and starting the cycle, Mohammed glanced outside at the steady rain.

This neighborhood that was so loud and rowdy at night was always quiet in the mornings, especially when it rained.

He had a routine, every Saturday while his clothes dried, Mohammed would buy a phone card at the store next door and call his family in Pakistan before they went to bed. Even though he was running late today, he still had a little time to catch them before bed.

He didn't feel like going back outside into the rain, but he knew his parents looked forward to hearing from him every week, and he also wanted to hear their voices.

Mohammed zipped his sweatshirt and put the hood over his head before going outside. He usually wore his brown blazer on the weekend, but decided to wear a sweatshirt today because of the weather, even though it didn't match what he was wearing.

He sloshed through a puddle in the sunken sidewalk on his way to the store next door.

Once inside the store, he took off his hood and greeted the old Arabic man behind the counter. "As-Salamu Alaykum."

The old man returned the traditional Muslim greeting, which was Arabic for peace be upon you. "As-Salamu Alaykum."

Mohammed only knew a few words in Arabic from when he was a child in Quran class, so he spoke to the man in English while buying a ten-dollar phone card and a bag of peanut M&M's for later. He thanked the man, put his hood back on, and hurried outside into the rain.

Back inside the laundromat, Mohammed fed a couple more quarters into his dryer and said hello to an old Haitian woman loading clothes into a washing machine. She smiled and said hello with a heavy French accent while continuing her wash.

Mohammed sat down and dialed the phone card number on his flip phone. He hoped his parents didn't already go to bed. He considered talking with his father or maybe his brother about his dilemma.

His mother answered the phone in their native language. "Hello?"

"Hello, Mother."

"I knew it was you, Mohammed. How are you?"

Mohammed wished he could ask his mother what to do about his situation as she would be the most sympathetic, but he didn't want to alarm her, so he kept the conversation simple. "I'm okay, a little tired, but okay."

"Are you sure, Mohammed? You sound different."

He knew he couldn't hide his feelings from his mother, and he knew if he didn't tell her something, she would keep probing him, so even though he hated to do it, Mohammed lied. "I have the flu, but it's nothing."

"Never say nothing, Mohammed. People have died from less. Make sure you drink plenty of tea and water, and don't over-exert yourself."

"Okay, I will." Mohammed asked, "How is Grandmother?"

"Much better now. She's a tough old woman. I think she will be with us for many more years."

"Thank God." Mohammed glanced outside at the rain.

"Your sister is ready for bed. Say goodnight to her first, then

I'll get your father."

"Okay, mother. Goodnight. I love you."

"Goodnight, Mohammed. I love you, too."

Mohammed's twenty-two-year-old sister, the baby of the family, got on the phone first. "Hi, Mohammed."

"Hello, Faiza. I heard about your high scores at the university. Congratulations. I am very proud of you."

Women in Islamabad enjoyed a bit more freedom than those in smaller cities and in the countryside. At first, their father was against Faiza going to college. He believed a woman's place was in the kitchen and in the bed. Mohammed agreed with his mother and other siblings that Faiza should make her own choices. Their father finally gave in.

Faiza told Mohammed, "I am just thankful I'm able to attend university. When I get into politics I will make sure all women in Pakistan have the opportunity to get an education."

"I know you will succeed, Faiza." Mohammed thought about his other sister, twenty-seven-year-old Safia. Safia lived with her husband and two children a few miles outside of the city. "So, have you seen Safia lately?"

Faiza said, "She was here this morning. She's as big as a house. The baby should be coming any day now. And the other two are so cute. They're getting so big so fast. I can't wait for you to come and see them."

"Me, too."

Faiza said, "I have to go to bed now. I'll put Ibrahim on the phone. I love you."

"I love you, too."

Mohammed's older brother, Ibrahim, got on the phone next. "Mohammed, the Yankees called me. I am coming to New York to play for them."

Mohammed laughed. "I wish you were coming here, Ibrahim."

"Why? What's wrong?"

Ibrahim was two years older than Mohammed and always took care of him when they were kids in school. He thought about telling Ibrahim about his dilemma, but changed his mind after remembering his older brother's quick temper.

Mohammed said, "Nothing is wrong. I cannot miss my brother?"

"Well, nobody told you to leave home and move to the land of the infidels."

"Now you sound like father."

Ibrahim laughed and said, "I know, that's why I said it. He's sitting right here next to me."

Mohammed asked, "So, did you meet that girl Safia was talking about?"

"I met her. She is nice, but not very pretty."

"You have to stop with this craziness now. Not every girl can be pretty. How could your younger brother get married before you? Think what people would say."

"I don't care what people say." Ibrahim said something to someone else then told Mohammed, "Father is ready for bed. I'll put him on the phone."

"Okay, goodnight, Ibrahim. I love you."

"Love you, too."

Mohammed's father got on the phone and said, "Hello Mohammed. Your mother tells me you are sick. I hope you remember what I told you when you left."

"Yes, father. I remember." Before coming to New York, Mohammed's father had warned him not to touch any American women. He said most of the infidels are on drugs and infected with disease. "It is just the flu, father. It is cold and raining here."

"Just be careful."

"Yes, father." Mohammed changed the subject. "So, tell me about my bride to be. How did she look the last time you saw her?"

His father answered, "Oh, she is beautiful, Mohammed. You will be pleased. I just wish you would come back to Pakistan. You don't have to work with your brother and me if you do not want to. There are other jobs. Maybe Safia's husband could get you into the police department."

Mohammed wanted to stay in New York, and his fiancée's family had already given permission for their daughter to live in New York with Mohammed after they were married. Mohammed's father, however, had different ideas. Mohammed decided to keep the phone call pleasant by humoring him. "I don't know, father, I may stay in New York, or I may move back to Pakistan. I have plenty of time to decide."

"Your mother and I are off to bed now, Mohammed. Say hello to your cousin for us."

"I will. Good night, I love you."

His father answered, "I love you, too."

Mohammed ended the call and began taking his clothes out of the dryer. As he folded his work shirts, he wondered if he should have told his father what was going on, but he didn't want to hear another lecture on how he should have stayed in Pakistan instead of moving to the land of the infidels.

After folding everything and organizing it into stacks, Mohammed placed the clothes into his laundry bag and tied it up tight. Before leaving, he wished the old Haitian woman a nice day and waved goodbye to the old Chinese man.

It was only a block and a half away, but Mohammed hurried home, trying to avoid his freshly dried clothes getting soaked in the rain. He carried the bag with two hands against his body. The rain in New York seemed colder than the rain in Pakistan, but it wasn't as heavy. Although there were sometimes thunderstorms, they were nothing like the saturating downpours of the rainy season back home, and he was grateful for that.

While hurrying home, the memory of the Egyptian embassy bombing once again invaded his thoughts. The memory had always been there, in the back of his mind, but after hearing those men talking about explosives, the memory surfaced more and more.

Once inside his apartment, Mohammed took off his wet shoes and sweatshirt and left them on the floor by the door. The kitten slept peacefully in its box as Mohammed unpacked his laundry and noticed a few items on top were damp from the rain. He spread the damp items out to dry across the two chairs and hung everything else up. He kept his socks and underwear in a cardboard box on the floor of the closet.

He wasn't ready to go back to Manhattan yet. He still had grocery shopping to do. He knew in the back of his mind he was making excuses, but he was still scared as hell. If the three men really were terrorists, who knows what violence they would be capable of if Mohammed confronted them.

CHAPTER 13—SATURDAY 12:25PM

Andrew drove to a posh neighborhood on Manhattan's Upper East Side, not far from Central Park. He circled a quiet block lined with five-story brownstone townhouses. He didn't know exact numbers, but he knew that brownstones in this neighborhood sold for millions of dollars, many millions.

After turning on Madison Avenue and passing a few expensive clothing boutiques and jewelry dealers, he turned another corner, going down another block lined with brownstones. He glanced over at the addresses and realized he went too far.

In the rearview mirror, he saw a fancy metal awning protruding from a twelve-story limestone building. He waited for a car to pass then backed up the SUV until he could get a good look at the address. This was it.

It was quite a surprise when a valet approached and offered to park the SUV. He double-checked the address before letting the valet park the car.

Stepping onto the sidewalk, he didn't need his umbrella. The huge awning with built-in heat lamps protected him from the elements as he entered the building.

This was the first time his supervisor, who was also the director of the DCTA, invited him for lunch. He didn't expect a greasy spoon, but he didn't expect anything like this either.

He gazed at the crystal chandeliers hanging from the ceiling and the ornamental columns and arches that adorned the walls.

The patrons all wore expensive clothes and jewelry, brands they didn't sell in the stores where he shopped. He knew he must have entered the wrong place.

Andrew double-checked the address on his Motorola, again. It was correct. He must have typed in the wrong number. He decided to go outside and call his boss.

Just as he turned around to leave, he heard someone call his name. When he turned around, two men approached him.

The first man was his boss, Agent William Grant, tall and thin with gray hair and gray eyes. His shiny black suit looked too expensive to belong to a government agent.

Andrew didn't know the second man, but recognized his face from a magazine article he'd recently seen on America's top ten richest people.

Agent Grant extended his hand to Andrew and said, "Agent Miller, punctual as usual."

They shook hands.

"I thought I was in the wrong place."

The second man was short, fat, and bald. He extended his hand to Andrew and said, "You must be that promising young man whom William has been telling me about."

Andrew shook his hand and said, "No, I'm Agent Miller."

The fat man laughed and said, "He's funny, too."

After checking the time on his diamond-covered Rolex, the fat man said, "Please excuse me. I'm late for a meeting." He shook both their hands again then left the restaurant followed by two huge bodyguards.

Agent Grant placed his arm around Andrew's shoulder and said, "I already have a table."

They walked a few feet and sat at a newly set table covered with a shiny white tablecloth and a flickering candle in the center.

Andrew said, "I saw that man in an article recently on America's top ten richest people."

Agent Grant said, "Really? That sly fox made it back into the top ten?"

The waiter brought them a bottle of white wine.

Agent Grant said, "I hope you don't mind me taking the liberty of ordering the wine."

Andrew didn't know much about wine, and besides, he was on duty. "Thank you, sir, but I'm still on the clock." Andrew sipped his water.

Agent Grant chuckled. "Of course you are." He poured himself a glass, smelled it, swished it around in his mouth, then swallowed it. "The bacon wrapped swordfish is delicious here. Shall I order for both of us?"

"Uh . . . okay." Andrew had never even heard of bacon-wrapped swordfish, but he didn't really care about lunch anyway. He wanted to jump right in and discuss his case.

Agent Grant called the waiter over and ordered for both of them, in French.

Andrew was curious about Agent Grant's impeccable French, but he was more interested in moving forward with his case. He waited for the waiter to leave then said, "Sir, the group has the fakes, and they're moving them upstate as we speak. They're planning to blow up some government buildings in Albany. I have a task force ready to assemble. I just need—"

Agent Grant interrupted, "Albany? You cannot send a task force to Albany."

"Why not?"

Agent Grant sipped his wine and answered, "It is not our jurisdiction."

Andrew was too surprised to conceal his feelings. "Jurisdiction? I've been working on this case for two months. I'm ready to lead these men—"

Agent Grant interrupted again, "Excuse me, Agent Miller, I did not hire you to risk your life unnecessarily. The men below you will do that. You are in the intelligence business now. This is not the police department." He sipped his wine then continued, "And in regard to jurisdiction, it is a formality that must be adhered to."

Andrew knew he had to follow the chain of command, and there was nothing he could do about it. He answered just as he did when he was in the marines, "Yes sir."

Agent Grant said, "It should not take more than an hour or two to transfer the files to Albany and get them up to speed on the case. Go home to your family after that. Enjoy the rest of your weekend. You deserve it."

"Yes, sir."

"I admire your ambition, Agent Miller. One of my Assistant Directors has a high profile case. He planned to give it to an ass-kisser named Jones. I will see you get the case."

"Yes, sir. Thank you, sir."

CHAPTER 14—SATURDAY 2:39PM

Mohammed trudged ten blocks in the rain while trying to keep his umbrella pointed against the wind so it wouldn't collapse, but then it was useless against the rain. His legs and feet were soaked by the time he reached his mosque on Bedford Avenue, a small brown windowless building on the corner decorated with tile mosaics and big brass double-doors engraved with Arabic writing.

He entered the black wrought iron fence that surrounded the entire building and closed his umbrella before hurrying inside.

After wiping his feet on the mat near the door, Mohammed removed his shoes and sweatshirt and then washed his hands and forearms in a water basin.

He proceeded into the main area and knelt next to a few old men who were already praying on the red and white checkered carpet. Glass bulbs holding lit candles hung in a circular pattern from the black and white checkered dome ceiling.

Mohammed performed his usual prayers then stayed in the prone position for a while. He asked God for guidance.

He started to think that going back to the building might be a waste of time. There was no guarantee he would find those three men, and if he did, he doubted he would have the courage to confront them.

His mind kept jumping back and forth between whether or not calling 911 with an anonymous tip would help. He considered trying it, and if they didn't take him seriously, he would tell them his name and explain everything.

He stayed with his face to the floor for a while longer, waiting for God to give him a sign.

CHAPTER 15—SATURDAY 4:00PM

In his office, Andrew Miller had already finished transferring his case files to the Albany division and speaking with the lead agent from that office about an hour ago, but instead of going home, he began reviewing his next case. He wanted to go home to his wife and kids, but also wanted to start putting a dent in terrorism and make a name for himself. His family wasn't expecting him home until late tonight anyway, so he figured he could stay an extra hour and still make it home in time for dinner.

Andrew's new case was high profile, but boring. Not what he had hoped for. He had to work with a banking expert, investigating donations from rich businessmen in the Middle East to mosques in America. The case centered on one particular terrorist from Syria, a man they believed was hiding somewhere in the New York area.

He knew what he was doing was important to national security, but he preferred to be out there in the middle of the action. Once a marine, always a marine.

Andrew put the folder into his file cabinet then powered down his computer. He closed his office door and locked it before heading down the almost empty hallway.

Downstairs, Andrew waved to the few security guards still working and wished them a good weekend before stepping outside into the rain with his umbrella.

He drove to the highway where traffic had quickly accumulated on both sides. Headlights and windshield wipers were all he saw for miles.

Andrew waited thirty minutes in a standstill on the FDR Drive. He called his wife and told her he was on his way home, but traffic was heavy.

The cars began to crawl, and it took another fifteen minutes to pass the Queens Bridge where traffic finally began to give way. Now he regretted staying the extra hour.

CHAPTER 16—SATURDAY 6:15PM

On his stovetop, Mohammed prepared some fried chicken and white rice. He sprinkled a few different types of curry powder over everything for flavor.

He glanced at the rain out the window and wished it would stop. His kitten had already eaten and was napping on the kitchen floor.

Mohammed knew he should have gone to the authorities by now, but he just couldn't find the nerve. He knew he shouldn't procrastinate, people's lives could be at stake, but he was still so scared.

After cooking, Mohammed ate, but he didn't eat much, and he didn't enjoy it. Fried chicken was his favorite, but he just didn't feel like eating.

After placing the leftovers into plastic containers and putting them into the refrigerator, Mohammed went into the living room to read his Quran.

He opened the book, but didn't read it. He just stared at the pages. The same words continued echoing throughout his head like a demonic chant getting louder. Explosives. Jihad.

He thought about a woman he had seen during the embassy explosion, just after he and his father and brother got out of their car. At first, he only noticed the blood and dust that covered her face and torn fancy clothes, then he noticed she was hopping on one foot. Her other foot was gone. A ball of flesh and material hung from her knee.

When Mohammed's mind returned to the present, he picked up his cell phone and stared at it. He wondered, if he did make an anonymous tip, could they trace the call? He didn't care anymore. He couldn't take the chance of letting people die in a terror attack.

Mohammed dialed nine. His body temperature rose as his fingers began to tremble involuntarily. He quickly pressed the next button: one.

Only one number left to go. His finger was already above it, he just had to press it one more time. His heart rate increased as lava ran through his veins. The trembling got worse, but he managed to snap his finger down on the button: one.

He stared at the three numbers on the cell phone screen: 911. He'd never called 911 before and had no idea what to expect.

Feeling dizzy, he held his still trembling thumb over the green button, but moved his thumb across and pressed the red button. He couldn't do it.

Part of his mind told himself he was a coward and the other part said he needed to survive, no matter what.

He thought about going downstairs to speak with his landlord, Nasir. Mohammed considered Nasir to be a wise man with a good heart. Nasir reminded him of a younger version of his own grandfather back in Pakistan. If anyone could help him, it would probably be Nasir.

CHAPTER 17—SATURDAY 6:49PM

Andrew and Amy had already finished eating, but they stayed at the table in their small kitchen while the kids watched TV in the other room.

Amy had made meatloaf, macaroni and cheese, and broccoli. "You didn't eat much tonight," she said. "Did you have a late lunch today?"

Andrew didn't want to tell his wife he had bacon-wrapped swordfish for lunch at a fancy French restaurant that he couldn't even pronounce the name of, but he didn't want to lie to her either, so he said, "You know I can't discuss my cases, honey."

She laughed. "Not even your lunch?" She laughed again and stood while taking the dishes from the table. "Sorry, I wouldn't want to blow your cover, Mr. Bond."

Andrew got up and took the empty glasses off the table. He followed his wife as she went to the sink. He stood behind her and kissed the side of her neck. In a Russian accent he said, "We have ways of making you cooperate." He put the glasses on the counter and grabbed her hips while kissing her on the back of the neck.

She laughed and dropped a dish into the sink.

When Andrew realized the kids were standing there watching, he stopped kissing his wife and said, "I thought you two were watching TV."

Stephanie looked like a miniature version of her mother: chubby cheeks, bright blue eyes, and blonde hair. A big space stood out where one of her baby teeth recently fell from. She asked, "Why were you kissing her?"

Brian giggled.

Andrew noticed the rain had stopped outside. It was easy to change the subject with kids. He pointed at the window and said, "The rain stopped! Who wants to go outside?"

Both jumped up and down and yelled, "I do. I do."

Amy laughed and said, "You guys go ahead. I'm going to get the dishes washed then get dessert going."

Brian looked like his father with brown hair and brown eyes. He was so skinny and hated to eat, but he loved sweets. "We're having dessert? What are you making, mommy?"

She bent down to whisper in his ear, but she didn't whisper. She said, "It's a surprise."

Stephanie laughed. Brian slapped her on the shoulder. Stephanie pushed him.

Andrew said, "If you two start fighting again, we're not going anywhere."

The kids stood still and silent while their father looked at them.

Stephanie said, "We'll behave, Daddy."

Andrew looked down at Brian. Brian nodded in agreement.

Andrew said, "Go get your jackets."

CHAPTER 18—SATURDAY 8:50PM

Mohammed woke up with his kitten still asleep in his lap. He didn't remember falling asleep, but the nap did leave him feeling refreshed.

He'd always paid his rent early, but never this early. It wasn't due until the first of the month, but he decided to pay it now, and that would give him an excuse to go downstairs to talk to his landlord, Nasir, a sixty-three-year-old man with a fifty-year-old wife and two daughters, both in their early twenties. The oldest daughter lived in a dormitory while attending the University of Pennsylvania.

Nasir had once asked Mohammed if he would be interested in his youngest daughter, Fatima, for marriage. Mohammed told Nasir he would have been interested, but his parents had already arranged his marriage. He had airline tickets to go to Pakistan in January and meet his future wife.

After reaching the bottom of the staircase, he stood alone in the silent lobby for a moment.

He couldn't do it. He started back up the stairs.

He stopped and stood in the middle of the staircase. He had to tell someone. This was driving him mad. He turned around and went back down.

After standing in front of Nasir's door for a few minutes, trying to get control of his nerves, Mohammed finally rang the bell.

He saw someone's eye look through the peephole, then three deadbolts snapped open.

Nasir opened the door and smiled. "Hello Mohammed."

"Hello, Nasir." Mohammed gave him an envelope full of cash. "The rent."

"The rent is not due for another week and a half."

"I do not like to be late."

"Yes, I see that. I wish all my tenants were like you." Nasir opened his door wider and motioned for Mohammed to come inside. "Please come in, eat something."

"Thank you. I already ate."

"You are welcome to eat with us anytime, Mohammed."

Mohammed smiled. "Thank you." He was trying to be polite, but couldn't stop feeling nervous.

"Is something bothering you, Mohammed?"

He hesitated, but then asked, "Can I speak with you alone?"

"Of course." Nasir brought Mohammed inside.

Mohammed savored the aroma that filled the entire apartment. It smelled just like his mother's cooking back home in Pakistan. The smell brought back memories of a time long ago, when the only things that were important to him were playing marbles with his friends and watching reruns of old American sitcoms on TV.

Nasir led Mohammed into his bedroom, closed the door, and rolled the computer chair out from under its desk. Mohammed sat on the chair and Nasir sat on the bed.

"What can I help you with, Mohammed?"

After telling him everything about the three men and what he'd heard, Mohammed asked Nasir what he should do.

Nasir patted Mohammed's hand and looked into his eyes. "It is a very difficult situation, and no man can tell you what to do. Only Allah can tell you what to do, and only you can know what that is. The truth is inside you, Mohammed, and I have confidence you will do what is right."

CHAPTER 19—SUNDAY 12:14AM

Detective Garcia drove an unmarked police car while Diane sat in the passenger seat smoking a cigarette, trying to blow the smoke out the window and away from her partner. She glanced at her face in the side mirror. Shiny ointment covered patches of scabs from her forehead to her chin. Even though it was only a surface wound, she worried about scarring.

Garcia turned right onto Webster Avenue, passing a row of four story buildings, all with stores on the ground level. The tax accountant was the only store that had its graffiti-covered steel gate down. The laundromat, barbershop, pizzeria, and grocery store were still open and full of people.

Diane pointed and said, "This is the place."

Garcia double-parked alongside a line of parked cars in front of the Jamaican Restaurant on the corner, then he and Diane got out of the car at the same time. Diane forgot to keep the pressure off her twisted ankle, but when the pain kicked in, she remembered.

A few old men smoking cigarettes, drinking beer, and playing dominoes on a makeshift milk-crate table glanced over at the detectives as they stepped onto the sidewalk and under the light of the streetlamp above. Diane threw her cigarette into the gutter.

The smell of marijuana floated along the cool breeze as a young Rastafarian with huge dreadlocks stood in front of the laundromat talking on his cell phone and puffing on a blunt. When he saw Diane and Garcia, he cupped the blunt in his hand and started down the block.

Garcia held the door open for Diane as she entered the Jamaican restaurant. The walls had three stripes painted horizontally: red, yellow, and green. A young couple eating curry jerk chicken turned their heads to look when Diane and Garcia entered. A chubby little Jamaican man in the corner gobbled down a stack of beef patties while talking in a heavy accent on his Bluetooth. He glanced for a moment at the two detectives, then took another bite and continued his conversation.

Diane tightened her ponytail, then she and Detective Garcia both showed their badges to the hard skinny woman behind the counter.

With a heavy Jamaican accent the woman asked, "How may I help you officers?"

Garcia said, "We're looking for Terek."

"Who isn't? That bastard son of mine owe me twenty dollar, dem."

Garcia said, "Do you have any idea where he might go?"

"Me don't know about them riff raff that he be spendin' him time with. That boy is trouble, just like his father. I never should have slept with an American."

Diane said, "A man who killed a cop last night is looking for your son. If he finds him before we do, he will kill him."

She looked at Diane directly in the eyes then turned her gaze on Garcia. After a moment, she said, "Me know he used to hang out with some white kid at Echo Park, but that was a long time ago. Terek called him Jon Jon." She wiped the counter with a rag.

Garcia asked, "Do you know his last name?"

"No, me only meet the boy once, and Terek called him Jon Jon, a skinny little dirty-looking white boy."

Garcia gave the woman his business card and said, "Don't hesitate to call me anytime."

"Are you asking me on a date, big boy?" She smiled and slipped his card into the pocket of her stained apron while giving him the eye.

Garcia didn't answer. He just smiled. Diane held her laughter while following him out of the restaurant. No one paid much attention to them on their way out.

They both laughed as they got into their unmarked cruiser.

PHIL NOVA

Diane drove while Garcia munched on some M&M's in the passenger seat.

She glanced at his bag of candy and said, "She must know how much you love chocolate. You gonna call her, big boy?"

"That chocolate expired years ago." He poured the rest of the bag into his mouth.

Diane kept laughing. "You know what they say, melts in your mouth, not in your hands."

Still chomping away at his M&M's, Garcia said, "You surprise me, Diane. I thought you had more class than that."

She laughed again while Garcia opened a bottle of Coke and guzzled half of it.

After driving for a while along a wide two-lane street lined with small apartment buildings and stores, Diane turned onto a small, dark, one-way street going uphill.

They cruised up the quiet street, passing a few six-story apartment buildings on the right and Echo Park on the left. Stone steps led up to into a grassy area that surrounded one of many stone mounds.

The street ended and another began. Diane turned right and cruised past a playground on the left, and more apartment buildings on the right.

At the end of the park, she pulled the car over in front of a fire hydrant and asked, "Around the other side? Or should we go for a stroll in the park?"

Garcia replied, "This is a lot of ground to cover. Maybe we should call the four-eight and see if they could pick up Jon Jon for us. This is their jurisdiction."

Diane put the car in gear, drove up the block to the next intersection, and turned right.

Garcia said, "Let's go check out my boy on Jerome Avenue."

Diane picked up the pace while Garcia contacted their captain and asked him to call the 48th precinct.

It took less than ten minutes to get to Jerome Avenue. Diane parked the car under the steel-framed elevated subway tracks then they hurried a half block to a hardware store with its gate down. Next to the closed gate was a banged up metal door. Garcia checked the doorknob. It was locked.

Diane rang the buzzer. No one answered. "He's probably high as a kite." She rang the buzzer again, this time holding down until someone answered.

A man's raspy voice whispered over the intercom, "Who the hell is it?"

Garcia said, "It's your fairy Godmother. Let me in."

The voice on the intercom said, "Shit."

The buzzer sounded. Diane pushed the door open and grabbed her gun. She kept the safety on, but she was ready to click it off at any moment.

Garcia closed the door and led Diane up the dark musty staircase to the third floor.

There were two doors, one on each side of the hall. Diane stood in the middle of the hallway at the top of the stairs.

Garcia knocked on one of the doors.

It opened just a little. The chain was still on. A skinny old man with dark circles under his big buggy eyes glared at Garcia and asked, "What are you doing here, man?"

Garcia said, "We need to talk to you."

"I told you not to come to my house. You trying to get me killed?"

Garcia pulled a twenty-dollar bill out of his pocket and held it up for the man to see. "Just a few minutes. It's the fastest twenty bucks you'll ever make." Garcia waved the twenty in front of him then folded it in half and began to put it back into his pocket. "Unless you don't need the money."

"Wait." He closed the door, released the chain, then let them in.

Diane followed Garcia into the roach-infested apartment, still holding her gun.

The man closed the door and asked Diane, "What's with the heavy artillery, Mami?"

Diane pointed her gun at him and said, "Don't call me Mami."

Stepping back, the man put his hands in the air and said, "Okay, okay, take it easy."

Diane lowered her gun and holstered it. The man exhaled.

Garcia asked, "You heard about what happened last night?"

"Yeah, I heard."

Diane lit a cigarette and asked, "So what do you know about it?"

"What do I know about it? I don't know nothing. What could

I know?"

Garcia said, "What have you heard?"

"I heard rumors, but I can't say if they're true. I guess that's why they call them rumors."

Diane said, "Stop playing games and tell us what you heard."

"Okay Mami, take it easy."

Diane grabbed him by the shirt and pushed him against the wall. "What did I tell you?"

"I'm sorry. I forgot."

She let him go and calmly asked, "What did you hear?"

"Okay, I heard the kid that killed the cop is from Manhattan, he's part of some gang in Harlem. He was supplying his cousin, the dead kid, and supervising the operation. That's what I heard. I can't promise it's accurate."

Diane stomped her cigarette out on the faded wood floor and said, "Thank you." She turned around headed for the door.

Garcia handed the man his twenty dollars.

The man whispered, but not quietly enough, "Why don't you help out your partner and give her some? She really needs to get laid."

Diane didn't know herself how she crossed the room so fast. She punched the man in the jaw. He fell backward, blood dripping from his mouth. Garcia grabbed Diane by the arm and pulled her out of the apartment.

From inside, the man yelled, "I should sue your ass, you crazy bitch!"

Garcia said, "What are you doing? We need him."

Diane didn't answer. She just lit another cigarette and went down the stairs and back to the car outside.

Garcia followed her onto the street and said, "Maybe you should let me drive."

"Whatever." Diane threw him the keys and then circled to the passenger side.

They got into the car and took off. Neither said a word.

A call came in on the radio: "Detective Garcia, the four-eight just called. They're holding some kid named Jon Jon for you."

Garcia answered, "Tell the captain that's where I'll be." He stepped on the gas and sped to the 48th Precinct.

Inside a small interrogation room, Detective Garcia and Diane sat on one side of a table while a skinny, dirty, white kid in his mid-twenties with red hair and freckles sat on the other side of the table. A young uniformed officer stood against the wall near the door.

Garcia asked, "Okay Jon Jon, where's Terek?"

Jon Jon shrugged and said, "I don't know where he is."

Diane asked, "When did you see him last?"

"A couple weeks maybe, I don't know. What's the difference?"

Garcia said, "We're looking for the guy who killed that cop last night, and that same guy is looking for Terek. You want your friend to die?"

Jon Jon shook his head.

Garcia said, "Then help us find him."

Diane asked, "Where would he go?"

"He's got a girl that lives by the concourse, on 181st Street. Her name is Ericka."

Diane said, "Son of a bitch. Two blocks from our precinct."

Garcia said, "What does she look like?"

"I never seen her. Terek says she's bangin', but Terek likes anything, fat ones, skinny ones, ugly—"

Diane interrupted, "We get the picture."

Garcia asked, "Is she white, black, what?"

"He didn't say. He did tell me she's solid, though, and what Terek calls solid, I call fat."

"Anything else?" asked Diane.

Jon Jon shook his head. "If I knew anything I else, I would tell you."

Garcia said, "You're free to go, Jon Jon."

Diane and Garcia thanked the captain on their way out of the 48th Precinct before heading back toward their own precinct.

Outside a small 24-hour grocery store on the corner of 181st Street and Grand Concourse, Diane and Garcia parked the car, then approached a bulletproof glass window and spoke through a revolving Plexiglas cube with a young Arab man behind the counter.

Garcia showed his badge and said, "Excuse me, do you know a big girl named Ericka?"

The man said, "Yes. She just bought some cigarettes about ten minutes ago. She was with her friend."

"Which way did they go?" asked Diane.

He pointed and said, "Around the corner."

Diane and Garcia turned the corner and hurried up the block. A few young men were hanging around in front of one of the buildings, but no one who resembled Ericka's description.

Diane said, "I wonder if he's talking about the same Ericka."

Garcia turned to the guys hanging around and asked, "Hey, any of you fellas know a girl named Ericka?"

They all shook their heads and said no.

Diane knew they wouldn't tell, even if they did know her.

Garcia stayed on one side of the street while Diane crossed to the other side. They walked up and down the block, looking in every building lobby they passed.

After a few minutes on foot, they got back into their car and circled the area. They circled the same block, then the surrounding blocks, but didn't find anyone matching Jon Jon's vague description of Ericka.

Diane hoped the other detectives were doing better than they were.

CHAPTER 20—SUNDAY 4:01AM

Wearing just his boxer shorts, Mohammed lay in bed staring at the wavy, cracked plaster ceiling.

He was exhausted after having nightmares all night and waking up almost every hour. All of his dreams consisted of bombs exploding. Some of the dreams were in Manhattan and some were a replay of the embassy bombing in Pakistan. After the bombing in his last nightmare, he saw the charred corpses of his family stacked in a pile, his mother, father, older brother, and both of his sisters. He could smell their burnt flesh in the air as buildings collapsed around him. Mohammed had awakened from that nightmare crying.

When he realized it was just a dream, he wiped the tears from his eyes, went to the bathroom, and went back to bed. Even though he knew he was awake and in his bed, he still had lingering emotions from his dreams. They felt so real.

Mohammed knew that if he did nothing, he would be just as guilty as the terrorists would, if something really did happen.

He sat up on the bed. He needed to clear his conscience. He picked up his cell phone and dialed 911. This time, without hesitation, he pressed send. The line rang only once.

A woman answered, "Emergency."

"Hello. I am calling to report three terrorists who might have explosives."

"Where are you located, sir?"

"Not here. The men with the explosives were in Manhattan, on Seventh Avenue. I heard them talking on Thursday. I was outside the window. I heard them say explosives. They were talking about jihad, and there was a backpack–"

The woman interrupted, "Sir, I need you to slow down. I have you located at 326 Nostrand Avenue in Brooklyn, apartment 3F, is that correct?"

"Yes, but you need to tell the police to go to Seventh Avenue in Manhattan, between forty–" Mohammed heard sirens outside in the distance. He looked out the window, but didn't see anything.

"Sir, are you still there?"

"Yes. I am here."

"Please verify your address."

Mohammed answered, "My address? 326 Nostrand Avenue."

"And what is your name, sir?"

"My name is Mohammed. Mohammed Ali."

"Someone is on their way to speak with you now, sir, but I need to ask you a few more questions before they get there."

"Yes. Okay"

The sound of sirens blared louder. It sounded like they were right outside.

Mohammed glanced back out the window and saw drug dealers scatter as two police cars screeched up to his building.

He stepped away from the window and said to the woman on the phone, "Yes. The police are already here. I will tell them everything. Thank you for your help."

The intercom buzzed. Mohammed pressed the 'door' button and let the cops in the building. He opened his apartment door and waited.

Four NYPD officers came up the stairs and entered the apartment. A fat old Italian cop with sergeant's stripes on his shoulder and a food stain on his shirt told Mohammed to wait in the living room.

Mohammed stood against the wall near the window while a Hispanic cop checked the bedroom, another Hispanic cop checked the bathroom, and a big black cop checked the kitchen.

The three cops returned to the living room. The sergeant told Mohammed that a federal agent was on his way to ask him questions. The cops documented his name, social security number, and other personal information.

Mohammed was getting restless and scared. He noticed the way the cops looked at him, and he didn't like it.

After hearing another car with sirens blaring speed down the block and screech to a stop in front of the building, Mohammed glanced out the window and saw a black sedan double-parked.

Within seconds, a pale white man in a shiny black suit entered the apartment. He was tall and thin with gray hair and gray eyes. He unbuttoned his suit jacket, revealing the handle of his gun. "Mr. Ali, my name is Agent Grant. Please have a seat."

Mohammed wished he'd put some clothes on before calling. He felt uncomfortable sitting there wearing nothing more than his boxer shorts. He had no idea they would arrive so quickly. He sat down and said, "I told the lady at the 911 that the terrorists are in Manhattan, on Seventh Avenue, in an office building between forty–"

The agent interrupted. "We will get to that, Mr. Ali. First, I need you to slow down and start at the beginning." He pulled the empty chair closer to Mohammed and sat down. After taking a gold cigarette case out of his jacket pocket, the agent held up a cigarette, stared at it for a moment, then put it back in the case. He slipped the gold case back into his jacket pocket and said, "You can begin now."

"Thursday after work, I went back up to the bridge because I forgot my lunch containers on the scaffold. I heard three men inside the building talking in Pashto. I already missed part of their conversation and it was hard to hear everything they said, but I did hear the words explosives and Jihad."

Agent Grant asked, "You should have called the police on Thursday. Why did you wait?"

Mohammed opened his mouth and hesitated, but then told the truth. "I was scared."

Agent Grant stared into Mohammed's eyes and held his gaze until Mohammed looked away. Agent Grant asked, "What did these three men look like?"

Mohammed's eyes still didn't meet the cold gray eyes of the agent in front of him. He looked around at the four cops in the room when he said, "They were wearing blue uniforms, maintenance uniforms. They looked Pakistani, but they could have been Afghani. All three of them had long beards like mine, and uh—"

The fat sergeant laughed. "So, they all looked like you. What a freakin' surprise that is!"

The other cops chuckled.

Agent Grant stood and turned to the sergeant. "Please wait outside, Officer."

Without an argument, the sergeant left the apartment.

The agent sat back down next to Mohammed and said, "I need you to come down and look at some pictures."

Mohammed asked, "At the FBI office?"

Agent Grant said, "No Mr. Ali, I am from another federal agency. We just need you to come down to the local precinct, it is only a few blocks from here . . . we will have you back home in no time. Go get dressed."

Mohammed's kitten was at his feet, meowing for her breakfast.

"I have to feed my cat first or she'll never let me get dressed."

Agent Grant said, "Please try to hurry." He stood and stepped out into the hall where the sergeant was standing.

The two Hispanic cops waited in the living room while the big black cop followed Mohammed into the kitchen and watched him open a can of cat food.

Mohammed heard the other two officers talking in Spanish in the next room. He was far from being fluent, but there were enough guys in the union from Spanish speaking countries for him to pick up a little. The thing that made him worried was their sarcastic tone, their use of the words pendejo and culo in the same sentence, and multiple references to Guantanamo Bay.

That's when Mohammed realized he was a suspect. That's when everything hit him at once, everything he'd ever heard about American soldiers torturing Muslims in Guantanamo Bay, even if they were innocent. What if it was all true?

He knew he fit the stereotype, a young Muslim immigrant from Pakistan living alone in America. He had a long beard and a copy of the Quran in his house. No one would ever believe him. He didn't know what to do, and he didn't have time to think about it. Instinct took over. He had to escape.

He noticed the big black cop getting irritated as the kitten went back and forth between the two of them, rubbing her back against their legs and feet, meowing for its food.

Mohammed squatted and emptied the food from the can into

a plastic bowl. The kitten pounced, trying to devour the food as quickly as Mohammed scooped it into the bowl.

His heart rate increased as he contemplated escape. He certainly couldn't fight his way out. He would never make it past the first man. Maybe he could talk his way out, but probably not.

Mohammed finished emptying the can of cat food then stroked the kitten on the back of its head. This was his only chance. He had to escape. Now.

The cop said, "Okay, time to go."

Everything seemed to slow down and speed up at the same time. Hormones and endorphins mixed with the blood in his veins. Even though he knew he was still in his body because he could feel it trembling, he felt like he was out of his body watching everything unfold, like watching a movie.

While pointing his finger, Mohammed spoke quickly, "The stove! Fire! Behind you!"

Just as the cop stepped away from the stove and turned around, Mohammed leaped out the open window.

CHAPTER 21—SUNDAY 5:12AM

Standing on the rusted fire escape outside his kitchen window, Mohammed climbed down the cold steel steps to the second floor, then without releasing it, he climbed down the ladder as far as it went. He heard the cop yelling at him from above. He just hoped the guy wouldn't start shooting.

With his feet dangling a few feet from the ground, Mohammed let himself drop. He hit the sidewalk and rolled into the street, scraping his bare arms, legs, and feet.

He raced up the block and across the street, toward the projects, his feet scraping and bleeding all the way there. The cold November wind felt like flames on his bare skin.

He didn't have time to think. He just had to move. In front of one of the project buildings, Mohammed put his hand into a hole next to the door where a window used to be and pressed the buzzer inside.

The door unlocked. He pulled it open and slipped into the graffiti-covered lobby that smelled of vomit. Peeking out the window opening, he watched as the two cop cars left his building with their lights flashing. One car went one way and the other car went the other way. The black sedan took off down Nostrand Avenue, heading away from the projects.

Mohammed wanted to wait a few minutes just in case they came back, but he heard one of the elevators moving, and he was worried about who might come out of it. He waited a few more seconds, took a deep breath, then stepped outside.

A bright spotlight blinded Mohammed as the black sedan skidded onto the sidewalk out of nowhere. He turned around and bolted back into the building.

The elevator doors opened and a skinny crackhead in a trance came out. Mohammed didn't look back. He pushed the crackhead out of his way and sprinted up the filthy stairs as his bare feet bled and stung.

While passing the second floor, he heard the echo of hard shoes against concrete below, someone climbing the stairs from the bottom.

He ran faster.

After reaching the third floor, Mohammed sprinted through the hallway, across the building to another staircase on the opposite side.

He kept going up the filthy concrete stairs, trying to ignore the pain in his feet. He got to the fifth floor and decided to take a chance. He entered the hall and pressed the elevator button.

He heard a noise. It sounded like something behind him. He turned around and raced back to the second set of stairs.

Mohammed stood against the wall inside the staircase, trying to figure out which way to go. He tried to contain the sound of his breathing as his entire body trembled. He couldn't believe this was really happening. He wondered for a moment if he was dreaming, but the excruciating pain in his feet reminded him that he was awake.

He heard something in the hallway. He recognized the sound; the elevator arriving and the door opening. Mohammed didn't hear anyone, so he peeked out into the hallway. The coast was clear. He sprinted back to the elevator just as the doors were closing. He could see it was empty, so he put his hand inside and hit the rubber edge. The doors bounced off his hand then retracted. He jumped inside and stood against the side wall, the doors stayed open.

For some reason he decided to go up. The highest floor was twelve. Mohammed pressed eleven. The doors closed and the elevator began on its way up.

It stopped on the ninth floor. Someone must have pressed the button. Trying his best to stay out of view, Mohammed stood flat against the side wall as the doors began to open. He held his breath while repeatedly hammering the 'close doors' button. The doors began to close.

Someone stuck their hand inside. The doors opened. His mind failed to produce a solution. Out of instinct, Mohammed clenched his fists, ready to strike. This was his last stand.

It was a young man, the punk who was bothering him for a dollar on the street. "Yo, that you, al-Qaeda?" He laughed as the elevator doors closed behind him. "Oh shit. What are you doin' here in just your drawers?"

Without a thought, Mohammed slammed his fist into the kid's nose. Blood sprayed everywhere. The kid covered his face with his hands. Mohammed gave him another hard shot to the temple. The kid's eyes rolled back in his head as he dropped to the floor. Mohammed's fist began to throb.

He pressed the elevator stop button just before arriving at the eleventh floor. He quickly undressed the kid. The kid was skinny, and his clothes were huge. They were big on Mohammed, but he had no other choice but to wear them. More pain rushed to his bloody feet as he squeezed into the sneakers that were a little too small. He couldn't lace them up, but at least his feet were covered.

As he turned his head, Mohammed caught a glimpse of himself in the faded metal elevator wall. He felt ridiculous. The kid's wardrobe was almost the same as it was the other day, with a few changes: orange and white Jordans, a huge orange baseball cap, and black jeans. What stuck out most was the oversized, bright orange hooded sweatshirt. He checked the pockets. There was a five-dollar bill in the kid's wallet, along with a learner's permit. He checked the address on the permit. It was on the ninth floor.

Mohammed released the stop button and the elevator continued up to the eleventh floor. He stood back against the wall and held his breath, trying to be silent.

The doors opened. Mohammed pressed nine repeatedly until the doors finally closed.

The elevator went back down to the ninth floor and the doors opened.

He dragged the unconscious kid out of the elevator and down the hall to the apartment listed on the learner's permit.

Mohammed rang the doorbell then sprinted down an adjoining hallway. He peeked around the corner while listening.

Children's cries filled the hall when a huge woman opened her apartment door and saw the kid wearing just his underwear, bleeding on the floor. "My baby! Oh, my God, what happened?" She touched the kid's bloody face. "I told you not to hang around with those hoodlums. Look what they did to my baby!"

Mohammed felt bad. He had never hit anyone before. He knew it wasn't right, but it was just instinct, survival instinct. Just like everything else he did since hearing the words Guantanamo Bay. It was too late now to change his mind. He had to get away.

He bolted down the adjoining hallway and entered another staircase. He didn't hear anyone, so he decided to go back down. While tiptoeing down the stairs, Mohammed checked each floor on his way down, hoping his new clothes would help conceal his identity if someone did see him.

He heard sirens in the distance so he picked up his pace. He ran down the stairs and hoped no one would be waiting for him at the bottom.

At the ground floor, he noticed the empty black sedan. No police cars yet, but the sirens were getting louder, closer.

He stepped outside and looked around before dashing across the street.

Trying not to attract attention by running, Mohammed strolled down a side street lined with old brownstone townhouses as a cop car pulled up to the project building with its sirens blaring. He heard another siren, coming down the block he was on, coming right toward him.

Mohammed ducked down on the side of a stoop as the sirens got closer. His heart pounded as he waited. It was an ambulance, and it kept going, down the block toward the projects.

Another police car arrived at the projects. Two cops jumped out of their car and raced into the building while unsnapping their holsters.

The black sedan skidded away from the projects and down Nostrand Avenue as sunlight began to appear in the distance.

Mohammed came out of his hiding spot and sprinted up the block toward the next avenue. He slowed down and walked for a few blocks while trying to catch his breath and at the same time trying to stay out of sight.

Finally, he reached the train station and went downstairs. Using the five dollars from the kid's sweatshirt, the only money he had, he purchased a two-fare Metrocard in the machine, swiped it at the turnstile, then went down another flight of stairs to the platform.

Not many people waited for the train. The few who were there were reading newspapers and yawning.

Mohammed stood all the way at the end of the platform. It wasn't long before the train arrived, but it felt like an entire lifetime.

The back of the train was almost empty. Mohammed sat down. The doors closed and he sighed with relief.

After a few stops, the train went above ground, then continued to climb until they were above the street. The sun was bright and the sky was clear. Mohammed gazed out the window at the downtown Brooklyn and Manhattan skylines in the distance. The rumble of the train was relaxing. His eyes began to close.

The train jerked when it stopped. Mohammed woke up startled. He was at his stop. The doors opened and he got out.

People stared at him as he exited the train onto the platform. He knew how ridiculous he looked, a bearded Muslim dressed like a street kid in bright orange. But what could he do? He tried to play the part. While heading down the stairs toward his next train, Mohammed pulled his pants down below his waist showing his boxer shorts and took one step at a time while limping to the side as if he were on MTV cribs.

People laughed at him, but that was good. At least they didn't suspect him as a terrorist.

After waiting for sixteen long minutes, the R-train arrived. Still playing the part, Mohammed strutted into the train and sat down as the doors closed.

At 77th Street, he got off the train, walked up the stairs, and scanned the area.

The sound of cars going both ways on Fourth Avenue wasn't enough to block out the sounds of the birds chirping in the trees above. He missed his old neighborhood.

He passed the apartment buildings that lined Fourth Avenue then turned on 78th Street. Some of the townhouses displayed paper turkeys and cornucopias in their windows.

At the corner of Fifth Avenue, he stopped and looked both ways. Most of the stores were still closed.

A police car cruised down the avenue. The cop turned his head and glanced at Mohammed, but kept going.

Mohammed slipped into a small coffee shop and stood by the

glass door. An old Greek man behind the counter watched Mohammed while a waitress carried two plates of breakfast to an old couple at a table. Mohammed smiled at the old man behind the counter then looked back out the window. He waited a few more seconds before heading outside.

The cop was farther down the avenue. Mohammed crossed the street quickly, but didn't run. He didn't want to bring attention to himself.

The smell of freshly baked bread followed him from a bakery on the corner as he strolled up another block lined with brick and stone townhouses.

He stopped at a small apartment building on the corner. The building he used to live in. Mohammed rang the buzzer.

His cousin, also named Mohammed, answered the intercom. "Hello?"

"It is me, Mohammed."

"Mohammed, what are you doing here?"

"Please, let me in."

The buzzer rang and the door unlocked. Mohammed went inside and waited in the small immaculate lobby for his cousin to come down.

Cousin Mohammed was a taxi driver. He had just finished his shift and was still wearing his work clothes, faded blue jeans and an old beige jacket. He also had a long beard and looked a lot like his cousin. "Why are you dressed in those crazy clothing, Mohammed? What is going on?"

"I need your help, please. I heard some men talking about explosives. I did not say anything at first, but then I called the police. They were going to arrest me. I heard them talking about Guantanamo Bay, so I ran away. I did not have any clothes, so I hit someone and took his clothes. I have to go somewhere. I do not know where, maybe back to Pakistan."

"This is crazy, Mohammed. You hit someone? You ran away from the police? Why would you do that? How could you do that?"

Mohammed didn't answer. He just watched his cousin shake his head and pace the small lobby.

Cousin Mohammed said, "What if they come here looking for you? I have a wife now, and you know she is pregnant."

"I am very sorry, I did not want to get you involved, but I need your help, please."

"You should turn yourself in."

"I can't."

They stood silent for a minute, staring at each other.

"Here." His cousin reached into his pocket and handed him a wad of cash and the keys to his taxi parked outside. "You must go."

Mohammed thanked his cousin and raced out of the building. He still didn't know what to do, but at least he had a car and some money.

After turning back for one more look at his old building, and his old life, Mohammed started up the taxi and pulled away from the curb.

The black sedan skidded up the block, going the wrong way on a one way street, right toward Mohammed.

Mohammed threw the taxi in reverse and stepped on the gas, burning the tires as he tried to control it going backwards, hoping another car didn't come in behind him. He scraped most of the parked cars on the block as the sedan sped up, getting closer.

The tires squealed as Mohammed spun out and turned backward onto the avenue. He threw the gearshift into drive. The car jerked. He slammed on the gas just in time, avoiding an oncoming car. He sped forward.

The oncoming car swerved to avoid the black sedan as it sped around the corner. The oncoming car clipped the sedan's rear bumper. The sedan started spinning out of control.

Mohammed stepped on the gas, but didn't make it far. Two cars in front of him began to slow down for the light that just turned red.

It felt like the longest red light in history. He ground his teeth and squeezed the steering wheel. Mohammed checked his rearview mirror and saw that the sedan had gained control and was moving forward. He looked ahead at the red light and thought about jumping out of the car and running.

The light turned green. Just when the two cars ahead of him were far enough way, Mohammed slammed the gas pedal to the floor, screeching around the corner and onto a side street with the black sedan right behind him.

He zipped across the next avenue, swerving hard to the left to avoid a turning bakery truck. He wasn't sure if there was enough space between the truck's grill and the mailbox on the corner, but he went for it.

He slammed the gas pedal to the floor. The engine roared and the transmission burned as he slipped through the small space ahead, staying as close to the mailbox as he could without touching it. The truck's grill was only inches away from the taxi door as he made the turn.

Mohammed turned the wheel just a little. The opposite side of the taxi scraped against the mailbox, leaving a yellow stripe of paint behind.

The truck driver slammed on his brakes and blasted the horn while yelling obscenities at Mohammed. His tires squealed to a stop, blocking the narrow intersection.

Mohammed checked his rearview mirror. The sedan was stuck behind the truck. Mohammed slowed down.

The agent leapt out of the sedan with a pistol in his hand and darted past the truck, onto the sidewalk, and toward Mohammed. He fired two shots at the taxi while running toward it. He was too far away. Both bullets missed.

Mohammed stepped on the gas and peeled out down the block without looking back.

CHAPTER 22—SUNDAY 8:30AM

After dressing the kids for church and bundling them up in their heavy coats, Andrew and Amy locked up their apartment, and the entire family took the elevator downstairs.

Outside, it was cool and breezy with a few dark clouds lingering overhead. They continued down the path to the carport then to Andrew's SUV. He lifted the kids up, placed them into their car seats, and strapped them in. He usually let them climb in on their own, but today he didn't want them to mess up their church clothes.

As a child, Andrew had never been in a church. His mother did speak of the wrath of God on occasion, but that was usually when she was drunk and angry. Amy's family, however, were devout Baptists, and after marrying Amy, Andrew started attending Sunday service every week with his wife and her parents. Since Stephanie and Brian were born, they attended Sunday school classes. After church, they all sat down to a big breakfast at Denny's. He didn't know of any Denny's in New York, so they settled for the local diner.

Andrew started the engine and waited a few minutes before turning on the heat. His Motorola rang. Amy looked over at him as he checked the caller ID.

He said, "It's my boss."

Amy didn't say anything, but she didn't have to. He knew what she was thinking.

Andrew answered the call, "Agent Miller here."

Agent Grant was out of breath. "Miller, we have a situation. I need you to come to Brooklyn."

"Brooklyn?" Andrew tried not to pay attention to the evil eye his wife was giving him. "When?"

"Right now, Miller. Meet me on 77th Street and 4th Avenue."

"I'm not familiar with Brooklyn, sir."

"That is why we gave you the GPS. Use it, and get here right away."

"Yes, sir. I'll be there right away." He hung up the phone and said, "I have to go to Brooklyn—"

"I know, I heard."

Andrew turned to his kids in the back and said, "Daddy has to go to work. You two go to church with mommy in her car."

Brian said, "But why do you have to go to work, Daddy?"

"I work for the government, Brian, I told you this before. Sometimes Daddy has to go to work when he doesn't want to. I'm sorry."

Stephanie opened the car door and climbed out. "I hate your new job, and I hate New York." She slammed the door and stormed to her mother's Camry while sobbing.

Andrew looked at Amy and said, "I'm sorry."

She said, "I know. Just go, and try to hurry home."

Andrew typed the location into the GPS while his wife and kids got into the Camry and drove away. He hated to leave them like this.

CHAPTER 23—SUNDAY 10:12AM

Mohammed had parked his cousin's taxi on the street near the 86th Street subway station. He was trying to throw the agent off his track, so he didn't take the train.

His cousin had given him about $120 in small bills. After getting a few dollars in quarters from a Russian woman in the laundromat on Fourth Avenue, Mohammed bought a cheese pie and a cup of tea at a small Arabic restaurant across the street.

He ate his breakfast while walking to 92nd Street, then used a payphone outside a grocery store to call his friend Amir who lived around the corner. Amir was his first friend in America. Mohammed had memorized his phone number in the days before he could afford a cell phone. It was Amir who got Mohammed into construction.

Amir sounded terrified when he answered the phone. "Mohammed, why do you call me? A government man woke me up and came inside my house. He ask me questions about you. He ask my wife questions, and he ask my children questions, too. He said I will be in very big big trouble if I help you. I cannot talk to you, Mohammed. I must go, please."

"Wait, Amir, wait." Mohammed pleaded with his friend, but the line was already dead.

Just as he hung up the pay phone, Mohammed noticed a white van with tinted windows parked across the street. His heart rate picked up.

He turned around and strolled up Third Avenue while trying to act natural then turned down the next side street and took a deep breath.

He stood there for a moment, in front of a quiet apartment building, wondering if he should just turn himself in. Maybe they wouldn't take him to Guantanamo Bay for torture. Maybe he overacted and they really did believe what he told them and they just wanted him to look at pictures, like they said. He could just surrender himself to whoever was in that white van and it would all be over.

But then again, Agent Grant did just shoot at him in the middle of the street. He could have killed him. He could have killed an innocent bystander. He wondered if Agent Grant had gone mad and was acting on his own or if he were acting under orders. It didn't matter. He had to keep running. He didn't know what else to do, but he knew he had to keep running.

After a few minutes, Mohammed stepped back onto the avenue behind a woman walking a Chihuahua. He stayed behind her, out of the van's view.

He glanced down the block and saw two men carrying giant spools of electrical cable out the side door of the white van. Electricians. Mohammed felt stupid, but relieved.

The woman's Chihuahua turned and barked at Mohammed as he followed too close. Mohammed jumped back. The trembling little Chihuahua growled and yelped. The woman spun around and glared at Mohammed.

Mohammed said, "I am very sorry. I did not mean to startle him."

The woman corrected him, "Her."

"I am sorry. I did not mean to startle . . . her." Mohammed stepped away from the woman and her crazed dog and waited at the curb for traffic to pass. He crossed the street and stood near a busy coffee shop while waiting for his heart rate to return to normal.

He had a few other friends, but their phone numbers were in his cell phone, which was in his apartment. For just a moment, he considered going home and sneaking in. Everything was at the apartment, his passport and driver's license, his wallet, his cell phone, and his cat. He wondered if the cat ran away or stayed there. He wondered if anyone fed her or gave her milk. She liked a lot of milk.

As bad as he wanted to go home, he knew he couldn't.

He continued walking for about an hour, all the way down Third Avenue until the stores ended and the old green, steel-framed Brooklyn-Queens-Expressway turned and ascended above the avenue. It was dark under the expressway even though the sun was in the middle of the sky.

Mohammed's stomach growled, so he headed up the street to Fifth Avenue and ate a Chicken Parmigiana sandwich from an Italian deli.

He called his cousin but no one answered, so he left a message. He told him that he'd parked his taxi at the 86th Street Station and that he would pay for the damages as soon as he could get his money from the bank.

Mohammed noticed The Alpine movie theatre a few blocks away and decided that would be a good place to hide until dark. He approached the window and bought a matinee ticket to a romantic comedy that had just started.

Inside, he passed two kids playing a video game in the corner, then glanced over at the popcorn and candy counter. The aroma from the popcorn was tempting, but Mohammed didn't want to spend any more time out in the open than he had to. The wall of glass doors on the front of the theatre provided a full view of the bright lobby. He just wanted to get out of sight and hide in the dark.

He approached an old man standing behind a small wood podium. The old man tore the ticket and told Mohammed what theatre to go to.

Mohammed proceeded down the hall and glanced back to make sure no one could see him. He slipped into another theatre where he heard children laughing. In his mind, he was being cautious. In case someone saw him enter the theatre and asked what movie he was watching, he wouldn't be there. Maybe that would give him a little extra time to escape.

He entered the dark room and saw a cartoon already playing on the screen. It took a couple minutes for his eyes to focus on the people and the seats. He sat in the back row, which was empty, and tried to pay attention to the movie.

Mohammed always loved American movies and television shows. As a child in Pakistan, his father occasionally took him and his brother to one of the few movie theatres in the neighborhood that showed American movies. The movies were censored, of course, but no one seemed to mind. The VHS rental stores, however, had copies of American and other foreign movies that were uncensored. Although Mohammed's father kept a strict eye on the tapes that Mohammed and his brother rented, he did allow more freedom than the government censorship bureau.

While trying to watch the animated movie, his mind kept drifting. He planned to go back to his building after dark and get into his apartment the same way he got out, the fire escape.

CHAPTER 24—SUNDAY 1:10PM

Andrew took a quick bite of his Whopper and a sip of iced tea while sitting at the desk in his office, looking at his computer monitor. Agent Grant paced back and forth in the small space near the door.

"Other than his cousin, Mohammed has no other family in the US, and you already spoke with his Pakistani friends here in New York." Andrew scrolled up and down staring at the same list of names and contact information on his computer. "I wonder if he has any American friends."

Halfway through Brooklyn, Agent Grant had called Andrew and told him to meet him in Manhattan, at the office. Andrew had arrived just after ten. Agent Grant was already there. Agent Grant had briefed Andrew on the man he was searching for, then they checked every government database. Andrew did his job without complaining, but he still hoped to get home early enough to spend some time with Amy and the kids.

Agent Grant continued pacing while his Whopper sat unopened in the paper bag that it came in. "Did his supervisor return our call yet?"

Andrew washed down another bite of his burger and said, "Yes, but he doesn't know Mohammed personally. He said we'd have to contact the foreman."

Agent Grant stopped pacing and asked, "Well? Did we contact the foreman?"

"I tried. He's upstate on a hunting trip. His wife said cell phones don't work up there in the deep woods. He'll be driving straight to work tomorrow morning."

Agent Grant said, "Finish your lunch. I will return in one hour." He motioned to the unopened bag on the desk and said, "Take mine if you like."

As soon as Agent Grant left the office, Andrew devoured the rest of his Whopper. He wasn't going to do it, but he also ate Agent Grant's Whopper.

Andrew already had Mohammed's immigration records on screen, but there was nothing out of the ordinary. He decided to take another look, just in case he missed something.

If the records were genuine, Mohammed Ali did not fit the typical profile of a terrorist. After high school, Mohammed spent four years in the Pakistani army as an assistant cook. He did one tour in Kashmir, but never saw action.

Mohammed applied for a visa to the United States upon his discharge. He worked for less than one year washing dishes with his father and brother in a fancy hotel in Islamabad before leaving his family in Pakistan to live with his cousin in Brooklyn. Mohammed drove his cousin's cab for three years before he began working in construction. After four years with the same company, he had the opportunity to join the union. He also passed his citizenship test and was sworn in last year.

Andrew had doubts about Mohammed Ali's involvement in terrorism. Maybe the man was mentally slow, or maybe he really did have information about a terrorist plot. Andrew wished he was there. He wished he could have looked into the man's eyes and spoken with him.

He left the office for the bathroom then returned to find Agent Grant waiting for him.

Agent Grant said, "I have a meeting. I will be back at three. I want to make another trip to Brooklyn this afternoon."

"Yes, sir." Andrew wanted to go home to his family, but he did ask for this. He said he wanted to be involved in the action, and now he had no right to complain.

Agent Grant glanced at his Omega watch while leaving the room.

CHAPTER 25—SUNDAY 2:00PM

Mohammed woke up just as the movie ended and the credits began rolling. It took a few seconds to remember where he was.

He waited until he was one of the last ones there then stayed close to the crowd on their way out, mostly mothers and a few fathers with their children.

A gawky teenage employee stood by the door, typing a text message on his phone.

Mohammed slipped into a theatre across the hall that was already full of people. He quickly sat in the back row as the coming attractions played on the screen. After what seemed like an eternity, the movie started. It was a fast pace action movie that kept Mohammed wide-awake. The film lasted more than two hours and ended with a bang.

Mohammed knew it wasn't dark outside yet, so he decided to sneak into one more movie. He followed the crowd into the hall just as he had done before and prepared to make his move.

Just as he was about to slip into the next theatre, a security guard spotted him. Mohammed knew the security guard saw him, so he snuck across the back of the room in the dark as a horror movie played overhead.

The security guard must have anticipated Mohammed's next move. He entered through the door that Mohammed was ready to sneak out of.

The guard shined his flashlight in Mohammed's face. "Do you

have your stub, sir?"

Mohammed reached into his pocket while trying to keep the light out of his eyes. He found his ticket stub and handed it to the guard.

The security guard shined his flashlight on the stub and said, "This movie is across the hall, and this is a matinee ticket. You'll have to come with me, sir." He opened the door and gestured for Mohammed to leave the theatre.

Mohammed walked into the hall with the security guard who looked like a forty-something-year-old junkie trailing behind him. He proceeded through the lobby and headed for the front door.

The guard grabbed his arm and said, "Not so fast. You're gonna have to talk to my manager."

Mohammed pushed him away, almost knocking him down, then continued for the front door as people waiting in line for popcorn moved out of his way.

The security guard yelled while following Mohammed, "Stop right there!"

Mohammed pushed the front door open and left the building as fast as he possible without running.

He crossed Fifth Avenue and hurried down a crowded street following the setting sun as the streetlights began to turn on.

He wondered how he was supposed to sneak back into his apartment if he couldn't even sneak into a movie theatre.

CHAPTER 26—SUNDAY 5:56PM

Diane sat next to her brother Tony at the table in their parents' dining room. She watched him soak up the last of the tomato sauce on his plate with a piece of Semolina bread.

Tony asked, "Could you pass me another meatball, sis?"

Diane had told Tony a million times that his eating habits could lead to a premature death. The doctor had already warned him about his high cholesterol and blood pressure, but when it came to food, Tony did what he wanted. She just handed him the meatball and watched as he stuffed half of it into his mouth and bit it off.

Tony and Diane's parents, Mr. and Mrs. Lasalvo, sat at the two opposite ends of their long rectangular table. The French provincial, cherry veneer dining set was forty years old, but looked brand-new. A matching cherry veneer china cabinet filled with fine china, fancy wine glasses, and crystal vases took up most of the back wall.

Next to the china cabinet, the family dog, a thirteen-year-old white Maltese named Fluffy, laid asleep in its bed, a wicker basket with a pillow inside.

Mr. and Mrs. Lasalvo both had thick black hair and dark brown eyes like Diane, unlike Tony's thin light brown hair and hazel eyes. Diane enjoyed teasing Tony when they were children. She said their parents found him in a garbage can and adopted him.

Tonight's dinner was quieter than usual. Everyone knew how

Diane was feeling about Officer Armstrong's death. Tony had asked her a few questions about it when dinner started, but Diane said she couldn't discuss the case. No one mentioned it again after that, but no one mentioned much of anything after that.

Diane decided to break the silence. She looked at Tony's wife across the table and said, "The meatballs were delicious, Angela."

"Thank you." Tony's wife, Angela, was short and plump with shoulder-length black hair that framed her round face.

Tony and Angela's daughters, eighteen-year-old Bianca and sixteen-year-old Maria, sat next to their mother. Both girls were thin and cute with long brown hair. Maria, however, had the same hook nose that her grandfather and her Aunt Diane had.

Bianca and Maria left the dining room when everyone except their father, who was still eating fried meatballs, started to smoke.

Tony inspected Diane's scabbed up face and said, "It's not that bad. Just keep the ointment on it. Remember that time I scraped up my whole forearm at work?" He showed her his arm and said, "Can't even tell."

Mrs. Lasalvo stood and put some table scraps into Fluffy's bowl as the ancient dog lifted its head to eat. She then took off her apron, headed into the kitchen, and returned with a deck of cards.

Diane looked at the new beige sweater with a brown turkey print her mother was wearing. "Where'd you get that sweater, Ma?"

Mrs. Lasalvo brushed a piece of lint off her black pants before looking at the sweater and said, "Lois made it for me."

Angela said, "Very cute."

"Thank you." With her cigarette dangling from her lips, Mrs. Lasalvo sat at the table, adjusted her glasses, and shuffled the cards seven times. She dealt seven cards each, placed the stack of cards in the middle of the table face-down, and turned one card over.

Tony's wife took a card from the top of the deck and slipped it into the cards in her hand. She flicked an ash off her cigarette before discarding, placing an unwanted card from her hand face-up on top of the single card next to the stack.

Angela looked at Tony and said, "Hey, Tony, what was the name of that new guy at your job? You know, the new supervisor."

Mr. Lasalvo drew a card from the top of the deck and studied the cards in his hand.

Tony said, "Who? James?"

Mr. Lasalvo discarded the same card he had just picked up.

Angela said, "Yeah, James." She turned to Diane and said, "He's a very successful and attractive man."

Diane took a card from the deck and kept it. Before discarding, she said, "That's nice." She knew what Angela was getting at, and she wanted to end it before it started, before her mother started on her soapbox about settling down, getting married, and having children.

Diane had already been married and divorced by the time she was twenty-one, but she never had children. She always said she would consider starting a family after she made it to detective. Now she was a detective and still didn't feel ready. Women were having babies in their forties all the time now. Why not her? What's the rush?

Diane changed the subject by saying, "Hey, Tony, what happened with those two guys on the scaffold the other day?"

Tony picked up a card from the deck and finished chewing the piece of Italian bread in his mouth before answering. "One guy died. The other guy lived, but he's a vegetable now. Can you believe it? Forty-six floors and the poor bastard is still alive." Tony threw a card down on the discard pile.

Mrs. Lasalvo said, "I hate to hear those stories. It always makes me think of you all the way up there. I wish you didn't have to do that damn job."

Tony spoke with his mouth full. "I gotta pay the bills right?" He took a sip of soda to wash down the food and said, "Don't worry, Ma. I'm a professional. I always got my belt hooked up. There's more chance of getting in a car accident than a scaffold accident." He pointed at the deck of cards on the table and said, "Your turn, Ma."

Mrs. Lasalvo picked up a card and looked at it.

Angela said, "I hate to hear those stories, too. You just better make sure you're safe up there, Tony."

Tony placed his hand on his swollen stomach and burped. "I'm safe, don't worry."

Diane and Angela shook their heads at the same time.

Mrs. Lasalvo continued staring at the card in her hand.

Mr. Lasalvo said, "How long are you gonna look at that card?"

Mrs. Lasalvo leveled her gaze. "I'll look at this card as long as I want to. You just shut up, old man."

"What did I tell you about telling me to shut up?"

Diane lit another cigarette, took a deep drag, then said, "Will you two stop already?"

They continued their game of Rummy 500 for about an hour.

After the game, Mrs. Lasalvo went to the kitchen and returned with a pot of hot coffee. Diane helped with the cups.

Angela opened a box of cookies and a box of pastries and placed them on the table.

Tony reached out for a pignoli cookie and called into the living room, "Girls! Dessert!"

His daughters came back in and surveyed the cookies and pastries on the table as their father swallowed his cookie, then stuffed a cannoli halfway into his mouth. The girls each took two seven-layer cookies and hurried back into the living room to watch TV.

Tony spoke with his mouth full. "Those girls never eat."

His wife said, "They eat plenty."

Diane said, "Just be grateful they don't eat like you."

Tony laughed. "I'd have to get a second job." He stuffed the rest of the cannoli into his mouth and licked the excess cream from his fingers.

After coffee and dessert, everyone lit another cigarette and filled the last few pockets of clean air with fresh smoke while Tony opened a window and forced a few extra cookies down his throat.

They hung around talking and drinking coffee until 9PM when Tony told his wife and kids to get their coats. Everyone hugged and kissed each other before Tony left with his family.

Diane locked the front door then helped her mother clean up in the kitchen before kissing her parents goodnight.

Trying to keep her weight off her twisted ankle, she proceeded up the stairs to her apartment on the second floor.

Diane's father retired from the sugar factory in Williamsburg last year, but he'd finished paying off the house years ago. They didn't want their daughter to pay rent, but Diane refused to live there free, so she paid them a small amount of rent, took care of her own utilities, and everyone was happy. It was just after she'd finalized her divorce and began working at the NYPD when she took the apartment over sixteen years ago.

Diane's furniture was also French provincial, and in the same perfect condition as her mother's furniture, but it was made of oak, and she kept it polished to a high shine.

Everything was in place and spotless. Family pictures covered most of the walls. A huge oil painting hung in the center of the living room wall that depicted a man rowing an empty gondola down a canal in Venice. She had gotten the painting on her honeymoon in Italy when she was nineteen years old. She always wanted to go back to Europe, but never got around to it.

A gigantic orange and white cat meowed when Diane entered the apartment. She bent down and stroked its back a few times. "Don't tell me you're hungry again." She poured a little dry food in the cat's empty bowl and refilled its water bowl.

Family time was over. Her mind went back to catching that cop-killer.

Diane strapped on her shoulder holster, loaded a clip into her 9mm service pistol, and checked the safety. She attached her NYPD detective's badge onto her belt then threw on the beige blazer that matched the beige pants she was wearing. She grabbed a big blue police jacket from the closet and took it with her. The bulletproof vest waited in her locker at the precinct.

CHAPTER 27—SUNDAY 10:30PM

At the edge of Brooklyn, across the street from a row of apartment buildings, Mohammed sat on a wooden bench overlooking the highway that ran along the coast. He shivered as an icy breeze shot right through him. He gazed ahead at the choppy water in the harbor and thought about how cold it must be. He could never make it to safety. Even if he did know how to swim, he would probably freeze to death.

He lifted his head and stared at the illuminated skyscrapers that made up the lower Manhattan skyline in the distance. The midtown skyscrapers were too far away to see, but the red, orange, and yellow Thanksgiving lights that illuminated the very top of the Empire State Building were visible all the way from 34th Street.

While gazing out at the city and the harbor, and thinking about his situation, Mohammed decided again that going home would be too dangerous. He thought the cover of night would make him feel more confident about going home, but it didn't. He was still scared.

As he tried to figure out his next move, his eyelids began to close. He fought to keep them open, but they tried to close again.

A cop car cruised down the quiet street behind him. Instantly awake, Mohammed tried to act natural and hoped the cop wouldn't notice him.

After waiting for the car to pass, he shuffled down a dirt slope that led to the highway below. Before reaching the concrete wall at the edge of the asphalt, he found a fence that blocked access to a garbage-filled area under a concrete pedestrian overpass. It smelled like urine, but he knew he had to get some rest or he wouldn't make it anywhere, and he had a feeling no one would find him here. He climbed over the fence, trying to ignore the stench.

At the base of the graffiti-covered concrete column, Mohammed curled up into a ball, pulled the orange hood over his head, and closed his eyes. He thought about the bearded old homeless man whom he saw on the train a few days ago and wondered how many homeless people were really fugitives with nowhere to turn. He didn't want this to be his new home. He needed a plan.

CHAPTER 28—SUNDAY 11:08PM

While lying in bed wearing just his briefs, Andrew watched the Channel 5 news on a 20-inch LCD TV. Two new pinewood dressers and nightstands sat against the off-white walls on either side of the bed. Amy's parents had bought them the bedroom set while vacationing in New York for Labor Day weekend. Amy's father owned a successful chain of tax accounting offices in San Diego and did quite well financially.

Andrew, however, didn't come from such a privileged background. His father left before he was born. He grew up in a trailer park in Arizona with his mother, who always had some new loser boyfriend. He watched her drink herself into oblivion until he was eighteen. That's when he joined the marines and never looked back.

Andrew tried to pay attention to the news on TV, but his mind was on work. Not only was he unhappy about his boring new financial case, but now his boss made him miss a Sunday with his family, for nothing. What kind of job was this? At least Agent Grant never came back at 3PM and Andrew was able to get home in time for dinner.

He was grateful that his wife supported him in his career choice, but he also felt guilty for taking her away from her family and friends.

A commercial finished and the news came back on. The weatherman gave the forecast: cold, but no rain, at least for a few days. Another commercial played, and Andrew began to fall asleep involuntarily.

The bedroom door opened and so did his eyes.

Amy strolled into the room in her heavy flannel pajamas. She closed and locked the door behind her before taking off her pajama top and revealing a tight black tank top. She said, "It feels warm in here tonight."

Andrew said, "Do you want me to lower the heat?"

"No," she replied. "I like it."

She climbed into bed and snuggled against him. Her freshly washed, creamy skin felt good against his body.

He kissed her and said, "I'm sorry I had to work today."

"It's okay. Just try not to make a habit of it."

He smiled, gave her another kiss, and held her close. Commercials continued to play on the TV while they continued kissing. He savored the sweet aroma of her shampooed hair and perfumed skin while she kissed the side of his face and neck. She caressed his bare chest and abs while his skin tingled and his mind drifted away into a peaceful slumber.

CHAPTER 29—MONDAY 12:00AM

Diane drove the unmarked gray police car up 181st Street on their way to look for Terek's girl, Ericka. It was only a few blocks to the Grand Concourse—three separate roadways separated by two concrete dividers. She turned and crossed all six lanes before double parking on the corner.

They went back to the store from last night and asked the man behind the counter if he'd seen Ericka tonight. He had not.

They sat in their car and waited, watching. Diane wondered if this was a waste of time, but there weren't any other leads, other than those the homicide detectives were already following.

Down the block, Diane noticed two big girls leaning against a parked car smoking cigarettes and laughing. She could see them clearly under a bright streetlight. "Either of those two could fit the description of Ericka."

Garcia looked over at them and said, "Let's check them out."

They drove up the block, double-parked, got out of their car, and approached the two girls.

Garcia pulled out his badge and asked, "Excuse me. Are either of you Ericka?"

Both girls stood away from the car and backed up, clearly scared.

Diane stood with her badge out and said, "We're not here for you. We need to find Terek. He's in danger. Serious danger."

The taller of the two girls, answered, "I know. Some guys

came by looking for him a couple hours ago."

"What did they look like?" asked Garcia.

"Three of them waited in the car. I only saw one of them. He was short, light skinned . . . said he was from the Lenox Avenue Homicides. He said he was going to kill Terek. I told him I didn't know where Terek was. He pointed a gun at me and said that I better not be lying or he would kill me, too."

The other girl said, "It's true, I saw everything."

Diane asked, "What kind of car were they in?"

"I don't know. I think it was orange or yellow. It was a little car."

The other girl said, "Yeah, it was orange, or, maybe it was . . . no, no, it was orange."

Diane could smell that the girls had been smoking weed, so she doubted the accuracy of their memories.

Garcia said, "If you see Terek—"

The tall girl said, "Terek was already here."

"What? When?" asked Garcia.

"About a half hour ago. I told him about the guys that were looking for him, and then he bounced. He didn't tell me where he was going, but I bet he went to that old abandoned building on Webster Av."

Diane and Garcia jumped into their car and drove a few blocks to Webster Avenue where they found a reminder of how the Bronx had looked thirty years ago, an old, condemned, three-story building rotting away. Broken concrete slabs covered the first floor windows and loose rotten sheets of plywood covered the second and third floor windows.

Garcia said, "Park across the street so we could scope it out."

Diane passed the building, made a U-turn at the intersection, then double-parked across the street. They sat and waited.

Just as she lit a cigarette, she noticed four young men wearing black skullcaps sitting in an old yellow Toyota parked on the corner at the far end of the block. Either they were there before, or she must have been too busy looking at the abandoned building to notice them pulling up. Without taking her eyes off the Toyota on the corner, Diane said, "Hey, Garcia—"

Garcia said, "There he goes."

Diane turned her head and saw Terek as he passed under a streetlight, going toward the abandoned building. She knew it was him because of his red down jacket and the way he looked over his shoulder constantly as he walked.

Garcia opened the door and stepped out of the car.

A young man jumped out of the Toyota and hurried with something in his hand toward Terek on the sidewalk.

Diane jumped out of the car as the Toyota pulled out of its spot. Her ankle still hurt a little, but it was healed enough for her to walk without limping. She pointed her gun at the man moving toward Terek and yelled, "Stop, Police!"

Everything seemed to happen so fast. The young man on the sidewalk sprinted toward Terek and fired a bullet into his face. Blood sprayed as Terek collapsed and went into convulsions on the sidewalk. The young man put another slug into Terek then pointed his gun at Diane and Garcia and started shooting.

Diving behind a parked car for cover, Diane and Garcia opened fire. The young man returned fire while trying to make his way toward the street where the Toyota had pulled up and was waiting for him.

The three men inside the car started shooting. Diane and Garcia stayed down while leaping onto the sidewalk and behind the car. There were too many of them, and they had no moral dilemmas about killing cops.

Diane saw her opening when the young man who shot Terek sprinted toward the Toyota. The door opened. Just as he tried jumping into the back seat, Diane peeked out and fired two shots. One missed, and one hit him in the shoulder making him lose his balance. She fired two more shots as the car moved forward. Both bullets hit him in the body. He fell to the street.

The men inside the Toyota continued shooting out their windows as they sped off into the distance, leaving their friend bleeding on the street.

A cop car with flashing lights sped toward the scene. It slowed down. Diane yelled, "Get that Toyota!" The cop car screeched away after the Toyota as Diane approached Garcia and the body on the floor.

Garcia said, "I got the plate." He picked up his radio and called in the license plate number while checking the young man's pulse. "He's dead."

"Let the coroner worry about this garbage."

Garcia said, "Give me the keys."

Diane threw him the keys on their way across the street and back to their car. She jumped into the passenger seat and loaded a fresh clip into her gun. Garcia burned the tires while making a U-turn and taking off the same way the Toyota went.

Diane felt her left arm stinging. She looked down. Blood dripped from her sleeve. She pulled the saturated material away from the wound and winced.

Garcia saw her arm and said, "You're hit."

The hole in her blazer revealed that the bullet just grazed her skin. "It's nothing, just grazed the skin. Keep going."

She turned up the police radio and listened for the Toyota's position. Police were in pursuit going north on Webster Avenue. Garcia threw the siren onto the dashboard and started it up while stepping on the gas.

It only took a few minutes to reach the chase in progress.

Two patrol cars chased the Toyota as it turned left on East Fordham Road, going the wrong way. Oncoming traffic steered out of the way to avoid colliding with the Toyota. A small truck smashed one of the police cars, both of them skidding out of control.

Garcia followed the other police car as it whipped around the corner. The concrete divider ended and the Toyota zipped over to the right side. Another patrol car joined the chase. They continued a few more blocks until reaching the Grand Concourse.

The Toyota spun around the corner, making a right turn.

The first patrol car turned too wide and smashed into the concrete divider with metal guardrails.

Garcia spun the steering wheel around as the car roared around the corner. Diane held the dashboard. She had no idea Garcia could drive like this.

The other patrol car slowed down while taking the corner.

It was a long straight run, one lane. The Toyota's small engine was no match for the big Chevy. Garcia held his foot down on the gas pedal and stayed glued to the Toyota's ass.

The guardrails ended at the intersection. The Toyota sped through the red light. Garcia followed. The Toyota continued forward as the lanes opened up. Garcia pulled up, almost next to them. Someone in the car started shooting. Garcia fell back a few feet. Diane wanted to shoot back, but didn't want to risk hitting someone in a passing car.

The light at the intersection was already red as they approached. Two pedestrians took their time crossing the street in the crosswalk. The Toyota kept going. It smashed into one of the pedestrians, hurling the body across the street.

Garcia stepped on the brakes to avoid the other pedestrian. The car screeched to a stop, but he lost control and smashed into a mailbox on the corner.

The patrol car behind him slowed down to check Diane and Garcia.

Diane yelled out her window at the cop in his car. "We're fine! Go get them!"

The cop peeled out up Grand Concourse as another patrol car pulled up to the scene.

Garcia pulled rank and took the young cop's car. He told the cop to call for an ambulance and stay with the injured pedestrian until help arrived.

Diane turned to Garcia and said, "I'll leave the driving to you."

They jumped into the patrol car and took off up the concourse with sirens blaring.

The woman on the radio reported that the patrol cars lost the Toyota when it crossed the divider onto the other side of the concourse. Two helicopters in the area were searching for them.

Diane said, "If the helicopters can't find them—"

"They must be under the L." Garcia made a left turn onto a two-way street with brick apartment buildings on both sides.

Jerome Avenue was only a few blocks away. They stopped at the corner and looked ahead at the steel tracks of the 4-train above.

Garcia turned the siren off. "I wonder which way they went."

"Maybe left," said Diane, "on their way back to Manhattan."

Garcia watched a car wait to turn as another car passed in front of it. "The right turn is faster, especially if cars are passing."

She took this opportunity to light up a smoke. "So go right." She pulled the fabric away from the burning wound on her arm and cringed as it took flesh and blood with it. "Just when my face is starting to heal up. I need this?"

Garcia approached the intersection, hesitated for a minute, then turned right. "They could have abandoned the car and took the train."

"That's true." Diane scanned the cars parked in front of the empty stores and quiet apartment buildings as Garcia cruised. She wondered who that pedestrian was. She could still hear the smack of the body against the Toyota's grill.

The woman on the radio said one of the helicopters spotted the Toyota on West Kingsbridge Road, crossing the expressway onto 225th Street.

Diane said, "How the hell did they get all the way up there so fast? And without anyone noticing them?"

Garcia turned the siren back on and picked up speed. After a few blocks, he made a left turn onto West Kingsbridge Road and sped past a gigantic red brick building that looked like a castle complete with turrets and a moat, the Eighth Regiment Armory. They sped past block after block of closed stores and restaurants, weaving in and out of the sparse traffic.

The woman on the radio said the helicopters last saw the Toyota turning north on Broadway, under the elevated train.

Garcia barreled forward, then whipped the patrol car around the corner, onto Broadway, following a few other patrol cars that were already on their way. Diane peered out her window, trying to spot the Toyota, but the only thing she saw were flashing police lights.

They followed the other patrol cars as they turned left on 240th Street. After a few blocks, the street ended, and so did the chase. The Toyota was wrapped around a tree, the driver's dead body hanging halfway out the window.

The other two men hid behind their twisted car and opened fire on the cops. The cops fired back. Bullets ricocheted off parked cars and metal fences.

Diane and Garcia got out of their car and hid behind it. They tried to get an open shot, but there were too many obstacles.

The two men sprinted up the asphalt path behind them.

The cops took one of them down, but the other one disappeared into the darkness.

Diane knew the man who got away was the tall thin man from the other night. She recognized him by the way he moved. The adrenaline in her blood masked the pain in her ankle and arm as she sprinted toward the smashed Toyota. She was the first cop to move.

Garcia yelled, "Diane, stop!"

She didn't stop. She knew she should stop, but the image of

Armstrong's corpse and the memory of her telling him to guard the staircase haunted her. It wouldn't bring him back, but Diane felt she owed it to him to bring his killer to justice.

Other cops raced after Diane as she followed the path up to a small, three-way intersection. Apartment buildings lined one side of the street behind her. The other two streets were dark and narrow and lined on both sides by trees. She looked ahead and didn't see anything but darkness.

Uniformed cops scoured the area with their flashlights.

Someone yelled, "Stop! Police!"

Two gunshots echoed throughout the quiet area as Diane instinctively hid behind a parked car. Cops swarmed as the helicopter spotlight illuminated everything.

The thin man raced up the street, toward a fence.

Diane yelled, "He's there!"

Everyone bolted forward. The man climbed over the fence. Some of the cops followed him, but many couldn't make it.

Another gunshot echoed throughout the night sky. Diane climbed over the fence and found herself on the roof of a small building. She tried keeping her balance on the slanted rubber roof. Below her stood a wall of metal vents, the wall from another building next door.

There were about a dozen of these identical little red brick buildings, all connected. Each building had one wall higher than the other, a sloped roof ended at the bottom of the next building's high wall. At the end of the row of buildings sat a bigger square building.

The helicopters continued to hover overhead, shining their spotlights, scanning the entire area. The killer was somewhere in the train yard below.

Diane shimmied her way down the slanted roof to the wall below. She tried to see over the wall, but she was too short. While balancing herself against the metal vents, she stepped closer to the front edge and looked down. Below her were a dozen train tracks, some empty, but most occupied by out-of-service subway trains. Two uniformed cops shined their flashlights while walking across the tracks, then stepped out of sight between two train cars.

Diane wondered how they got down there. She noticed that each small building had a cast iron pipe coming down from the roof for drainage. She decided to give it a shot.

Before climbing down the pipe, she scanned the area below once more, then thought about what her mother would say if she knew what she was doing. But she wasn't doing this for nothing. This was for Armstrong.

While holding onto the pipe, she got down on her butt and slid her body off the roof. With her feet against the wall, she shimmied down the pipe.

She was already almost down when she heard another gunshot. She let go of the pipe and let herself fall down the last few feet, landing on her back, and knocking the wind out of her lungs.

On the ground, she rolled over onto her belly, took out her weapon, and released the safety while scanning the area.

The lampposts and helicopters above provided plenty of light, but that didn't help her see between the trains. She stayed down, looking around. She was on a concrete sidewalk that ran in front the little brick buildings. The sidewalk ran parallel with the tracks ahead. Diane couldn't see anything below the tracks, but she knew the entire train yard was elevated above the ground at least twenty feet.

Why didn't the helicopters see anything? Maybe he was inside one of the buildings. She glanced both ways and noticed that only one building had a door, a solid steel door. Each of the other buildings had vents in front of them, but they were all in place. How else could he have gotten in? She wondered if he might have gotten into one of the trains.

Two gunshots rang out. The sound came from the tracks. Then two more. Even with the chopper blades above, the blasts shattered the silence and lingered on in the cold night air.

Diane stayed down, looking under the trains. She saw a shadow. She saw movement. Her blood pumped faster.

She sprang to her feet and bolted across the tracks. The pain in her ankle returned, but she didn't care. She moved forward, jumping over the third rail that she knew carried 770 volts, but hoped would be out of service now. She held her breathing in while sneaking around the train car ahead. Someone came at her. She fired. It was a cop. She hit him. The cop went down.

"Shit!" Diane raced toward the cop and knelt next to him. He was alive. "Stay down." She noticed the bullet buried in his shoulder, and she knew he was in pain, but he would live.

A cop from the helicopter yelled over a loud speaker, "Drop

your gun!"

Diane thought they were talking to her. Maybe they didn't know she was a cop. If she had to drop her gun, she would be wide-open to the thin man. Before her mind had a chance to assess the situation, the helicopter spotlight passed over her and settled behind her.

She spun around, gun in hand. The thin man stuck his head out from between two trains and fired at Diane. At the same time, a cop hanging out of the helicopter door with a rifle shot at the thin man. The thin man missed Diane and the helicopter sniper missed the thin man.

Diane knelt and fired two shots as the thin man lunged back into his hiding spot between two trains. Both shots hit steel and echoed as they ricocheted away. She grabbed the cop on the ground and helped him to his feet. "Take cover."

Both helicopter spotlights focused on the same area where the thin man was hiding. Diane knew if they had a shot, they would have taken it already. It was up to her and the injured cop. More cops should be on their way, but even a few seconds could mean life or death.

The injured cop hid between two trains, holding his gun with his left hand while his right arm hung limp at his side. He yelled to Diane as she hid behind another train car on the other side, "I can't shoot with my left hand!"

Just as Diane motioned with her finger for him to be quiet, the thin man jumped out and fired twice. Diane was just about to return fire when she heard the rifle from the helicopter—three consecutive shots—each shot leaving behind a sonic boom.

She peeked out and saw the thin man under the helicopter's spotlight, lying across the tracks, dead.

CHAPTER 30—MONDAY 5:30AM

Andrew had already been up for an hour. He was showered, dressed, and ready to walk out the door. He kissed his kids while they slept then he headed into his room to kiss his wife before leaving.

Amy was awake when he entered the room. He leaned down to kiss her, but she rolled over, away from him, avoiding his kiss.

He knew why she was mad. "Honey, I'm sorry I fell asleep on you last night. I've just been so exhausted."

She didn't say anything. He went around to the other side of the bed, but she turned away from him again.

He quickly kissed her on the back of the head before she could move away farther then he said, "I'm going to work. I love you."

She didn't answer, so he went to the door, opened it, and stepped out of the room.

Just as he closed the door, he heard Amy say, "Andrew."

He opened the door and peered in at her.

She said, "I love you, too. But I'm still mad at you."

Andrew smiled as he turned around and left.

Outside, a thick cold fog made everything invisible. He could only see a few feet ahead while walking, and it wasn't much better when driving. The streets and highways were deserted. Even going slow, Andrew made it to the city early.

Maintenance people were just finishing up for the night when

Andrew entered the glass office building downtown.

He showed his ID while passing security then headed into the elevator.

Upstairs, he approached Agent Grant's office and noticed the door partially open. The office was still quiet as a few people stared like zombies at computer screens in their cubicles.

He noticed the sound of heavy breathing coming from inside. It sounded like someone sleeping. He snuck a look inside the office and saw Agent Grant snoozing on a recliner chair in his plush oversized office. The desk and bookcases were solid oak, the recliner and the sofa against the wall were black leather, and the hardwood floor appeared as if it had been polished daily.

Agent Grant got out of his chair as if he'd never been sleeping. Like a vampire from his coffin. Startled, Andrew stepped away from the door.

The door opened. Fully awake, Agent Grant said, "Come in, Agent Miller."

Andrew stepped into the office.

Agent Grant opened a mini-refrigerator in the corner. He took out a bottle of Perrier and offered one to Andrew.

Andrew showed Agent Grant a pair of thermoses, one full of coffee and one of water. "Thank you, sir, but I brought my own."

Agent Grant tried to straighten out the wrinkles in his expensive pants then put his jacket on. "All set, Agent Miller. Time to get to work."

CHAPTER 31—MONDAY 8:23AM

Mohammed woke up to the long deep sound of a cargo ship's foghorn echoing throughout the dense mist. Another foghorn, slightly higher pitched, answered the first, then another, and another. It sounded like whales singing to each other. He knew the ships were close, but the only thing he saw was fog.

Heavy traffic crawled on the highway just a few feet below. Mohammed could barely see the cars, but he clearly saw their lights and heard their horns. The sun was out, but scarcely visible between the fog on the ground and the clouds overhead. He could smell and taste the moisture in the air.

Balled up under the filthy concrete overpass, shivering from the cold, he tried to forget the nightmares he had throughout most of the night. There were no bombs exploding this time. It was always Mohamed running for his life. Sometimes cops and agents chased him, other times terrorists chased him. The faces in his dreams seemed to morph back and forth, people constantly changing their identities. Mohammed died in a few dreams, but in one of them, he flapped his arms as if they were wings and flew away like a bird. Although he wished he really could fly away, he knew that was only possible in dreamland. In real life, he needed money.

He decided he had no other choice but to go home for his bankcard and his cell phone, if they were still there. Even if the cops did take everything, he still had five hundred dollars in cash hidden inside a rolled up pair of socks in his closet. He hoped they didn't find that.

After climbing over the fence, he tried to brush the filth off his clothes the best he could before trudging back up the dirt slope through the trees to the bench-lined sidewalk of Shore Road. He crossed over to the other side of the street and headed east while passing numerous four and six story brick apartment buildings.

Mohammed shivered then sneezed. His head was congested. He knew he was getting sick. There couldn't be a worse time. He remembered lying to his mother about being sick. Now the lie had come back to him.

After a few blocks, spacious houses with expensive cars parked in their driveways lined the streets between the avenues. Most of the houses were over-decorated for Thanksgiving, as if there were a competition in the neighborhood.

It took almost thirty minutes to reach the train station on 4th Avenue, where once again, apartment buildings and stores dominated the landscape. He still heard the sound of foghorns signaling each other in the distance. The thick fog reminded him of the winters back home.

Before going down the stairs to the subway, Mohammed glanced at himself in a store window. The bright clothes were already faded and filthy, his thick black hair and beard were matted, and his face was dirty.

The stairs, the station, and the trains were all crowded with people going to work, and they all kept their distance from Mohammed.

It took about twenty minutes on the R-train to reach 9th Street, where he exited the train and climbed four flights of stairs along with the crowd of commuters.

Hundreds of people scampered in all directions as Mohammed waited for the G-train to arrive on the elevated platform.

The F-train arrived first. Mohammed stood back against the wall while people got off the train and other people got on.

As the noise from the departing train faded away, only the rhythmic sound of hard wood tapping on concrete remained. A tall Russian girl with long blonde hair, wearing a short skirt and tall boots, sashayed down the platform, leaving a trail of perfume all the way to the stairs. All of the men and some of the women stared as she passed.

Mohammed remembered the only time in his life he'd ever been with a woman. He was nineteen and in the Army. Recently stationed in Kashmir, a group of young soldiers took him to a brothel. They didn't tell him where they were taking him, and he didn't figure it out until it was too late. Upon entering a dark room full of women lounging on big sofas and chairs, a beautiful South Indian woman clamped onto Mohammed and led him into a small room with a mattress on the floor. His mind turned off and his animal instinct took over.

He'd always felt guilty for that night, and now, hypnotized by this tall blonde, he felt the same lust and the same guilt. He asked God to forgive him. He wondered if everything that was happening to him now was punishment for that one night of fornication.

The platform began to rumble below his feet. Mohammed glanced up and saw headlights. The G-train was on its way. The train screeched to a stop and the doors opened. After waiting for one crowd to exit, Mohammed followed another crowd into the train. The doors closed.

The train rumbled along the elevated tracks to one more station before descending underground. After a few stops, they arrived at Hoyt-Schermerhorn, where Mohammed got off.

The A-train was already there with its doors still open, waiting for the commuters from the connecting G-train. Mohammed hurried onto the A-train and stayed away from everyone while watching for his stop, Nostrand Avenue.

Once he was outside on the street, Mohammed had to look around for a moment before knowing which way to go. This wasn't the same train station he usually used. The G-train let him off at Nostrand and Lafayette, a few blocks from where he lived. Now he was on Fulton Street, at least fifteen, maybe twenty blocks from where he lived. He decided to come this way in case anyone was looking for him at his usual station.

Most of the stores' gates were still down. The only stores open at the time were a small coffee shop and a small grocery store. The only people on the streets were commuters going to the train or the bus, mostly going into Manhattan.

Mohammed turned the corner and headed north on Nostrand Avenue.

A skinny young girl with bloodshot eyes approached

Mohammed and said, "Hey, baby, need a date?"

Mohammed knew she was a prostitute, and she looked sick, so he tried to stay away from her without being rude. This was the type of woman his father had warned him about. He passed her, staying a few feet away, and said, "I don't have any money."

She responded by saying, "Your loss."

Mohammed picked up the pace as he continued north on Nostrand Avenue. He thought about how dirty he looked and knew that girl must have been desperate to approach him.

He stopped a few streets before his building and went around the block to the next avenue where he waited for two women to pass before climbing a fence into an empty lot. He searched through the garbage people had dumped there: toys, clothes, boxes, a broken sink. After finding a couple milk crates, Mohammed turned one over emptying the garbage from it, then he looked around.

Through the fence he saw a few people strolling by on the sidewalk. They didn't even pay attention to him. He looked like a homeless man doing homeless man things.

With one of the milk crates in his hand, Mohammed dashed through the tall weeds of the vacant lot to another fence on the opposite side. He waited for an old man to pass then threw the milk crate over as gently as possible.

He looked around. Cars zipped by on the street, but the sidewalk was clear. Before going over, he stood there for a moment, wondering if this was a mistake. Maybe he should turn back. He considered his options and decided he had to take the risk. Mohammed climbed over the fence.

Standing on the sidewalk on the side of his building, just outside his landlord's kitchen window, Mohammed stood the milk crate on its side and used it as a step. It caved in on itself just as he jumped up and grabbed the bottom rung of the fire escape ladder.

He pulled himself up then climbed the ladder until he was on the second floor platform. There was no one above him, so he stood against the wall and let his body rest for a moment before tiptoeing up the metal stairs to the third floor.

Standing against the wall outside his kitchen window, Mohammed waited for his heart rate to slow down, but it never did. He peeked into the window at the latch. It was unlocked.

Before opening it, he waited to see if he could hear or see

anyone inside. The lights were off, but the sun gave him enough light to see. The apartment seemed to be empty. He wondered if it really was. He considered how much money it would cost to keep someone here twenty-four hours a day. Maybe there was no one here. Once again, he thought about turning back, but after thinking it over for a few minutes, he decided to continue with his plan and just have faith that God would protect him.

After a few minutes, Mohammed built up enough nerve to open the window. He pushed his hands flat against the glass to get it started then inserted his fingers under the old wood frame. He eased it up, trying not to make any noise.

With the window halfway open, he moved away, against the wall. His entire body trembled. He inhaled then exhaled, trying to calm himself. He just wanted to get it over with.

After peeking inside one last time, Mohammed eased the window the rest of the way up, then climbed into the kitchen. He surveyed the empty kitchen while creeping toward the living room entrance. While standing there, he heard something move in the other room, and it didn't sound like his kitten. It was too late go back outside now. If someone was there, he would have to fight.

He stepped back and slowly opened a drawer next to the stove where he kept the knives. He didn't want to kill anyone, but he was willing to stab someone in the arm or the leg if it meant avoiding capture.

Someone came in and turned on the light.

Mohammed snatched the biggest knife from the drawer and held it up, ready to attack.

He lowered his weapon when he saw it was his landlord, Nasir.

Nasir stepped back, startled, bumping into the wall.

A voice came from the other room. "You okay in there?"

Nasir motioned with his finger against his mouth for Mohammed to be quiet then answered the man in the other room, "I'm fine." Nasir opened a cabinet, took out a can of cat food, and closed the cabinet.

Mohammed was near the window, still grasping the knife, ready to jump out onto the fire escape.

Before leaving the kitchen, and without making a sound, Nasir pointed at himself, then at the floor, then at Mohammed and the fire escape.

Mohammed knew what Nasir was telling him. He snuck out the window and made his way back down the fire escape to the first floor, trying not to make any noise. He didn't lower the ladder. He climbed down and let himself drop from the bottom rung, but this time he planned it better, and he was wearing something on his feet. With his knees bent, he landed on the sidewalk about a foot away from the crushed milk crate, without injury.

He looked both ways before throwing the milk crate back over the fence then tapping on Nasir's kitchen window. No one answered. He waited a few seconds, then tapped again, a little harder.

Nasir's twenty-one-year-old daughter, Fatima, opened the blinds and jumped back. She looked closer then opened the window and asked, "Mohammed? What are you doing out there?"

"Your father told me to come."

She opened the window and held Mohammed's arm as he climbed into the kitchen and over the counter. She closed the window and the blinds. Fatima was a bit chubby, but pretty. Although her Hijab covered her hair, her thick lips, high cheekbones, and big brown eyes were mesmerizing. Not only was she pretty, but she was also a sweet and intelligent girl. If he were not already engaged, Mohammed certainly would have considered her for marriage.

She asked Mohammed if he wanted something to drink. He asked for water. He knew she wanted to ask what happened in his apartment, but she never did.

Within just a few minutes, Nasir came into the kitchen and said, "There is a man in your living room, there is always one there. They just sit on your sofa and wait for you to come back."

Mohammed said, "I did not want to come back, but I need my bank card, and my cell phone, and my passport . . . if it is still there."

Nasir motioned for his daughter to leave the room. She did.

He turned to Mohammed and said, "Everything is gone. I saw them take it. I woke up early yesterday morning and heard the police upstairs. What happened?"

Mohammed told Nasir everything that had happened since they last spoke.

Nasir gave Mohammed a piece of flat bread.

Mohammed ate the bread and said, "Thank you. How is my

baby cat?"

"I am taking care of her. She is in your bedroom. They let me go your apartment to give her food and water twice a day. You are very lucky I was there when you snuck in."

"I asked Allah to protect me."

"And he did." Nasir took some money out of his pocket and counted it, a little over sixty dollars. He handed it to Mohammed and said, "Here, it's all I have on me."

Mohammed took the money and thanked him.

Nasir asked, "What will you do?"

Mohammed thought about it for a moment then answered, "I don't know what to do, but I cannot run forever."

Nasir said, "You must find the real terrorists. Only then can you prove your innocence."

Nasir gave him more bread and some chicken from the refrigerator. Mohammed devoured it. He didn't care that it was cold.

He thanked Nasir then snuck out the way he came in, through the window and over the fence.

After walking for about fifteen minutes, Mohammed passed Fulton Street and noticed shoppers beginning to fill the streets and stores. He decided to continue another block or two then wait for the bus. Without anyone's phone number, he would have to go find his other good friend and ask for his help in person. He didn't want to put anyone at risk, but he had no one else to turn to.

He crossed Atlantic Avenue under the steel tracks of the Long Island Railroad and stood at the bus stop on the corner of Nostrand Avenue. The morning rush hour crowd was gone, but there were still quite a few people waiting for the bus. Grocery stores and dollar stores were full of shoppers while barbershops and restaurants were just rolling up their gates.

The bus arrived and Mohammed let everyone else on first before getting on behind them. He inserted his Metrocard into the slot then stood near the front of the bus holding onto the metal pole above his head. Knowing how bad he looked, he tried to stay away from everyone.

The bus took off down Nostrand Avenue, passing grocery stores, nail salons, and Laundromats, miles and miles of stores with apartments above them.

It took about an hour before finally arriving at Avenue U

where Mohammed got off the bus and went around the corner to wait for another bus.

There wasn't much going on around there. Most of the one-story commercial buildings were empty except for a drug store, a small grocery store, and a gas station. A few cement lots occupied space between the graffiti-covered vacant stores.

Mohammed started to feel better as the fog began to dissipate and the clouds were on their way out to sea.

The bus arrived after about fifteen minutes and Mohammed got on behind two other people. He checked the map posted behind the driver to make sure he was going the right way then stood near the front door.

After about twenty minutes of peering out the window at a dead area, Mohammed noticed the neighborhood changing. A Mexican delivery boy got off a bicycle with a pizza in his hand. Two old women pushed their shopping carts down a side street. A group of firemen entered their firehouse with bags of groceries.

Mohammed looked up as the F-train thundered into the station overhead. He glanced up at the street sign, McDonald Avenue. He knew he was getting close.

He glanced at the huge salamis and cheese wheels hanging in the window of an Italian deli. A pizzeria occupied every corner, and he'd never seen so many hair and nail salons.

The bus finally came to the last stop at the end of Avenue U and opened its doors.

Mohammed heard seagulls squawking overhead when he got off the bus on Stillwell Avenue. He stayed below the elevated tracks of the D-train until reaching 86th Street. The train rumbled by overhead and screeched to a stop at 25th Avenue.

Mohammed continued forward. He was getting hungry. He passed a gym and a real estate office then followed the smell of fried food to McDonald's.

CHAPTER 32—MONDAY 1:19PM

Andrew sat in the passenger seat of Agent Grant's black sedan while Agent Grant drove along the FDR Drive going to their office downtown. Traffic was heavy. They both stayed silent listening to 1010 wins, all news. Andrew thought about starting a conversation, but Agent Grant never seemed approachable. They had never spoken about anything that didn't pertain to work.

The morning fog had completely disappeared and bright sunrays now warmed the clear sky. Just after passing rows of brick housing projects on the right, Andrew looked left past Agent Grant and out the window at the East River. He noticed heavy traffic going into Brooklyn on the Williamsburg Bridge above.

As they inched their way downtown, he noticed traffic on the Manhattan Bridge and the Brooklyn Bridge, going both ways. The unseasonably warm weather must have brought out all the early Christmas shoppers.

Andrew and Agent Grant were on their way back from midtown Manhattan. They had started at 7AM and spent the next six hours interviewing Mohammed's foreman and co-workers at the building where he worked on Seventh Avenue. Everyone at the job had said the same thing: Mohammed was a good worker and a nice guy who kept to himself. Agent Grant had spent quite a bit of extra time questioning Tony Lasalvo, Mohammed's scaffold partner. Tony had nothing but good things to say about Mohammed.

They had also interviewed the building manager, the

superintendent, and the daytime maintenance men. They all remembered seeing Mohammed, but none had ever spoken with him. The security guards on duty all remembered Mohammed quite well. They all voiced their suspicions of him based on his race and religion, but they didn't have anything bad to say about him otherwise.

At 1PM, Agent Grant had decided to get a cup of coffee then go back to Brooklyn.

They never made it back to Brooklyn. Agent Grant received a phone call and said he had to get back downtown for a meeting. Agent Grant told Andrew to go back to the office and work on his financial case for the rest of the day.

Andrew was upset yesterday about having to miss church and spend a Sunday away from his family. But today, he was happy to be out in the field. It was better than being stuck to that computer screen in the office. There were only a few hours left in the day, so it wasn't so bad. Andrew hoped Agent Grant would take him back out tomorrow.

CHAPTER 33—MONDAY 1:44PM

Mohammed already finished his Quarter Pounder value meal at the crowded McDonald's and was still sitting there, nursing his soda. Two old men sat at the table behind him drinking coffee and a rowdy group of high school kids, who were probably supposed to be in school, sat at the table across from him.

A friend of his from work, also named Mohammed, lived a few blocks down the street in an apartment above a store. He knew his friend wouldn't be getting home from work until around 4:30, and he knew he couldn't stay too much longer in McDonald's, so he spent another ten minutes on his soda, then decided to walk around outside a little.

The streets were crowded with cars and the sidewalks were crowded with shoppers taking advantage of the unseasonably warm day. Mohammed followed 86th Street under the elevated subway tracks. People moved out of his way when they saw him. The warm sun brought out the aroma from his clothes that he had absorbed from the urine-saturated concrete column he'd slept under last night.

While passing the windows of a few clothing stores, Mohammed thought about buying some new clothes, but even if he bought the cheapest clothes he could find, he needed everything from shoes to underwear, not to mention a shower. The cash he had would be gone in no time. He still needed money for food and transportation, for who knows how long. He decided to stay dressed the way he was and try to avoid people as much as possible. Maybe the fact that he looked like a bum would help keep him safe from the authorities. He browsed the store windows on both sides of the street.

He sneezed, still congested. He had enough problems without getting sick. While approaching a newsstand on the corner, Mohammed decided to invest a few dollars in some cold pills and a bottle of water to wash them down. While standing there looking at all the different brands of medicine on the back shelf, he glanced over at the phone cards. He thought about buying a five-dollar phone card, but decided to get a ten-dollar card. There was still plenty of time to kill.

After swallowing the cold pills, he found a busy Chinese takeout place and used one of the two pay phones outside to call Pakistan. He knew it was around 1AM there, and he knew his parents would be sleeping, but he needed someone to talk to, and he had a feeling this might be his last chance to speak with them, so he called. Just the thought of there being a possibility that he may never see or speak with his family again made his inner organs cringe.

After a few rings, Mohammed's father answered in a groggy voice. "Hello?"

They spoke in their native tongue.

"Hello, Father."

"Mohammed, are you okay? Your cousin said—"

Mohammed tried his best to hold himself together. "I am fine. It was only a misunderstanding."

"You don't sound fine."

Mohammed turned his head away from a couple coming out with Chinese food. He didn't want them to see the tears he was unsuccessfully trying to hold back. He cleared his throat and said, "I am fine. I still have the flu, that's all. I will explain everything to mother. There is nothing to worry about. Go back to sleep. I know you have to work in the morning. I love you." Mohammed knew his father would ask too many questions, but his mother would believe anything he told her.

"I love you, too," replied Mohammed's father.

Mohammed's mother got on the phone. "Mohammed, thank God you're alright. Your cousin called us. He said you were in trouble."

"I am fine." Mohammed didn't want to lie, but he also didn't want his mother to worry. "Someone stole my wallet and my cell phone, so I reported it to the police. I did not have any money, and my bankcard was in my wallet, so I asked Cousin Mohammed for some money. I needed a ride home, but he was tired, so he told me to take the taxi. Everything is fine, mother. There is nothing to worry about."

Mohammed's mother sounded relieved. "Thank God, we all thought you were in trouble."

"I am very sorry to call late and wake you. I just wanted to tell you that I am okay."

Mohammed and his mother continued talking until his phone card time expired.

Time passed quickly on the phone. It was already after four. Mohammed strolled back toward his friend's apartment and waited across the street at the bus stop. The bus pulled up to the curb and people got on. The bus driver looked at Mohammed. Mohammed shook his head and waved the bus away.

Within the next fifteen minutes, another group of people waiting for the bus had formed. Just as a bus was ready to pull over and pick up its passengers, Mohammed spotted his friend across the street. He was few years younger, with the same bushy beard, and dressed in his dusty work clothes.

Mohammed leaped in front of the bus as it was slowing to a stop. The bus driver slammed on the brakes and the horn at the same time.

Mohammed yelled, "Sorry!"

The bus driver stuck out his middle finger as Mohammed disrupted traffic again while crossing 86th Street.

Mohammed's friend turned to see what all the commotion was about. When he saw Mohammed, he turned and hurried toward his door.

Mohammed yelled while running toward him, "Mohammed!"

His friend continued to ignore him and unlocked the door to his building. The screeching and rumbling of the subway overhead drowned out the sound of the cars on the street.

He called out again, "Mohammed!" But he could barely hear his own voice.

Mohammed got to the building just as his friend was stepping inside. He put his hand on the door and said, "Wait! It is me, Mohammed!"

His friend said, "I do not know you. Please leave me alone." He pushed Mohammed away and slipped inside.

Mohammed pulled his hand away from the frame just in time. His friend slammed the door in his face. The last feeling of hope drained from his body. His two best friends in America, both from Pakistan, both turned their backs on him. He knew a few other Pakistani men from work, but didn't know where they lived. He wasn't as close to any of them as he was with Amir and Mohammed. He thought he'd be able to count on his two best friends.

The roar of the train above faded away as it continued on its track toward Coney Island. The busy sound of people and cars filled the air once more.

Mohammed wanted desperately to run back to Pakistan and hide, but he knew that even if he did make it, they could find him there just as easily as they could here.

The sun was on its way out and the streetlights were beginning to come on. Mohammed didn't have any place to go. He proceeded west on 86th Street, looking for a secluded place to spend the night and regroup his thoughts. Stores and restaurants lined both sides of the four-lane street and two-story attached townhouses occupied the one-way side streets.

After the subway tracks overhead turned north and followed New Utrecht Avenue, Mohammed passed a car wash and some auto mechanic shops. Although the area wasn't as busy as where he had just come from, he still didn't feel safe spending the night anywhere around there. It just felt too open.

As much as he hated it, Mohammed decided he would be safest sleeping under the urine-saturated overpass in Bay Ridge.

He waited for the bus and took it all the way down 86th Street to Fourth Avenue where he had to walk the rest of the way toward the coast.

It was already dark when he made his way toward his disgusting resting place. Mohammed gazed up at the clear night sky, hoping for some help from God.

Hundreds of bluish-white lights in the distance caught his attention. It took a few seconds to realize what he was seeing, the Verrazano-Narrows Bridge, the huge gray double-decker suspension bridge connecting Brooklyn and Staten Island.

He thought about his scaffold partner. Tony lived in Staten

Island. He seemed like a nice guy, and they always got along at work, but why would he help a wanted Pakistani immigrant?

Mohammed continued forward, toward the overpass, but the illuminated steel monster looming in the distance felt like it was trying to tell him something.

Even if he called Tony and Tony didn't want anything to do with him, he still wouldn't be any worse off than he was already.

At a payphone, he dialed 411 and asked for Tony Lasalvo in Staten Island. The operator gave him two phone numbers, both of which he remembered.

The first was a seventy-eight-year-old man.

He called the second number and a woman answered. "Hello?"

Mohammed tried his best to replicate a New York accent. "Hello. Is Tony there?"

"Who's calling?"

Mohammed hadn't planned this far ahead. He didn't want to use his real name, so he used the first name that popped into his head, the name of their foreman at work. "This is Patrick."

"One minute, Patrick. I'll get him."

Mohammed looked around. The traffic was getting lighter. He started to worry. He tried to think of what to do next if Tony wouldn't help him.

Tony answered. "Patrick?"

"Tony, it is me, Mohammed."

"Mo?" Tony began to whisper. "What's going on? The feds were at the job today, asking all kinds of questions about you. There's rumors going around that you're a terrorist."

"It is not true, Tony. I called the police because I heard some terrorists talking inside the building when I went back up to the bridge for my thermos on Thursday. That's why I lost my head on Friday. They were talking about explosives. It is not me, Tony. I promise. I am not a terrorist."

Tony stayed quiet for a few seconds then said, "I believe you, man."

"Will you help me?"

"How?"

"I don't know." Mohammed began to cry, but he pulled the phone away from his mouth and covered it with his hand.

"Are you crying, man?"

"No." Mohammed wiped the tears from his face. "No, I'm not. It is okay, there is nothing you could do. I am sorry to bother you, my friend."

"I can give you some money, maybe some food, or something . . . but I can't stick my neck out, Mo. I got a family."

"I understand."

"Where are you?"

Mohammed looked around. He wasn't sure if he should say where he was. Maybe they tapped Tony's phone. Then he realized that if they did have Tony's phone tapped, they already knew where he was anyway.

"Mo, you still there?"

"I am here, Tony. I am in Bay Ridge."

"Can you get to Staten Island?"

"I think I could take the bus on 92nd Street."

"Okay. I live at 45367 Burbank, six blocks west of Hylan Boulevard. Call me when you get here and I'll come outside."

"Thank you, Tony."

"You got it, kid. Later."

"Goodbye." Mohammed hung up the phone and held his stomach. He was getting hungry already.

He headed down the avenue toward some stores, he was planning to get something to eat then take the bus over the bridge to Staten Island.

Mohammed bought a cup of tea and a bagel with butter from a small deli at 101st Street. It wasn't much, but it was better than nothing. He ate while continuing toward the bus stop.

Just as he stepped off the curb to cross the street, the black sedan screeched toward him. Mohammed dropped his tea and bagel and sprinted down the sidewalk.

The sedan roared down the avenue after him.

Mohammed raced to the next block with the sedan right next to him. It was the same gray haired man, Agent Grant.

At the corner, the light turned red. The sedan stopped as traffic turned right, entering the ramp to the highway ahead.

Mohammed raced across the street, zigzagging through the oncoming cars as they beeped their horns at him.

The sedan inched forward, the engine revving, waiting for the heavy traffic to pass.

Mohammed darted toward the pedestrian overpass. He

glanced down and across the highway at the water and Staten Island on the other side.

He looked to his right and saw a footpath leading down. Mohammed wasn't sure how far the path went, and it was too hard to tell at night. Instead of going down, he ran forward, along the sidewalk next to the onramp. A wire fence sitting atop a short stone wall lined both sides of the overpass. The fence ended, but the short wall below it continued. Mohammed glanced over his shoulder. The light changed. Traffic moved. He leaped up onto the short wall and jumped over.

His feet and knees hit the hard grassy slope at the same time. He rolled downhill while the sound of tires screeched to a stop on the onramp above. Mohammed's chest slammed into a small tree, bending its weak trunk and knocking his breath out.

Cars on the ramp above leaned on their horns. Mohammed figured the agent probably stopped traffic with his car and was now on foot, on his way either down the footpath or over the side of the ramp after him.

He crawled to the concrete wall below the overpass and made his way down the slope while crouching as low as possible. He still didn't see the agent. The cars above continued to blare their horns, but then he heard a car screech away and the horns stopped.

Mohammed was at the edge of the highway with cars coming toward him. He heard the car above screech to a stop again. He had only one move to make, so he made it. Standing with his back flat against the wall, Mohammed made his way along the side of the highway as cars zipped past him, the wind whisking past his face. A van almost sucked him away from the wall with the vacuum it created while speeding by. His skin tingled, hoping no one would lose control and take him out. Little by little, he inched his way under the concrete overpass.

Finally, on the other side, he raced up the grassy slope to the street above. An onramp and an off-ramp separated Mohammed from Agent Grant's car now. He looked across the two ramps trying to spot the agent, but didn't see him. He must have taken the downhill footpath.

Zigzagging through traffic, and almost being hit a few times, Mohammed raced across another ramp then across the street to Fourth Avenue. Trying to suck in as much oxygen as possible, he sprinted up the avenue, passing the old cast iron cannon and cannonballs that sat in John Paul Jones Park.

Up the block, a woman got out of a car service with two bags of groceries in front of an apartment building. Mohammed stopped the car just before it took off. "Please, I need to get to Staten Island." He glanced toward the overpass, but still didn't see anyone.

The driver said, "I can't do it. I got another fare."

Mohammed knew the toll was thirteen dollars, but he also knew the trip over the bridge was only ten minutes. He showed the man two twenty-dollar bills and said, "Just over the bridge. I know this will cover the toll. And you will still have time to get your next fare. Please, my friend. It is an emergency."

The driver saw Mohammed's dirty clothes and hesitated. He looked again at the money in his hand and said, "Just over the bridge."

CHAPTER 34—MONDAY 8:07PM

Wearing her navy blue dress uniform, police hat, floor shined shoes, and bright white gloves, Diane got out of her silver Volvo SUV. The pain in her ankle was back, and it was a worse since waking up this morning. She limped down the block to the funeral home, a big glass-faced building with a green awning that stood alone on the corner with its own parking lot. The entire area was crowded with cops, all in dress uniform.

She scanned the hundreds of faces as she approached the building, looking for someone she knew. While joining the single file line of people waiting to get inside, Diane noticed a few young officers from her precinct. They shook hands, but didn't know each other well enough for anything more than small talk.

Inside the funeral home, everyone was silent except a few people crying and wiping their noses. A mahogany veneer casket with both lids open stood against the back wall, in front of a long beige curtain. Dimly lit chandeliers hung from the ceiling casting a warm glow over the beige walls and brown pews.

Each guest approached the coffin then approached the family of the deceased in the front row. Twenty-six-year-old Reginald Armstrong was born and raised in the Bronx. He'd been a police officer for four years. He left behind a wife, a six-year-old daughter, and twin four-year-old boys.

Diane stepped up to the coffin and looked down at the lifeless body. They did a good job covering the bullet hole in his neck. She could still hear herself telling him to watch the staircase.

She wiped the tears from her eyes, made the sign of the cross, and turned away.

She shook the widow's hand and offered her condolences. The broken woman accepted Diane's sympathy. Diane glanced over at the children. The little girl stared ahead, looking at nothing. The boys were fidgeting in their seats, but stayed quiet. Diane glanced at the young widow's pained face one more time before stepping away. She wondered if the widow knew she was the one who told Armstrong to guard the staircase.

In the carpeted lobby, Diane took a tissue from a fancy metal box and blotted away the moisture from her eyes. She checked her face in the mirror on the wall. The scabs were getting better, but she still wished it would heal faster. Thank God for the dim lighting.

She went outside, walked away from the crowded entrance, and lit a cigarette by the parking lot. The grazed skin on her arm burned as she placed her lighter back into her pocket. She turned her head after hearing a familiar voice. Three women, also cops in dress uniform, crossed the street coming toward her.

The taller of the three women had blonde hair, brown eyes, and shoulders like a linebacker. "Holy shit. If it isn't Diane Lasalvo. Still smoking those things? You know they'll kill you, don't you?"

"Hey, Kelly." Diane stood on her toes to give the big woman a hug and a kiss on the cheek. "This job is what's gonna kill me."

Diane said hello to the other two women even though she didn't know them.

Kelly said, "You keep chasing down perps like that guy in the train yard, what do you expect? I heard you took one in the arm."

"Just barely grazed the skin. My face looks worse than my arm, believe me."

Kelly said, "You go inside yet?"

"Yeah. It sucks. His wife is devastated. I can't imagine her pain. And now those poor kids have to grow up without their father. Makes me happy I don't have any kids." Diane puffed her cigarette.

Kelly replied, "Well, I don't know about you, but I don't plan on dying anytime soon. I'm looking forward to spending many years with my children and eventually my grandchildren."

"I wish I had your optimism." Diane took another puff.

Kelly looked over at the line of people and told her two

PHIL NOVA

friends, "We better get over there before that line gets any longer."

"Go ahead. I'll see you later." Diane finished her cigarette and stomped it out on the sidewalk. She headed back toward the funeral home and stopped before the entrance.

She noticed Armstrong's partner coming out of the building, the woman who was holding his hand when they put him into the ambulance. She also noticed the woman's real 'partner,' another woman. For just a moment, even though she knew it was wrong, and she would probably go to hell for even thinking such a thing, Diane wished she had told Armstrong to guard the other staircase. At least his children would have a father to raise them.

Garcia caught up with Diane as she crossed the street and lit another cigarette. "Can I have one of those?"

"What, a cigarette? Since when do you smoke?"

Garcia pointed at the funeral home across the street and said, "Since that."

She took a cigarette from her pack and handed it to him. He lit it, took a deep drag, then coughed uncontrollably. Diane chuckled. He took another hit, but didn't cough as much.

Diane said, "You better not start smoking."

"I smoked a whole pack at my brother's funeral."

CHAPTER 35—MONDAY 8:56PM

After going over the Verrazano-Narrows Bridge to Staten Island, Mohammed had gotten out of the taxi and taken the bus up Hylan Boulevard past hundreds of strip malls and parking lots until reaching his stop.

Once outside, he scanned the area for any signs of the sedan or anything else that seemed suspicious before following a quiet suburban street parallel to Tony's street. He picked up the pace a few times when dogs in back yards began barking at him. At the end of five blocks, he turned down another street that led him to Burbank, which he then followed west for another block.

The entire neighborhood consisted of identical two-story suburban houses, each with their own land and garage. Some were brick-faced, but most were covered in aluminum siding. Lights were still on in most of the houses, but many were already dark.

Watching the addresses, Mohammed stopped just before Tony's house. The bay window in front had its blinds down, but the lights were on. He surveyed the area. Everything seemed normal.

The sound of a car engine in the distance became louder as Mohammed approached the house. He didn't want to take any unnecessary chances, so he sprinted around the side of the house and into the back yard. He hid in a small space between Tony's garage and fence. He peeked out and saw a black sedan slow down as it passed.

The sedan continued forward, then made a U-turn and came

back up, slowing down again as it passed the house. A few houses away, the sedan double parked on the opposite side of the street and turned off its lights.

Mohammed waited, trapped between the garage and the fence, his stomach growling and his head throbbing. He was scared for his life, but he was exhausted at the same time. He didn't have room to kneel, but he closed his eyes and prayed silently.

After about an hour of hiding between the fence and the garage, the sedan finally took off, and in a hurry. It looked like the same sedan that had been chasing him all over Brooklyn. He wondered if that was still Agent Grant after him. Didn't that man ever sleep? He also wondered why the police or any other agents didn't seem to be after him.

Mohammed's muscles ached from not moving. When he was confident the sedan wasn't coming back, he quickly shook some blood into his numb limbs, then snuck toward the house and peeked in through the back windows. All the rooms were dark. He went around the side. The only thing he was able to see was a night light through a small frosted window. He knew it was the bathroom, and he knew that after an evening of sports and beer, Tony must make more than one trip to the bathroom. Mohammed sat on the grass next to the house and waited.

His eyes went back and forth between the street ahead and the bathroom window. Finally, he heard something.

The bathroom light turned on and a heavy stream of urine splashed against the water in the bowl. Mohammed knew Tony lived with his wife and two daughters, and that sounded like a man. It had to be him.

Mohammed tapped lightly on the glass. The heavy stream of urine continued. Mohammed tapped again, a little louder. The stream stopped.

"Who's there?" It was Tony's voice.

Mohammed whispered, "It is me, Mohammed."

The window opened, and Tony stuck his chubby red face outside. "Mo? I told you to call me, and that was hours ago. What the hell are you doing out there?"

"I am very sorry, my friend, but your phone is tapped, and the agent was parked across the street. I had to wait."

"My phone is tapped? Are you smoking crack or what?"

"Please, Tony, you must believe me. People are trying to kill me."

Tony flushed the toilet. "Meet me by the garage."

"Okay." Mohammed went to the garage and waited on the side, stuck between the wall and the fence again, watching the street.

A few minutes later, Tony came out in dirty sneakers, loose sweatpants, and an old faded Mets jacket. He looked around and whispered, "Mo, where are you?"

Mohammed stepped out of his hiding spot.

"Come on." Tony unlocked and opened a door on the opposite side of the garage and brought Mohammed inside.

Tony's four-year-old brown Chevy Tahoe took up most of the garage along with a few dusty bicycles and beach chairs. A rolling toolbox stood neglected in the corner, the top open, tools thrown in haphazardly.

Tony turned on a small overhead light and closed the door. "What's going on, Mo?"

"I called the police, but they didn't believe me, and those two cops talking Spanish, laughing every time they mentioned Guantanamo Bay. I had to run. I had no choice."

"I still don't understand what's going on, Mo? Why did you call the cops in the first place? You said you heard someone talking while on the bridge?"

"Yes. After work on Thursday, I went back up to the bridge for my container . . ." Mohammed told Tony the entire story from the beginning.

Tony listened, then stayed silent for a moment, examining Mohammed's face.

Mohammed wondered if Tony believed him.

Finally, Tony said, "My sister is a detective in the Bronx. I could call her."

"No, please."

"I won't tell her where you are. I'll just say you called me. Maybe she could find out what's going on, why this guy is trying to kill you instead of arrest you. She might be able to help, and you need as much help as you can get right now if you wanna find the real terrorists."

Mohammed nodded. He knew Tony was right, but he was still scared of the police after everything that had just happened.

"And you're not gonna get far lookin' like that, neither. I'll give you some clothes, and you gotta get rid of that beard."

"I cannot cut my beard."

"One day you'll be wishing you shaved that beard . . . one day when some sadistic bastard is ripping your fingernails out in a concentration camp in some third world country."

Mohamed knew he had to do whatever it took to stay alive and to stay in one piece. "Okay. I will remove my beard."

"I'll get some scissors from the house and some other things. You hungry?"

"Yes, I am."

"I'll get you something from the kitchen. I think there's some leftover meatballs from last night. Don't worry, there's no pork in them."

Mohammed smiled.

After about fifteen minutes, Tony returned with a big black garbage bag full of something. He handed Mohammed a Ziploc bag with a few warm meatballs. "I nuked them."

"Thank you." Mohammed smelled the garlic as soon as he opened the bag. He ate the meatballs as fast as he could get them into his mouth.

Tony opened the garbage bag and retrieved a pair of scissors, a razor, shaving cream, and a handheld mirror. He took down one of the dusty beach chairs and wiped it off with an old rag.

Mohammed sat down and closed his eyes.

Tony cut Mohammed's hair and beard with the scissors then shaved Mohammed's head completely bald. He shaved his face, but left a thin mustache and goatee.

Mohammed's bare skin felt like rubber.

Tony gave him the mirror.

Mohammed held it up and was shocked. He couldn't believe he was looking at himself. He checked his profile from both sides. He turned the mirror up, then down, examining his face from every angle.

Out of the corner of his eye, Mohammed saw a small flame. He turned his head and leaped off the chair when he saw Tony heating a sewing needle with a lighter. "What are you going to do with that?"

Tony showed Mohammed two small gold stud earrings. "You want a disguise, don't you?"

"Not as a homosexual."

Tony laughed. "A lot of men wear earrings. Look at Jose at the job. He has an earring, and nobody gets more women than Jose."

"But Jose only has one earring."

"Alright, so I'll just do one ear. The left."

After the needle was red hot, Tony took the lighter away from it. He handed Mohammed a cotton ball and a bottle of alcohol. "Hold this for a minute." He held the needle up, waving it around to cool it down.

Mohammed couldn't believe what was happening. If they saw him in Pakistan with an earring, they would probably stone him to death.

He winced as Tony pushed the hot needle into his earlobe from the back. Tony put the earring against the needle and pushed it in while at the same time pulling the needle out. Tony did not have a delicate touch. Mohammed felt more pain from the earring going in than he did from the needle. Beads of sweat formed on his freshly shaved head.

Tony wet the cotton ball with alcohol and cleaned the blood from Mohammed's earlobe. Mohammed released his grip on the chair and exhaled.

Tony took some folded clothes out of the bag. "Here, these should do. I haven't worn them in years. They're too small. They were like new, so I kept them around in case I lost weight, but it doesn't look like that's gonna be happening anytime soon."

Mohammed took off the street kid's filthy clothes and put on Tony's clothes, a pair of blue jeans, a white T-shirt with a picture of a woman bathing in a giant champagne glass, a black and orange Mets jacket, and a matching Mets baseball cap. The clothes were a loose, but they fit.

Mohammed's feet were scabbed up and swollen. Tony gave him a bottle of water and a rag, which Mohammed used to clean his feet the best he could before putting on a clean pair of white cotton socks. He gave him a used pair of white Nikes that would have been a good fit, but felt tight because of the swelling.

Mohammed looked at himself again in the mirror and realized he might really have a chance of going unnoticed.

"I would let you take a shower, but my wife would kill me if . . ."

Mohammed said, "You have done more than enough."

Tony said, "Now, you just have to try and get rid of that accent."

Mohammed spoke with a New York accent, or his version of one anyway. "How you doin', babe?"

Tony said, "Try not to talk if you don't have to."

Mohammed laughed.

Tony gave Mohammed some money—five hundred dollars.

Mohammed stared at the money and said, "I owe you my life, Tony."

"No, you don't. But you do owe me five hundred bucks."

"I have the money in the bank."

"I know you do. But we'll talk about that later, after you get everything straightened out."

"What if they capture me and take me away?"

"Then, I guess I bet on the wrong horse again. Wouldn't be the first time." Tony took two iPhones from his jacket pocket. "These belong to my daughters. They're prepaid. They've been bothering me for months about getting the latest model, so as long as I give them enough money tomorrow morning to buy what they want after school, they won't even miss these. I'll call you when I hear from my sister." Tony kept one iPhone and gave the other to Mohammed. "You have Maria's phone, I have Bianca's. The number is programmed in there. Whatever you do, don't call on any other lines."

Mohammed nodded.

"And keep the phone turned off or Maria's friends will blow up the line. Just check it once in a while for a message from me."

Mohammed didn't understand what Tony meant when he said blow up the line, but just nodded and knew he should keep the phone off.

"You can sleep in my truck. When I leave the house in the morning, just stay in the back seat and stay low. I park in the Ferry parking lot. You can get out there." Tony took a clean folded blanket from the garbage bag and gave it to him.

Mohammed held the soft blanket and said, "Thank you, Tony."

CHAPTER 36—MONDAY 11:39PM

Diane sat on her sofa watching Saturday Night Fever and eating a pint of Haagen Dazs, both of which she always had when she was feeling down. Somehow, watching a young John Travolta dancing disco in his white suit cheered her up.

She remembered that her Blackberry was still off. She had turned it off before entering the funeral home, but forgot to turn it back on. She powered it up and noticed she had two messages. Her brother Tony had sent her a text message at 11:20 asking if she was busy. At 11:30, he'd sent another text message asking her to call him tonight.

The first thing that came to her mind was that Tony had been gambling again and needed money. Why else would he be calling her when he should be sleeping? The last time she got him out of trouble, she swore if he didn't learn his lesson, she wouldn't help him again.

While sitting there eating her ice cream, she wondered why he was calling her? What if it was something important? What if something happened to him? What if something happened to Angela or the girls?

She sent Tony a text message that read: are you still up?

It took about a minute for him to respond with a text message: I'm up, call me.

She called him.

It rang once then Tony answered, "Diane."

"What's wrong, you okay? The girls okay?"

"We're fine, everybody's fine. It's a friend of mine. He's in trouble."

Diane was relieved and a little annoyed. "Your friend? You have got to be kidding me. What is he, a gambler?"

"He's my partner on the scaffold, and he doesn't gamble. His favorite sport is cricket, for God's sake."

"Cricket? What the hell are you talking about, Tony?"

"Alright, this is what happened . . ." Tony told Diane everything that Mohammed had told him. He also told Diane Mohammed's name and address.

Even though her mind kept drifting back to the image of Armstrong's corpse and his crying wife, she was still listening to what Tony was telling her.

Diane was suspicious of the whole story. She didn't believe a federal agent would recklessly shoot at someone in the middle of the street. Although she didn't want to admit it, she had trouble trusting a Muslim, especially after losing so many friends on September 11.

Diane planned to check out Mohammed's story, only because Tony asked her to. She also planned to check into Mohammed's background and his immigration status. She did not want her brother implicated in some kind of terrorist plot. "I'll check it out, Tony . . . but I'll be able to get more information tomorrow."

Tony asked, "Are you going to call Jack?"

"Jack? Jack works in organized crime. Why would I call Jack?" Diane didn't like when people tried to play matchmaker, not even her brother. "This better not be some ploy to get me and Jack back together again."

"It's not," Tony assured her. "My friend is really in trouble. Everything I told you is true. It's just that I thought . . . maybe Jack would have more resources."

Diane replied, "The NYPD has just as many resources as the FBI. I will speak to you tomorrow."

CHAPTER 37—TUESDAY 4:30AM

Andrew cranked out his morning sit-ups in his dark living room then performed some push-ups. After a few minutes of stretching, he jumped into the shower, then got dressed.

He kissed his wife and kids while they slept, then, after drinking a protein shake instead of breakfast, he headed out the door an hour earlier than usual.

Andrew left early to get a head start. He was on schedule with his primary case, but he decided to try to get it over with early, hoping something more exciting would come along. He wondered how Agent Grant was doing in his search for that Pakistani guy.

The dark streets and highways were desolate. Andrew wondered how many people took extra time off before the holiday. He wished he could take some extra time off to spend with his family, but at least he had Thanksgiving off, hopefully.

CHAPTER 38—TUESDAY 5:50AM

Mohammed woke up shivering in the back seat of Tony's truck when the side garage door opened, then closed. It took a few seconds for him to realize where he was. He heard footsteps getting closer to the truck and hoped it was Tony. He clenched the blanket like a child.

It was Tony. He opened the truck door and gave Mohammed two corn muffins and a switchblade. "Sorry I didn't bring you any tea. My wife knows I don't like tea. She would have been suspicious."

"I do not need tea. You have done enough for me already. I thank you again." Mohammed stared at the closed knife in Tony's hand.

"You don't have to use it, but keep it with you, just in case." Tony handed it to him.

Mohammed took it and tried to open it like a regular pocketknife.

Tony said, "It's a switchblade."

"A what?"

Tony took the knife and pressed the button on the side. The blade flew open, startling Mohammed. Tony closed the knife and gave it back.

Mohammed pressed the button and the blade flung open. He closed it and switched it open again.

"We gotta go. Stay down. You'll have to eat on the way." Tony got in the driver's seat and started the engine.

Mohammed stayed down, trying not to make crumbs as he ate the corn muffins. He hoped he lived long enough to tell his father a swine-eating infidel helped him. He remembered the suspicious look Tony used to give him when they first started working together, but after a few months, they knew each other well, and he no longer had that look in his eyes, but he never expected Tony to go to these lengths to help him.

Tony pressed a remote control that opened the front garage door, then rolled the truck out into the street as the door closed behind him. He turned right, easing toward Hylan Boulevard.

From where he was, Mohammed could only see Tony and the dashboard, but he wanted to see what was going on outside. The only thing he saw out the windshield from his angle was clouds and sky, and the only thing that calmed his nerves was the thought that God was up there in those clouds, watching out for him.

Tony stopped and waited while sipping his coffee. He adjusted his rearview mirror.

Mohammed tried to see what was happening in the mirror, but from his angle, he couldn't see anything.

The light changed and Tony turned. After a few seconds, he picked up his cell phone and put it to his ear without calling anyone. "I think you're right, Mo."

Mohammed whispered, "What? What happened?"

Tony continued pretending to talk on the phone. "A black sedan that was parked across from my house just made the turn behind us. He's two cars back. I only see one man, the driver, but I can't tell what he looks like."

Mohammed wondered if it was Agent Grant again or someone else. Would he follow Tony to Manhattan or stay with the truck after Tony took the Ferry?

Tony still had the phone to his ear. "I have to lose him."

Mohammed whispered, "How?"

"I don't know yet. There's a cop." Tony let the phone drop to his side.

Mohammed thought about the whole scenario. What if Tony was pulled over for talking on the phone and the cop found a bald Pakistani with an earring hiding in the back seat? Mohammed stayed silent as his heart beat faster.

The cops must not have noticed the phone, because Tony kept driving. He turned on the radio. It was all talk, then a commercial. He turned the station . . . more talk and more commercials. He popped in a CD.

Mohammed caught a glimpse of the name on the disk, Highway to Hell. His heart began to race as the back seat started to feel like a coffin. He closed his eyes and prayed for protection.

The music began with a single electric guitar banging out chords, then another guitar, then drums joined the guitars. Tony picked up speed gradually as the singer's raspy voice joined in with the music and sang phrases Mohammed didn't understand.

The song's tempo increased as the double electric guitars got louder. Tony turned the volume all the way up and slammed his foot down on the gas pedal.

Mohammed tried to hold on as g-forces pushed him back.

Tony screeched down the street. He slammed the steering wheel to the left, screeching and skidding, then to the right, peeling out.

Mohammed heard tires screeching and horns blasting as Tony's speedometer kept moving up . . . fifty, sixty, seventy. Tony slammed the wheel to the right. The truck spun around. Mohammed felt the corn muffins swishing around in his stomach as his body bounced up and down on the seat. Using his arms against the front seat to brace himself, it took all of his strength to keep from falling on the floor.

Something smashed into them. They screeched down the street sideways. They hit something. It sounded like another car. Mohammed's head jerked as he fell from the seat to the floor. His stomach smacked against the bump on the floor, pushing out all of his air.

Tony's entire body slammed back into his seat. He lost control of the wheel. The truck spun out of control.

Mohammed stayed down as the sound of electric guitars continued to blare over the speakers. His head spun the same direction as the truck while sweat poured off his freshly shaved head and down the sides of his face. The food in his stomach began to rise. He tried hard to keep it down.

Tony grabbed the wheel, jerked it to the right, and stepped on the gas. He sped forward, made a hard left, and picked up speed again. They skidded around a half circle, skidded to the left, then continued forward for a few minutes.

Tony turned right and slammed on the brakes. He turned to

Mohammed and said, "Get out here!"

Mohammed froze.

"On the other side of those trees is a cemetery. Just follow it east back toward Hylan Boulevard until you reach the train tracks on the other side. Follow the tracks either way to a get to a station. The train will take you to the ferry. Hurry up. I'm not sure I lost them."

Mohammed jumped out of the truck and looked ahead at an area dense with trees and bushes. Across the quiet street, a row of ranch style houses sat back from the street under the cover of trees.

Tony peeled out down the block.

Mohammed stumbled into the woods, his head and stomach still spinning.

Trekking through brown and orange leaves that had recently fallen from their branches and watching the squirrels as they scurried around, Mohammed remembered he was still in New York City when he noticed a red fire hydrant fifty feet into the mini-forest.

It felt like fifteen minutes before he reached the end of the woods.

He scanned the area before stepping out onto another quiet street with ranch houses on the other side. The coast was clear, no people, no cars, only houses.

After crossing the street, Mohammed followed the sidewalk toward the rising sun, glancing across at the tombstones that were only occasionally visible through the black iron fence and the wall of trees behind the fence.

After following the cemetery for a while, Mohammed found himself in another residential neighborhood. He thought he was lost, but after walking another block, he noticed the street ended ahead. At the end of the street, he found a fence. The fence blocked access to the railroad tracks below.

Mohammed turned left and proceeded along the sidewalk across the street from the fence, following the tracks for another ten minutes before reaching the train station.

The station was just a small concrete corridor that led to a Metrocard machine and a turnstile, then a staircase that led to the tracks in an open trench below. Mohammed refilled his Metrocard at the machine then swiped it at the turnstile. He followed the stairs down the platform and waited for the train to the ferry.

On the opposite side, a southbound train rumbled into the station. Mohammed noticed it was the same as the metallic trains used on the regular subway.

After only a few minutes, the northbound train arrived and Mohammed got on with a group of commuters. He took the train to the last stop, St. George.

Upon exiting the train station, he followed the long line of commuters down an enclosed concrete walkway to a set of glass doors.

Inside the Staten Island Ferry Terminal, he followed everyone to a large open area where hundreds of people waited, sitting, standing, reading newspapers, and drinking coffee.

Mohammed stayed in the center of the crowd to avoid the eyes of the many police and security guards scattered around. He wanted to buy a cup of tea from the vendor next to the newsstand, but there were too many cops there, so he stayed where he was and waited for the boat to arrive.

Finally, two of the doors ahead opened. A small group of people who had just come in from Manhattan entered the terminal through the double doors.

The rest of the doors opened and the herd moved forward through the doors, outside to the cold windy dock, then onto the boat. Just before boarding the ferry, Mohammed glanced over the side and saw cars driving onto the lower level.

Once inside the boat, he sat on one of the long wooden benches and glanced out the window at the choppy water. He didn't have much experience on boats, and the few experiences he did have weren't good. If he just held down those corn muffins during the Tony's version of the Duke boys, a ride on the Staten Island Ferry should be nothing.

As the boat gently rocked, an old woman almost lost her balance while trying to sit on the bench next to Mohammed. He stood and grabbed her arm, helping to hold her up.

The woman caught her breath and said, "Thank you, young man."

"You're welcome." Mohammed helped her sit down then sat next to her. "Are you okay?"

"I'm fine, thank you so much."

Mohammed smiled.

The woman said, "I'm going to see my son in Manhattan.

He's a lawyer."

Mohammed smiled again.

She continued, "We're having lunch today. I know, it's early, but I haven't been to the city in years, so I thought I might walk around a bit, get a cup of coffee, do a little window shopping, you know?"

Mohammed knew she was a kind old woman, but he didn't feel like getting into a long conversation with her. At the same time, he didn't want to be rude. "That sounds nice."

The boat released from the dock with a jerk. The old woman closed her eyes and held on to the bench with both hands.

Mohammed asked, "Are you sure you are going to be okay?"

"Yes, I'll be fine. I just don't like the water." She opened her eyes and released her grip as the ferry moved forward at a steady pace.

Mohammed said, "I know how you feel. I don't like boats either."

She smiled at Mohammed and said, "I'm going to sleep a little. I don't mean to be rude."

"Not at all. I understand completely."

She smiled at Mohammed then folded her hands on her lap while lowering her head and closing her eyes.

A cop strolled down the aisle and out of sight.

Mohammed hoped his disguise would work.

While gazing out the window at the choppy water, he noticed the Statue of Liberty and Ellis Island in the distance, both becoming larger, then smaller as the ferry passed them. He had taken a trip to both of them when he'd first arrived in New York. He remembered his trip there and for a little while, he forgot someone was hunting him.

Mohammed didn't remember falling asleep. He was surprised to find the old woman waking him up by tapping him on the shoulder.

She said, "We're here, young man"

Mohammed stood and said, "Oh. Thank you."

He followed the old woman and the rest of the crowd out of the boat and onto the dock. They entered a set of double doors into the huge terminal full of people scrambling around. The police presence was much more pronounced than on the Staten Island side. Not only did cops and security guards fill every crack and crevice, but a few National Guard patrolled with M-16 assault rifles.

Mohammed turned to the old woman as they exited the terminal and said, "Have a good day."

"Thank you." She said, "You, too, young man."

Mohammed smiled at her and tried to keep his smile while passing a group of police with German Shepherds. He knew dogs could smell fear, so he tried to act natural, but the harder he tried to act natural, the more nervous he got.

He finally made it out onto the street and looked up at the glass skyscrapers towering above, trying to get his bearings. Mohamed wasn't familiar with the named streets and narrow blocks of the downtown area.

Just across Whitehall Street, he saw the green post of a subway station. He waited for the light to change then crossed with the crowd.

Mohammed headed down the concrete staircase to a crowded subway station, swiped his Metrocard, then sprinted to the waiting R-Train. He made it just before the doors closed.

He squeezed into the packed train and stood during the entire trip, wondering if he was doing the right thing by going back to his job. He knew there was good chance the agents or police would be waiting for him there, but he hoped his new look would conceal his identity.

He was still trying to come up with a plan when he almost missed his stop, 49th Street. He put his hand in the door as it was closing. The doors bounced open. Mohammed got out of the train and the doors closed again behind him.

After leaving the busy station, he climbed the stairs to the crowded street above. The sound of car horns echoed between the buildings as a traffic-directing cop blew his whistle.

Mohammed knew exactly where he was. Most of the jobs he did were in midtown, where he knew his way around.

With Times Square just ahead, he strolled down Seventh Avenue, hoping no one would recognize him. He felt safe surrounded by the rush hour crowd, people of all shapes and sizes, from decaying junkies to executives in thousand-dollar suits.

Mohammed stopped when he noticed the black sedan parked directly in front of the building that he worked on. How did they get here so fast? Or was it another black sedan? It looked like the same car. He wondered if they finally took him seriously and came back to the building to find the real terrorists, but he wasn't sure, and he couldn't count on it. He knew he had to proceed as a wanted man and try to find the terrorists himself. He decided to get the license number of the car then at least he could hopefully figure out how many there were.

Standing against the wall of the building next door, Mohammed took out the iPhone that Tony had given him. He turned it on and waited for it to power up. While trying to figure out how to enter picture mode, a Lady Gaga ringtone began to play. He fumbled to press the ignore button. He peered through the passing crowd at the sedan, which was still parked.

After finally figuring out how to mute the ringer and take pictures, Mohammed turned around and pushed his way through the crowd to the curb. His heartbeat increased as he prepared himself mentally.

Standing behind a man smoking a cigarette at the curb, Mohammed held the phone slightly above his waist and snapped a quick shot of the car and its license plate. He turned his body a little and pretended to type a text message while saving the picture. He turned back toward the car and took another picture. With his trembling hand, he turned the phone off and stuffed it into his pocket while scurrying down the block.

He zigzagged through the crowd, wondering if anyone saw him taking the pictures. He wanted to look back, but was too scared. He continued forward.

A few blocks away, Mohammed stepped into a common area between two buildings, a concrete floor and metal benches with a small fountain in the center. A few office workers drank coffee and smoked cigarettes as a security guard stood against the wall. A sleeping homeless man occupied a bench far from everyone else. He was glad he didn't look like that anymore.

Mohammed sat on one of the benches and checked the pictures on the iPhone. Only one was clear enough to make out the license plate, an official government plate with a triangular logo in the upper left corner that read: DCTA. The license number was 2211.

He didn't send the picture to Tony yet. He didn't want to call or text him until he had more information, just in case they found out about these phones and were able to trace them. He planned to wait for the sedan to leave then sneak into the building and look for the three men.

CHAPTER 39—TUESSDAY 8:41AM

Wearing a black pants suit with a beige shirt, Diane tied her hair into a ponytail and wiped the excess ointment off her face. The scabs were barely visible, but she still worried about scarring. After closing her windows, she headed downstairs to her parents' apartment.

She entered the kitchen where her mother and father were sitting at the table drinking coffee and smoking cigarettes. The channel-five morning news played on a small TV on the counter.

Diane kissed them both on the cheek then poured herself a cup of coffee from the glass percolator on the stove. She opened the window a little and lit a cigarette, adding to the heavy cloud of smoke already lingering.

Mrs. Lasalvo opened the refrigerator and took out some eggs. "You going to work now?"

"Have to go see the shrink, make sure I'm not crazy yet."

"Don't talk like that." Mrs. Lasalvo put the eggs on the counter. "How's your arm?"

Diane said, "It's fine. Just changed the gauze."

Mr. Lasalvo said, "I thought you were making pancakes."

Mrs. Lasalvo barked, "You want pancakes? You make them. I'm having eggs."

"You did promise him pancakes today, Mom."

"Go on, take his side again." She put the eggs back into the refrigerator and took a large mixing bowl from the cabinet. She took a bottle of maple syrup from another cabinet and slammed it on the table.

Mr. Lasalvo said, "So, what about that guy from Tony's job? He's a supervisor."

Mrs. Lasalvo listened while mixing the batter.

"Come on, Dad. I am not dating anyone from Tony's job. I wish everyone would stop telling me I have to settle down. Men invented marriage so they could control women. Why do you think they say love, honor, and obey. Keyword, obey." Diane puffed on her cigarette.

While pouring the batter onto a large griddle, Mrs. Lasalvo said, "You're reading too much into it. Don't you want children? You're gonna be forty this year."

"I know how old I am, ma. But thanks for reminding me."

Her mother added, "You always said you would settle down after making detective, and you've been detective for five years already."

"Four years." Diane finished her cigarette and put in out in the overfull ashtray.

"Four, five, whatever."

Mr. Lasalvo said, "Let's just enjoy the pancakes. Forget I said anything."

CHAPTER 40—TUESDAY 9:35AM

The air was cold, but the sky was sunny and clear. The midtown Manhattan streets and sidewalks were still crowded.

Mohammed had been looking out the window while waiting in a greasy old coffee shop a few blocks from his job. He only had a cup of tea and a bagel with cream cheese. He wanted to order eggs, but noticed the old Greek man behind the counter cooking the eggs, bacon, and ham all on the same grill. He couldn't take a chance of pork juice dripping into his eggs.

A young Polish waitress poured him another cup of tea and added it to his check that was already on the table. After finishing the tea, Mohammed paid his bill then headed out of the coffee shop and back toward Seventh Avenue. He stopped across the street and looked around. The sedan was gone. He crossed the street.

Mohammed passed the building and turned down a busy side street. He went the long way around and ended up at the side entrance of the building, the loading docks.

He snuck between two trucks, keeping his face down, and hoping that if the cameras saw him, they would only pick up his hat and jacket.

Peeking out from between the two trucks, Mohammed saw the security guard sitting in a chair, smiling while typing a text message on his phone.

Mohammed quickly climbed onto the concrete dock and grabbed a cardboard box from a stack. After hoisting it onto his shoulder, he placed the box in a way that it blocked his face from the camera and the guard. He passed the security guard, hoping the guard didn't notice the sneakers.

After making his way through a long metal hallway, Mohammed put the box down on the floor next to the freight elevator. He knew he needed a pass to get inside the elevator, and he was still worried someone might recognize him, despite his new look. Mohammed opened the door to a staircase and slipped inside with his head down.

He hurried up the stairs to the third floor where he knew he would find a door with a broken fire alarm.

Once inside, he headed down a carpeted hall as men and women working in cubicles glanced over at him. He hurried to the passenger elevators and pressed the down button. While waiting, he noticed the receptionist watching him from behind her desk. He tried to act natural, and at the same time, tried to stay out of view of the cameras. Even though he no longer looked like a Muslim, a rapper, or a homeless man, he still did not look like he belonged in an office.

The elevator door finally opened and Mohammed stepped inside. Out of the corner of his eye, he noticed the receptionist pick up the phone.

There were a few people already in the elevator. Mohammed tried not to make eye contact with anyone. He stood against near the wall and faced forward. The first floor button was the only one lit up. Mohammed pressed two as the doors closed. The elevator descended one floor and Mohammed got out.

Finally, on the second floor alone, Mohammed examined everything. Old cubicles still sat in their places with frayed wires hanging out of the floors and ceilings. A few old computer chairs were scattered around, and rows of file cabinets stood empty against the walls.

Mohammed thought about the three men. They must work in the building. He'd never seen them before, but he spent most of his time outside, on the scaffold.

He glanced out the window at the sidewalk shed—the bridge, as he and the other workers called it. Fortunately, no one was near the window. He couldn't see the traffic on Seventh Avenue, but he could hear it, even through the window. That's when it hit him, the Thanksgiving Day Parade passed right down Seventh Avenue, and this would be a perfect place for a terrorist to plant a bomb. Thousands of people would die while millions of people watched the whole thing on national television. Two days from now.

Mohammed tried to get his mind back on track. The receptionist upstairs probably called security, and it was only a matter of time before someone found him. He tried to think back to Thursday. He knew this was the floor where he saw the three men, but an empty floor didn't leave much hope. He decided to go into the corner office anyway just in case they left any clues behind, or maybe even stashed a bomb.

He followed the quiet hall around a corner to an office door with four spots of glue where a sign used to hang. He turned the doorknob. It was unlocked. He opened it slowly while peeking inside.

The office was completely bare except for a hunchback computer chair. The walls were bare except for tiny holes from screws and nails. Mohammed stepped inside and looked around. He glanced up at the ceiling and saw big foam tiles resting on metal tracks. They could have easily placed a bomb in the ceiling.

Just as he considered pulling a file cabinet into the room so he could climb up and check the ceiling, Mohammed heard someone talking on a walkie-talkie.

He stepped out of the office and looked both ways before hurrying down the hall, away from the sound. After turning a corner, he heard another walkie-talkie. He stopped for a second, wondering if he should have gone another way. It was too late to turn back now. He continued the way he was going, hoping they wouldn't spot him.

His hand involuntarily went into his pocket and grasped the switchblade Tony had given him. Mohammed surprised himself. He let the knife go and took his hand out of his pocket. Hitting someone was bad enough. There was no way he was going to stab anyone. He just couldn't do it.

A fat security guard saw Mohammed and said, "Excuse me, sir. Do you work in the building?"

He almost froze, but then a lie came out of his mouth a little too naturally. Trying to conceal his Pakistani accent, Mohammed spoke with his best British accent, the type of English he'd learned in Pakistan. "No, I do not. My lady friend works here. I must have gotten off at the wrong floor. Would you point me to the elevator, please?"

"What company does she work for?"

Mohammed almost stuttered. "She works for . . . Alpha Financial."

A tall security guard approached from behind. "There's no Alpha Financial in this building."

"I'm sorry. Maybe I got the address wrong." Mohammed started back toward the elevators, hoping they would just let him go. He'd seen both of these men before, and they had seen him before, but they didn't recognize him now.

The tall guard said, "May I see your visitors pass, please?"

"Visitor's pass? I do not have one."

The fat guard asked, "How did you get in the building?"

Another lie. "Why, through the front door, my good man."

The tall guard asked, "And security didn't stop you?"

Mohammed continued to spin his web of deceit. "I waved to the security guard, but he was reading the paper. He didn't even look up, just waved me through."

The tall guard asked the fat guard, "Who's working the lobby today?"

The fat guard responded, "Old man Ross. But we can't report him. He's got two weeks left 'til retirement."

The tall guard hesitated for a moment, then said, "Alright, let's just get this guy out of here before it's our asses." He pressed the elevator button.

The two security guards followed Mohammed into the elevator, down to the first floor, and through the spacious lobby to one of the front doors. They watched him until he left the building and was out of sight.

Mohammed walked down Seventh Avenue for a few blocks then turned a corner and headed down a crowded, one-way street. He continued all the way around the block then back up the avenue until he was at the building again.

Watching from a block away, he observed the scaffolds on the side of the building. He could spot Tony from his shiny green hard hat. He saw someone else on the scaffold with Tony, but they were too high for Mohammed to see who it was.

He felt like all hope was gone while watching the men work. He wished he could go back to work, and back to his normal life.

After about an hour of random thoughts and regrets,

Mohammed decided to buy a cup of tea to keep him warm during his stakeout. He might be waiting here forever, but he didn't know what else to do.

Just as he stood and started toward a deli in the middle of the block, he noticed a small young man with a huge beard, one of the three men he'd seen in the office. The young man came out of the service entrance still dressed in his maintenance uniform.

Mohammed tried not to think about the federal agent who was after him and tried to concentrate on following the maintenance man. He stayed at least a block away as he followed the man to the subway station.

CHAPTER 41—TUESSDAY 12:02PM

Diane's Blackberry began to vibrate while she drove over the Whitestone Bridge to The Bronx. She took the phone out of her small black leather purse and saw the name, Tony. She answered the call and put him on speaker. "What's up, Tony?"

"On my lunch break. You hear anything about Mo?"

"No, nothing yet. I'm on my way to the precinct now. I'll call you as soon as I know something."

She followed the bridge over the water then through hills covered with grass and trees. Traffic was light, so she only had to slow down a little on her way through the EZ-pass lane of the tollbooth at the end of the bridge.

The Expressway led her north to a series of ramps going in different directions. She followed a ramp that led her up to the elevated Cross-Bronx Expressway then followed that west through trees and hills until apartment buildings dominated the landscape.

She took the Webster Avenue exit and drove past a few auto shops and grocery stores on her way to the precinct.

Just as she got to the building, a patrol car pulled out of an angled parking spot on 181st Street close to the entrance. She parked her Volvo SUV and threw her half-finished cigarette on the street before entering the building.

On the second floor of the precinct, detectives filled out arrest reports while perpetrators sat in holding cells. With fifteen minutes to spare, Diane sat at her desk and started up her computer. She looked up Mohammed Ali's immigration records.

There was nothing out of the ordinary. He seemed like a typical immigrant to her.

She used the phone at her desk to call Police Plaza.

A recorded voice answered, "Welcome to . . ."

Diane typed in a four-digit extension and the recording stopped.

After a low beeping sound, a woman's voice answered, "Sergeant Campbell."

Diane said, "Hey, girl."

The woman on the other side of the phone spoke quietly. "Hey, girl. I heard they want to give you the medal of valor. They should give you the medal of honor if you ask me."

"I wish you were the one giving out the medals."

Sergeant Campbell laughed. The two women had known each other for ten years. They worked in the same Manhattan precinct for a few years and kept in touch by phone. They didn't spend much time together, however, as Sergeant Campbell was usually busy with her husband and four children in Jamaica, Queens.

Diane said, "I need a favor. Can you check out what happened in Brooklyn Sunday morning at 326 Nostrand Avenue? Two patrol cars were dispatched and a federal agent was there."

"Hold on a minute."

Diane heard fingers tapping a keyboard. She waited and checked her watch. She still had a little time, but not much.

"Did you say 326 Nostrand?"

"That's right."

"I don't see anything here. No patrol cars were dispatched to that address."

"Anything else, anywhere around there?"

"There was a shooting in the Marcy Avenue Projects, but nothing out of the ordinary. Definitely no federal agents on our records."

Now Diane really wanted to find out what was going on. "Thanks, girl. I'll call you later. I have an appointment with the shrink now."

"Okay. Talk later."

Detective Garcia came out of an office and headed toward Diane as she hung up the phone. Garcia said, "Your turn."

Diane threw a couple Tic-Tacs in her mouth to try to kill the smell of cigarettes then tightened her ponytail and entered the room.

Fortunately, Diane hadn't had many appointments with the police shrink, but the few times she did, she had spoken with one of two people, a skinny old man with thick glasses, and a large woman in her forties who waited for her now. Diane preferred the old man.

The large woman greeted Diane with a big smile and a handshake. "Hello, Detective."

"Hello, Doctor." Diane sat down and tried not to look at the time. She wanted to get out of there so she could get something to eat and hopefully get a little sleep before coming all the way back up to the Bronx for another night at Armstrong's wake, then it was back to work after that. Diane knew she could probably ask the shrink to get her the night off, but then the shrink would try to probe her even harder for hidden emotions.

The woman asked, "First, I'd like to congratulate you in advance for your medal."

"Thank you. But I had to do it. I owed it to Armstrong."

"So, Detective. Does that mean you feel personally responsible for Armstrong's death?"

"I told him to guard the staircase."

"What would you have done differently?"

Diane didn't have an answer.

The woman said, "Officer Armstrong knew that police work is dangerous. He was willing to risk his life from the moment he joined the academy."

"I know you're right. But, it still bothers me."

"That's normal, and it will take time. Have you been having any nightmares or trouble sleeping?"

"I had nightmares the day after Armstrong was shot, but that was it."

The woman looked through Diane's file then said, "I see you're not married. Any particular reason?"

"Just haven't got around to it yet."

"Part of my job is determining whether or not the duty of the officers is affecting their personal lives."

"Well, you don't have to worry about me. I'm just taking a break from men right now."

The woman spent the next twenty minutes trying to probe Diane, but Diane gave her just enough information to keep her satisfied. She didn't like having to share her personal feelings. Doctor or not, the woman was still a stranger.

Garcia was waiting at his desk when Diane came out of the office. "What do you say we go for lunch?"

Diane smacked him on the shoulder. "Come on, I'm buying."

Garcia smiled. "I can't say no to that."

Just as they started toward the stairs, a woman in a lieutenant's uniform appeared. "Detective, someone wants to speak with you."

Diane and Garcia glanced at each other.

The woman specified, "Detective Lasalvo."

Diane asked, "Who wants to see me now? I just finished my interview."

The woman responded, "Someone from Homeland Security would like to ask you a few questions." She gestured with her hand and said, "He's waiting for you in the captain's office."

Garcia asked, "Homeland Security?"

Diane shrugged and told Garcia, "Wait for me." She patted his belly. "Don't worry, I'm still buying." At first, she thought it must be a mistake that Homeland Security would be here for her. Then she thought of Tony's friend and wondered if this had something to do with him. She hoped to God Tony didn't get himself into trouble.

Garcia sat at his desk while Diane followed the woman to the captain's office.

Inside the office stood a tall man with gray hair and gray eyes wearing an expensive black suit. The captain was not in his office, nor were any other police officers.

The tall gray haired man extended his hand. "Hello Detective. I am Agent Grant."

Diane shook his hand and said, "Nice to meet you Agent Grant. How can I help you?"

Agent Grant opened his gold cigarette case, held up a cigarette, stared at it for a moment, then put it back in the case. He slipped the gold case back into his jacket pocket.

Diane watched every move he made, trying to figure out what was going on.

Agent grant asked, "Detective, do you know a man named Mohammed Ali?"

"I know of someone with that name, a guy that works with

my brother. Why?"

"That man is a dangerous terrorist."

"I looked up his records. I didn't see anything in there about him being a terrorist, or even a suspect. He seemed clean to me."

Agent Grant nodded. "They always seem clean, Detective. That is how they infiltrate us. This man is a dangerous terrorist and should be considered as such."

Diane asked, "Why haven't any bulletins gone out?"

"We do not wish to alarm the public. We believe we can apprehend the suspect quietly and without any publicity. The Pentagon prefers it that way."

"My brother said a federal agent shot at his friend on the street in Bay Ridge on Sunday morning."

Agent Grant looked her in the eye and without hesitation said, "That would be reckless and irresponsible, Detective. I assure you that no such thing could have happened."

Diane nodded. She didn't trust this guy. There was something about him. Although, it did seem a far-fetched that a trained federal agent would shoot at a suspect in the middle of the street like a Texas Ranger in a western movie, she knew he was lying about something.

Agent Grant said, "I must ask you about your brother, Tony."

Diane said, "My brother is just trying to help out a friend from work. He's a good family man. All he did was ask me to look into it."

"Your brother works with Mr. Ali, and quite closely, Detective. The law requires me to ask. Do you or your brother know the whereabouts of Mr. Ali?"

"No, I do not. Am I under suspicion, Mr. Grant?"

He corrected her, "Agent Grant."

Diane glared at him. Agent Grant glared back at her. Eye to eye, neither blinked, neither looked away.

Agent Grant broke the silence, but never lowered his gaze. "At 5:58PM last night, Mohammed Ali called your brother's house from a pay phone in Brooklyn. Your brother said he could help him with food and money."

"You tapped my brother's phone?"

Without answering her and without releasing her gaze, Agent Grant continued, "Your brother sent you two text messages, Detective. One at 11:20PM and one at 11:30PM. You returned his call at—"

Diane was pissed. "You tapped my phone, too, you son of a bitch? What gives you the right?"

Agent Grant answered, "The Patriot Act."

"What? What about the Constitution? You can't just go around spying on American citizens, tapping our phones without warrants."

"Yes, I can, Detective, and it is The Patriot Act that gives me the right. The Constitution is obsolete."

She wished she could punch him right in his smug face, but it wasn't worth her career. "Get out." She spoke sternly, but without raising her voice. "Get the fuck outta here right now, you son of a bitch."

He placed his business card on the desk. "If you would like to speak after you calm down . . . here is my card"

That comment and his indifference boiled her blood even more, but she didn't say anything. She clenched her fists and held back her anger as Agent Grant turned around and left the office.

She waited until he was gone before picking up the card. She felt like tearing it in half, but she kept her cool and read it, Agent William Grant, Homeland Security, DCTA Division. On the top left corner was a triangular symbol. On the bottom right corner were three telephone numbers, each with a different area code, 202 for Washington DC, 212 for Manhattan, and 917 for a New York cell phone.

Diane took the card and stormed out of the office, passing right by Detective Garcia. She needed a cigarette.

"Hey, Diane!" Garcia stood, grabbed his jacket, and followed her down the stairs. "Don't forget about lunch. Hey, slow down!"

CHAPTER 42—TUESDAY 12:55PM

Mohammed had stayed on the R-Train to Queens and followed the bearded maintenance man as he got off the train at the busy Queensboro Plaza station.

While walking along the platform, he was able to catch a glimpse inside the young man's unzipped jacket. He saw a name patch that read Omar.

Up the stairs to the ground level then up two more flights of metal stairs to the elevated train platform, Mohammed stayed far enough back that he was out of sight, but close enough not to lose him.

The neighborhood below consisted of two and three-story brick buildings, fast food restaurants, medical offices, and a few stores.

The elevated platform began to vibrate as the sound of metal wheels screeching against metal tracks got louder. The 7-train pulled into the station. The doors opened and a few people got off.

Mohammed entered the same train car as Omar, but through the doors on the opposite side. He stood, peering out the window at the neighborhoods below for most of the trip, occasionally glancing over to see when Omar would be getting off. At one point during the ride, Omar looked directly at Mohammed, and Mohammed nervously looked away. Mohammed tried not to look directly at him after that.

He stared at the ads on the walls, trying to act natural. He read advertisements for lawyers, churches, dermatologists, and

New York Times bestselling novels. Out of the corner of his eye, Mohammed checked to make sure Omar was still there. He was.

After the Mets stadium, the elevated tracks turned and descended underground. The train continued through the dark tunnel until reaching Main Street in Flushing, the last stop.

Mohammed followed everyone out of the train and onto the platform. Omar was behind him. They continued toward the exit.

Just before going up the stairs, Mohammed decided to turn around for a quick look. Omar slipped into the train on the opposite side of the platform just as the doors were closing. The train took off back the way it came and Omar was gone.

Mohammed wondered when Omar realized he was following him. It must have been when he looked directly at him, or maybe even before that. He wondered if Omar even lived in Queens or if this whole trip was just a trick.

Now he definitely knew the man's name, and he knew Omar definitely worked at the building on Seventh Avenue, but he had a new problem. Omar knew what Mohammed looked like, and that would make it practically impossible to follow him again.

Mohammed's first thought was to call the cops. But, he knew he needed some kind of evidence against Omar before accusing him. He thought about calling Tony and telling him about Omar, but not yet. He still couldn't be sure if the iPhones could be tapped and he wasn't in the mood for another incident tonight.

He decided to go upstairs to the street, use the bathroom, get something to eat, and plan his next move.

CHAPTER 43—TUESDAY 1:45PM

Diane and Garcia sat at a booth in a small coffee shop. They had already eaten. Diane had a chicken salad and Garcia had a cheeseburger deluxe.

The waitress left their bill and picked up their plates.

Garcia said, "So, are you gonna make me ask?"

"Ask what?"

"Ask you why someone from Homeland Security would want to talk to you."

"Oh, that. Just some immigration questions about some Pakistani guy at my brother's job. I never even met the guy." Diane trusted Garcia completely, but she saw no point in bringing up her entire conversation with Agent Grant, which would only get her aggravated again.

They stood, put on their jackets, then each put two dollars on the table.

Diane paid the bill at the cashier while Garcia waited by the front door gawking at a wall covered with framed photographs autographed by minor celebrities.

Once outside, Garcia said, "Thanks for lunch."

"Don't mention it. See you tonight." Diane lit a cigarette and crossed the street to her SUV while Garcia headed to his car.

She got in and started the engine. The memory of Agent Grant was still fresh in her head. She didn't like his attitude, and she didn't like when people tried to play her.

Diane finished her cigarette then pulled out of her parking spot. She was exhausted. She just wanted to get home and get as much sleep as possible before coming all the way back up to the Bronx.

An accident on the Whitestone Bridge caused traffic to stop. Diane turned on the radio, but every station had either talk or commercials, so she turned it off.

Her Blackberry vibrated. It was a text message from Tony that read: any news on Mohammed?

She texted him back: Nothing. I'll call you later. She instantly deleted the message. She didn't even feel comfortable having Mohammed's name on her phone.

The motion of the windshield wipers and the fact that traffic wasn't moving was driving her crazy, and making her head hurt. She smoked another cigarette, but that just made her feel worse. She wanted to tell Tony to stay away from Mohammed, to forget the whole thing, but she also wanted to find out what was going on. She beeped her horn at the stopped traffic ahead then smacked the steering wheel.

It was then she considered calling her ex-boyfriend, Agent Jack Sullivan from the FBI. She hadn't spoken to Jack since their break up in May, and she didn't feel comfortable talking to him now. They did not have a bad break up, no one cheated or became violent, but Diane was a little hard on Jack, and she knew it, but at the time, she thought it was necessary. She still loved Jack and knew that he still loved her, even though they weren't together anymore.

After beeping the horn a few more times at the stagnant traffic ahead, Diane finally swallowed her pride and decided to call Jack. She picked up her Blackberry and scrolled through the phone book until finding his name. She had thought about deleting it on more than one occasion, but didn't. Her stomach twisted a little more with each ring. She thought about hanging up.

Jack Sullivan's booming voice answered, "Hello, Diane, this is quite a surprise."

"Hi, Jack, how are you?"

"I'm fine. How have you been?"

"Fine." She knew she couldn't waste all day with small talk, no matter how nervous she was. "I need some help, Jack."

"Are you alright?"

Diane smiled. "Is that concern I hear?"

Jack chuckled. "I guess it is."

"I'm alright, just that some federal agent came to see me today at the precinct, and I didn't like his attitude."

"You don't like most people's attitudes."

"I knew I shouldn't have called you." She was about to hang up.

"I'm just trying to break the ice, Diane. I haven't heard from you in six months and now you call me out of nowhere."

"I'm sorry. It's just been a rough week."

"I know. I heard. You're quite the hero these days."

Diane would never admit it, but after hearing Jack's strong but gentle voice, she wondered if she didn't make a mistake by dumping him.

"Diane? Are you still there?"

"I'm here."

Jack said, "Whatever you need, I'll do my best to help."

"Ever hear of the DCTA, a division of Homeland Security?"

"No, but I'm sure I can find out something."

"The creep's name who came to see me was Agent Grant."

"Why would Homeland Security come to see you in narcotics?"

"Because of some guy who works with my brother, a Pakistani immigrant named Mohammed Ali. My brother said that a few uniforms and a fed chased Mohammed through the projects in Brooklyn then the agent shot at him in Bay Ridge. They tapped Tony's phone and my phone too, the bastards."

Jack asked, "What do you mean, he shot at him?"

"I mean he took out his gun and opened fire, in the middle of a residential street in Bay Ridge, at eight o'clock in the morning, on Sunday. I asked Agent Grant about it, but he denied it. I don't trust that smug bastard. I know he's got something to hide."

"And this Mohammed, what's his story?"

"He appears to be clean. He just became a citizen last year, and he was working with Tony on the scaffold until Friday. Mohammed told Tony that he called the police to report a terrorist plot he discovered and the police thought Mohammed was lying. I know it sounds fishy, and you know I never trusted those people, but this Agent Grant's story smells even fishier than Mohammed's. And, I promised Tony I would check it out."

Jack agreed. "Something doesn't sound right. I'll have someone from counter-terrorism look into it."

Traffic finally started moving again. Diane stepped on the gas and headed over the bridge. It was only a minor accident, but she was past it now. Traffic flowed, and her blood pressure returned to normal.

Jack asked, "So, would you like to meet for lunch?"

"I just finished having lunch with my partner."

"How is Minnelli, anyway?"

"Minnelli retired a few months ago. I have a new partner now, Detective Garcia."

"Garcia? Oh, Garcia, the fat guy with the donuts."

"Be nice."

Jack chuckled. "So, what about dinner later?"

"I have the wake."

"Of course, how could I forget? Such a shame to see a good cop die. Did you know him?"

"Not personally."

Diane wanted to have dinner with Jack. She missed him, but she didn't want to go down that road again. She knew he would ask again, so she lied. "I'll see if I could squeeze dinner in next week sometime."

"That would be nice. I'll call you after I find out about your brother's friend."

CHAPTER 44—TUESDAY 2:33PM

Andrew had been working on his boring financial case all day and his vision started to blur. He rubbed his eyes and finally decided he needed a break. He thought that by starting early, he would finish early, but now he wasn't so sure about that. The numbers just never seemed to end.

After putting his computer to sleep and locking up his office, he took the elevator downstairs for a late lunch.

He waited for the light to change then crossed the three-lane street to the concrete island with the cast-iron pylon in the center. He approached a food cart and ordered a sandwich.

An old Greek man chopped some chicken and threw it onto the scalding hot grill. An old Greek woman filled a pita bread with lettuce, tomatoes, onion, and white sauce. Andrew asked for a can of iced tea and paid the woman for his lunch while the old man seared the chicken on the grill and placed it into the bread.

With the sandwich in a paper bag, he strolled to the small park next to the concrete island and found a vacant bench facing the old government buildings opposite from his office building.

He ate his sandwich while watching the traffic and the bustling crowds of people go about their business. The air was cold, but the sky was clear and sunny.

After finishing his lunch, Andrew dialed his wife and waited while it rang.

Amy answered, "Hi, baby."

"Hi, honey. What are you up to?"

"Just finished talking with my mother. Getting ready to pick up the kids now. What about you, Mr. Bond?"

"Taking a late lunch. I'm working on the most boring case. Hope it's over soon."

"Why didn't you wake me this morning?"

"I left an hour early, wanted to let you sleep. I did give you a kiss, though."

"I don't remember it."

"So I'll give you two kisses when I get home."

"I can't wait," said Amy. "Sorry, baby, but I have to run to get the kids. I don't want to talk and drive."

"Okay, honey. I'll see you tonight. Love you."

"Love you." Amy terminated the call.

Andrew put his phone away, stood and stretched, then took a deep breath of the crisp cool air before going back up to the office for more boring computer work.

He didn't seem to need any experience in following money. The accounting expert showed him how to sift through bank account numbers, transactions, and donations. A robot could have done the job.

Back in his office, he typed in his password to take his computer out of sleep mode. His head and eyes still hurt, so he massaged them, then glanced at his family in the picture on the desk before turning back to his computer screen.

His mind drifted. He thought about Agent Grant and that Mohammed guy he was searching for. He wondered if Agent Grant caught him.

CHAPTER 45—TUESDAY 3:14PM

Standing on the corner of Main Street, Mohammed observed the bustling Queens neighborhood that smelled of fried food and carbon emissions. Some of the stores had signs in English, but more than half the signs were in Chinese, or maybe Korean.

Cars beeped their horns at each other while fighting their way through traffic at the huge intersection. People shopping and eating and vendors selling things on fold-out tables crowded the sidewalks.

Mohammed's stomach was empty, so he crossed the street and went into a Chinese restaurant. Inside, the place was small, but crowded. He studied the pictures of meals above the counter while waiting behind a few people who were ordering. Many of the dishes looked good in the pictures, but he didn't know much about Chinese food, and he didn't want to take a chance of eating anything with pork in it. He ordered something clean and simple, steamed chicken and broccoli with white rice.

All the tables were taken, so Mohammed ate his food while standing at the counter against the wall. Two chubby construction workers that smelled of beer stood next to him at the counter scarfing down food Mohammed had never seen before.

After his meal, Mohammed headed back outside and proceeded south along Main Street trying to figure out what to do. He wanted to go back to the building tomorrow and follow Omar. But what if Omar spotted him again? What if Omar had the other two men with him? What if Omar didn't even work tomorrow?

Mohammed's head was spinning with possibilities.

He stopped when he saw a men's clothing store that had a sign outside: SUITS $79. Mohammed knew he would look a lot less like a terrorist in a suit, and he hoped he could fool Omar by wearing a suit, so he went inside to see if they were really only $79.

A young Jewish man wearing a black yarmulke cap greeted Mohammed as an old Jewish man sat behind the counter, half-asleep.

"May I help you?" asked the young man.

"Are the suits really $79?" Asked Mohammed.

"Some of them are." The salesman showed him one rack and said, "These suits are $79." He pointed at another rack and said, "These are $99." He pointed at another rack and said, "These are $129."

Mohammed couldn't tell the difference in quality by looking at them, but he'd never owned a suit before. He browsed through the $79 rack and saw a few dark gray suits with light gray stripes. He pointed at one of them and said, "I like this style."

"What size are you?"

"I don't know," answered Mohammed. "This is my first suit."

The salesman took one of the jackets off the hanger and said, "This is a forty. Try it on."

Mohammed put the jacket on, but it was a little tight in the back and the sleeves were a little short. "Do you have another one like this, a little bigger?" He took it off and gave it back.

The salesman found a 42. The jacket fit perfectly, so he tried the pants on in the fitting room. They were also a perfect fit. No alterations were necessary.

Mohammed said, "I need a shirt, too, and shoes. I need everything."

The salesman gave Mohammed a white shirt, a gray tie, and a pair of black shoes. "I'll give you everything for $160. A special price, only for you."

Mohammed thought about the money. If he had to keep running, the five hundred dollars Tony had given him wouldn't go far, especially with one-sixty gone at once. Then again, if those men really were planning to bomb the Thanksgiving parade, he only had less than two days left anyway. He decided the suit would be a good investment, a good disguise that would give him an advantage while following Omar tomorrow.

He stood there wearing the entire outfit and pointed at a selection of fedoras on the wall. "How much is that hat on the wall, the gray one?"

"I'll give you that hat for $25."

"Give me everything for $170."

"I can't. $180 is the lowest I can go.

Mohammed pulled out his money and said, "$175, cash." He counted out $175 and handed it to the salesman. "No tax."

The salesman hesitated a moment before taking the money. "You have a deal."

"Thank you." Mohammed put the hat on and strutted out of the store in his new suit with the clothes Tony had given him in a plastic shopping bag from the store.

Outside, he took the earring out of his ear and rubbed his red infected earlobe.

While passing an Irish pub, a short chubby Colombian man handed Mohammed a business card and said, "Chicas."

Mohammed had heard about these chicas before. They were prostitutes. He didn't intend to get a prostitute, but he knew this man could help him with something else, so he said, "I need a hotel, a cheap one."

The man said, "Go down two more blocks then make right at the taco stand. After another block and a half, you'll see it. It's $20 an hour, or $80 for the night. Then you call the number on that card when you're ready for your chica, or chicas . . . if you can handle more than one." The man laughed and slapped Mohammed on the shoulder.

Mohammed said, "Thank you," then followed the man's directions.

After he turned the corner, Mohammed threw the business card into a garbage can. He bought a bottle of rubbing alcohol and some fruit for later from a small Korean grocery store on the corner then headed to the hotel.

The hotel lobby was nothing more than a dingy hallway with a staircase and an enclosed bullet-proof glass booth at the end.

Mohammed approached the Indian man inside the booth and spoke through a small metal screen. "One night please." He slipped four twenty dollar bills into the slot at the bottom of the glass barrier.

The man slipped him a key that read 402 and said, "Fourth floor. Eleven AM checkout."

Mohamed took the keys, thanked him, and climbed the stairs. On the way up, he smelled mildew and marijuana and heard people in different rooms moaning, laughing, and arguing.

The second of six doors on the fourth floor was Mohammed's room. The key went into the lock easily, but he had to jiggle it a little to get it to turn.

A full-sized mattress on the floor took up most of the room. It wasn't the cleanest place in the world, but it was much better than the urine and graffiti-covered overpass, and there was a shower.

After squeezing the puss from his infected earlobe and washing it with alcohol, Mohammed took off his shoes and socks. His feet were still scabbed up and swollen, and infected. He washed them with soap and water then with alcohol until he couldn't stand the burning any longer.

Before taking a shower, he filled the tub and soaked his throbbing feet for a while. He felt much better now that he was clean, but his feet were in more pain than before.

Wearing just his boxer shorts, Mohammed got down on his hands and knees on the floor next to the mattress and prayed for about twenty minutes before turning off the lights and lying down on top of the blankets.

His mind raced, thinking of how he would go after Omar tomorrow, thinking of every possible scenario.

CHAPTER 46—TUESDAY 4:41PM

At home, stretched out on her sofa, Diane had only slept an hour and a half when her phone rang. She glanced over at the screen and saw it was her mother calling. She answered the phone, "Yeah, Ma."

"Are you up?"

"I am now. Why?"

"Your Cousin Connie is here with the baby."

Diane wanted to see the baby, but she also wanted to sleep. Connie lived in Long Island with her husband. This was her first child. Diane's parents drove out there to see the baby four months ago, just after Connie gave birth. Diane had to work that day and promised she would make it out to see the baby another time. Now Connie was here, and Diane didn't have any excuses. "I'll be down in a few minutes, Ma."

She checked the gauze on her arm then threw on a clean pair of sweatpants and an oversized T-shirt. She grabbed her cigarettes then remembered she can't smoke with a baby around.

Once downstairs, Diane kissed and hugged her Cousin Connie, who was at least thirty pounds heavier than the last time she saw her.

Before she even had a chance to look at him, Mrs. Lasalvo shoved the baby into Diane's arms. The baby cried as Diane tried to hold him in different positions. Mr. Lasalvo sat in his chair laughing at Diane's difficulty.

Connie helped position Diane's arms and adjusted the crying

baby boy. "He likes to be held like this."

The baby reduced its sobbing then eventually stopped completely.

Mrs. Lasalvo said, "Now, don't you wanna have one of these?"

Connie chimed in, "Just one?"

Diane smiled at the helpless baby as he wrapped his tiny hand around his finger. "He is cute. But I prefer other people's kids. I could enjoy them without having to change any diapers."

She did want a baby of her own, instinctively anyway. Women were having babies older than ever these days, but she also knew the risks would increase with age. If she were going to have children, now would be the time. What she didn't want, however, was to raise a child in such a cruel and corrupt world. How could she guarantee her child a good future? What if she didn't make it home from work one night, like Armstrong? The child would have to grow up without a mother.

Still holding Diane's finger, the baby giggled. She smiled and brought the baby closer to her face to savor his aroma. She didn't want a baby, but at the same time, she did. His newborn baby smell penetrated her brain through her nostrils and unleashed a flood of emotions inside her. She knew the feelings were just the result of hormones and her ticking biological clock, but it didn't matter, the feelings were still there.

The baby hiccupped. Everyone laughed. He hiccupped again, but this time milk projected out of his throat and onto Diane's T-shirt, breaking the spell that temporarily held her. She held the baby away from her clothes while her father laughed louder than everyone else.

Connie took the baby and wiped his mouth with a cloth.

Mrs. Lasalvo looked at the vomit on Diane's shirt and said, "It's just milk. No big deal."

"I'm going up to change. I have to get ready for the wake anyway."

Connie said, "Oh . . . Sorry to hear about what happened. Were you close?"

"I didn't know him personally. But it's always hard to lose a fellow officer."

"I could imagine." Connie wiped the baby's face.

Diane kissed her cousin then headed back upstairs.

CHAPTER 47—TUESDAY 5:43PM

Andrew turned off his computer, stood, and stretched his legs and back. He turned the light switch off before closing and locking the office door behind him.

Just before heading down the hallway, he noticed Agent Grant turn the corner.

Agent Grant approached him and said, "Hello, Agent Miller. I hear the case is going well."

"Yes, sir. We discovered two deposits into an American bank account from an offshore account."

"Keep up the good work, Agent Miller." Agent Grant passed Andrew and continued down the carpeted hall without another word.

Andrew was still curious about that Mohammed character who made him miss a Sunday with his family, but he didn't ask. He continued down the hall, passing people who were still working in offices and cubicles. He turned the corner and pressed the button for the elevator, which he then took downstairs.

After leaving the huge marble lobby, he headed outside, happy the long day was over and he wouldn't have to think about this place again until tomorrow morning.

It was already dark outside, and the temperature had dropped drastically since the afternoon. A cold breeze shot right through Andrew's clothes and penetrated his flesh. His mind drifted back to the warm San Diego sun. He wondered if he should have just stayed there. His wife had her family and the kids had their friends, they were happy there.

Andrew knew he should have been satisfied with his job at the police department and his life with his family in sunny San Diego, but something inside him kept pushing him forward, pushing him to do greater things, and he just couldn't resist the urge.

CHAPTER 48—TUESDAY 7:00PM

Thousands of cops flooded the entire neighborhood, many times more than last night. Diane parked a few blocks away from the funeral home, checked her dress uniform in the mirror, then headed down the block.

After crossing the intersection, she noticed another cop in dress uniform getting out of his car across the street. She knew him. She waited for two cars to pass then crossed over to the other side just before the man made his way down the sidewalk, a distinguished older man with captain's bars on his shoulder and an impressive collection of medals on his chest.

Diane called out, "Excuse me, sir."

He turned around and looked at her face for just a moment before responding, "Diane Lasalvo? Is that you?"

"Hello, Lieutenant . . ." Diane glanced over at his captain's rank and said, "I'm sorry . . . Captain Gagliano."

Gagliano was Diane's first sergeant when she was fresh out of the academy and working in Manhattan. She knew he had a crush on her, and she had one on him. But, not only was he at least ten years older than she, he was also married. He transferred to Brooklyn after his promotion to Lieutenant.

Gagliano said, "Look at you, all grown up."

"And you don't look a day older."

He smiled. "Oh, I'm older alright. I'm a grandfather now."

"A grandfather? I can't believe it."

"Neither can I sometimes." He scrolled through some

pictures on his phone and showed her three little boys, each a year older than the next.

"Wow, your son has been busy."

"He has his father's genes."

Diane laughed.

"So what about you, Lasalvo? Any kids?"

"No. I've been too busy."

"Well, you better get started soon."

"Thanks."

"Not that you're old. I mean . . . you are still a beautiful girl. Not that I ever noticed—"

Diane laughed. "You better stop while you're behind."

"Right."

They made their way through the crowd to the funeral home. Diane looked at the long line of people waiting to get in. It wrapped around the corner. She dreaded having to go back in there again and face Armstrong's family. That was worse than looking at his lifeless body.

Gagliano said, "I have to tell you, Diane, there's nothing like the joy you get from children . . . except the joy you get from grandchildren."

From behind her, Garcia called Diane's name.

She turned around and saw him waddling over in his tight dress uniform. "Slow down, you might bust a button."

Garcia said, "Even at a funeral you make fat jokes?"

"Garcia, do you know Captain Gagliano?"

Garcia said, "No. We've never met."

The two men shook hands.

Gagliano's cell phone rang. He reached for it. "Hello?" He held the phone down and said, "I'm sorry, I have to take this call. I'll see you later?"

Diane said, "Okay."

Gagliano crossed the street as Garcia and Diane joined the line to get in.

CHAPTER 49—TUESDAY 10:01PM

Barely awake, Andrew lay in bed watching TV while his wife lay next to him reading a novel.

On the TV, an attractive middle-aged woman reported the first story: "A sting in Albany brought down four terrorists and has five others on the run. The nine men are members of a domestic terrorist organization from Long Island known as The Second Revolution."

Andrew's eyes widened as he lifted his head from his pillow.

The woman on TV continued: "Federal agents in New York sold the terrorist group fake bombs, which they then transported upstate to Albany. Undercover agents from Albany moved in and arrested the terrorists when they tried to detonate the fake bombs this morning at various government buildings, including the IRS."

Andrew said, "I can't believe it."

His wife lowered her book, looked at Andrew, then at the TV.

The news report continued: "Federal authorities stated that the public was never in any danger. When detonated, the fake bombs released a stream of harmless white smoke into the air."

Amy asked Andrew, "What's wrong?"

"That was my case. I set the whole thing up then had to transfer it to Albany because of jurisdiction guidelines."

On the TV, a round-faced man with salt and pepper hair began to speak. "Tonight in the Bronx, funeral services began for fallen Officer Reginald Armstrong."

Amy said, "I thought you weren't supposed to talk about your cases."

"It doesn't matter now, it's over. And I've been stuck staring at numbers for the past day and a half."

"Don't worry, baby. You'll get your chance to save the world."

Andrew turned off the TV. The small reading lamp on Amy's night table was the only light in the room.

Amy moved closer to Andrew and said, "Hey, Mr. Government man, I'm feeling a little naughty. Why don't you come and arrest me?"

Andrew rolled her over and jumped on top of her, pinning her hands to the bed. He kissed her with a hundred little kisses as she giggled then he let her hands go. She wrapped her arms around him and pulled him closer.

CHAPTER 50—WEDNESDAY 2:15AM

Diane and Garcia sat at their desks at the precinct, typing information into their computers. The only sound they made was the tapping of keys on the keyboard.

Garcia yawned and stretched his arms over his head. "I could use a cup of coffee."

"I could go for one myself. And a cigarette, too."

Garcia pressed enter on his keyboard. "I just sent something to the printer. Some old lady complained about people selling drugs on her block."

Diane stood and said, "So, let's go check it out."

Garcia got up, approached the printer in the corner, and waited for his document to finish. He removed it from the paper tray and glanced at it before following Diane out the door.

Outside, the cold wind made it hard for Diane to light her cigarette, so she waited until they got into their unmarked cruiser.

Sitting in the passenger seat, she rolled down the window, lit her cigarette, then asked Garcia, "Do you ever worry about not coming home to your wife and kids, like Armstrong?"

"Of course, I worry," replied Garcia, "but I try not to. Life is too short. I just enjoy the time that I do have with my wife and my son. I can't spend my entire life worrying about death."

Diane steamed her cigarette while staring out her window. "But our job can be dangerous."

Garcia made a right turn and pulled over in front of a twenty-four hour coffee shop. He double-parked the car, turned off the ignition, and said, "Life can be dangerous. Remember when that van flew off the expressway and landed in the Bronx zoo, killing seven people? What can you do? Never go to the zoo again?"

CHAPTER 51—WEDNESDAY 5:59AM

Andrew had already finished a three-mile run around the sleeping neighborhood and was back at home in his bathroom. He took a towel and a floor mat from the cabinet then turned the shower on and took his clothes off.

A set of decorative lavender towels hung on one wall just under a few pictures of horses. A basket of potpourri sat on the toilet tank next to a candle in a glass jar.

Amy stumbled into the bathroom, her eyes barely open. "Good morning."

"Good morning." Andrew kissed her before stepping into the shower. He knew she wasn't a morning person, but she always pretended for his sake. He thought the gesture was cute.

She sat on the toilet.

He spoke to her while lathering himself up with soap. "I was thinking about San Diego yesterday."

"What do you mean?" she asked.

"I was thinking we never should have left."

She flushed the toilet and washed her hands. "Now you say that? I never wanted to leave in the first place. We came here because of that job, because you want to save the world."

"I know. It's just not turning out the way I thought it would. And I know you and the kids hate it here." He quickly scrubbed himself down with a washcloth.

She opened the shower curtain as he rinsed the soap off his face. "So let's go back."

"We can't go back just like that. I wouldn't even have a job."

Amy said, "You know I could get my old job back, and I bet you could, too."

"What if I can't?"

"What if you can?" She asked, "If they give you your job back, can we leave this cold, God-forsaken place?"

Andrew laughed while rinsing himself off. "Maybe. Let's talk about it more later."

Just as he was about to turn off the water, Amy let her pajamas drop to the floor and got into the shower with him, closing the curtain behind her. She stopped him from turning the valve and kissed his chest.

Andrew didn't want her to stop, but he didn't want to be late for work either. "Stop, honey. I'm going to be late."

"Who cares?" She said, "We're going back to San Diego anyway."

"Maybe," said Andrew, laughing while half-heartedly trying to resist her. "I said, maybe. That doesn't mean yes."

She giggled and began to lather him up again with soap.

CHAPTER 52—WEDNESDAY 8:17AM

After leaving the filthy hotel and scarfing down a bagel and a cup of tea at a deli, Mohammed strutted down Main Street feeling like a new man. His new suit and hat looked good on him, and he liked the way he felt in it. While passing a store window, he glanced at his reflection and adjusted his tie. He felt hope. He was going to find the terrorists, clear his name, and go back to living his life.

Before entering the staircase to the train station below, Mohammed walked over to a newsstand and bought a copy of the New York Times. He knew it would be the perfect accessory, and he could use it to hide his face when necessary.

Light drizzle began to fall, so Mohammed hurried to an old Chinese woman who was selling umbrellas in front of the subway entrance. She had small plastic-handled umbrellas for four dollars and large wood-handled umbrellas for eight dollars. Mohammed bought a large one to help keep the rain off his new suit and to help hide his face.

He went the opposite way on the same trains that he'd taken while following Omar to Main Street the day before.

He got off the train at 49th Street in Manhattan and climbed the stairs to the street. The rain was light, but steady. People walking in all directions crowded the sidewalks, and their open umbrellas made it even harder to move. Taxis zipped back and forth with their windshield wipers going side to side while trucks with their lights still on fought for space to make their deliveries.

Mohammed approached a coffee cart parked on the corner

and waited behind a few other people in a single file line. When it was his turn, he bought a tea with milk. Just after buying, he realized he probably shouldn't have. He had one tea already and no place to use the bathroom. He just tried not to think about it.

While holding his umbrella overhead, Mohammed tried to sip his tea from his other hand. A young man bumped into him. Mohammed pulled his body back just in time. The tea spilled straight down, onto the sidewalk, without touching his clothes or anyone else.

That was enough of a warning. Mohammed turned around and went back down the stairs and into the train station.

He sat on a wood bench and drank his tea while waiting for Omar.

CHAPTER 53—WEDNESDAY 10:00AM

Diane stood at attention next to Garcia along with thousands of other cops in dress uniform. They stood on one side of the closed street while thousands more stood at attention on the other side. Although the rain was light, Diane knew she would be saturated by the end of the funeral.

The NYPD motorcycle honor guard rumbled down the street, through the parted sea of police officers. Diane heard them before she saw them, two single file lines of refined police officers riding Harley-Davidsons.

Dressed in blue kilts, with green knee-high socks and white shoes, The Emerald Society played a slow march on the drums as they followed the motorcycles.

A black Cadillac hearse flanked by four police officers on each side trailed the drummers on their way to a huge limestone church.

The hearse and the drums stopped at the same time.

The Emerald Society began playing their bagpipes while the eight honorary officers removed the casket from the hearse. An American flag lay draped over the coffin. The officers carried it into the church and then there was silence.

Diane and Garcia were too far away to hear the service inside the church and the mayor's speech afterward. They just stayed at attention along with the thousands of others.

After the service, the bagpipes played again while the honorary guard brought the casket back outside and loaded it back into the hearse.

The rain came down a little harder while the funeral procession headed down the street, toward the cemetery. Limousines and police cars followed the hearse as they passed block after block of saluting officers.

CHAPTER 54—WEDNESDAY 11:00AM

Andrew had made it to work ten minutes late that morning, but nobody said anything. He looked like a typical agent in a black suit this morning, not to impress Agent Grant, but because most of his other suits were at the cleaners and he felt like wearing something different today.

Sitting in his office, at his computer, he needed a break from all the numbers on his screen, so he went to the bathroom to splash some water on his face. The more time he spent on the computer, the more he hated it. He knew Agent Grant was right. He had a family, and it was safer to let the grunts do the dangerous work, but, if not on the front lines, he still wanted to do something more exciting than this. How much of this type of work was involved in this job?

Andrew headed back to his office and logged onto his computer. When the numbers and names of banks and transactions popped back up, his mind began to drift again. He thought about Agent Grant and the man he was chasing, Mohammed Ali.

He thought back to Mohammed's records. How could someone fake everything all the way back to his family history in Pakistan? It just didn't seem plausible, not without some serious help.

He remembered hearing Agent Grant mention that Mohammed had called 911 at 4AM on Sunday morning. Andrew pulled up the records for all 911 calls around 4AM in Brooklyn, which were easy to find. Anything was easy to find using a

Homeland Security computer.

After scrolling through the list of calls, he noticed there were some calls listed as classified. His clearance allowed him access to those calls. Andrew pinpointed Mohammed's address on Nostrand Avenue. He downloaded the file and listened to a recording of the call. Mohammed had mentioned a building on Seventh Avenue, probably the building where he worked at. He also mentioned three men in maintenance uniforms. Could he have been telling the truth?

Andrew checked his watch. He knew he should be working on his primary case, but this was much more interesting. He decided to check out one more thing, then get back to work.

He pulled up the file on the building where Mohammed worked and scrolled through a list of employees. Most had English, Spanish, or Italian names, except for a fifty-six-year-old Albanian man and a twenty-two-year-old refugee from Afghanistan named Omar Kadir. He knew it was racial profiling, but he couldn't help it. He pulled up Omar's records first.

Omar Kadir, twenty-two years old, the son of a poppy farmer in Afghanistan. Omar moved to the US after a bomb killed his entire family. He was out playing soccer with friends at the time. The US blamed the Taliban and the Taliban blamed the US.

Omar had an uncle in Queens who had been living there for over twenty years. Omar went to live with his uncle and enrolled in high school, knowing only a handful of English words. When Omar turned eighteen, his uncle got him a maintenance job where he worked at the building on 7th Avenue. Omar's uncle died two years ago.

Omar lives alone and never married. He usually works the night shift, but Thursday afternoon, he came in early and worked a double to replace one of the other maintenance men who was on vacation.

Andrew read Omar's record twice and was surprised Agent Grant could have missed something like this. This is the classic profile of a terrorist.

He searched the list again. Mohammed said there were three men. He pasted the list of building employees to the DMV data banks and searched. He looked at all the pictures. None of the other employees resembled Omar or Mohammed in any way. Maybe the other two men didn't work there.

He couldn't help thinking Mohammed was right and Agent Grant was chasing the wrong man. Agent Grant seemed too smart to make a mistake like that.

He wanted to call Agent Grant and tell him what he discovered, but what was his excuse for ignoring his duties and butting into somebody else's case? He didn't call Agent Grant. He just went back to work, staring at the numbers on his screen, but still thinking about Omar Kadir.

CHAPTER 55—WEDNESDAY 11:40AM

Mohammed had waited on the hard bench for so long he had to stand to stretch his legs and give his butt a break. The trains ran less frequently with fewer passengers on them. Mohammed had felt safe on the bench in his suit reading the New York Times during the morning rush hour, but not anymore, now he felt out of place and out in the open.

He turned his head slightly and glanced back when he saw a cop on the platform.

The cop looked right at Mohammed, and Mohammed got nervous and turned away. He knew he shouldn't have done that, but it was too late. He wasn't very good at this cloak and dagger stuff. The New York Times was still open on his lap, so Mohammed lifted it and tried to concentrate on one of the articles, hoping the cop wasn't suspicious of him.

As the platform began to rumble, Mohammed glanced over. First, he saw the headlights, then he heard the wheels grinding against their tracks as the train pulled into the station and stopped. The doors opened, and the cop entered the train behind a few other people. Mohammed exhaled then buried his face back in the paper.

After the train pulled out of the station, Mohammed glanced over at the digital clock hanging from the ceiling near the stairs. It was already 11:50AM, and Omar still wasn't there. Mohammed wondered if he'd already missed his opportunity. He didn't want to feel that all was lost, but as time went on, it did begin to feel that way. He thought about what he would do if he didn't find Omar. His only choice would be to go to the building tomorrow and hope to stop Omar and the other two terrorists during the parade.

He turned the page, and out of the corner of his eye, Mohammed spotted Omar standing on the opposite end of the platform. He must have walked right behind him, and neither noticed each other.

Mohammed tried unsuccessfully to control his heart rate. He knew he had to stay out of sight, but at the same time, he had to get closer to Omar.

He waited about ten minutes until he heard the next train on its way. He stood and strolled along the platform toward the other end where Omar was standing. With his fedora tipped slightly in the front and using his long umbrella as a cane, Mohammed continued forward with his newspaper under his arm, hoping Omar wouldn't recognize him.

Omar glanced in Mohammed's direction, but didn't pay much attention to him. The disguise worked.

Mohammed didn't get too close. He stopped about fifty feet from Omar.

The train pulled in and opened its doors. Mohammed stepped into the far side of the car that was behind the car Omar got in.

He strolled to the subway map posted on the wall and looked at it for a moment. He turned and walked toward the door at the end of the car. Glancing out the window, he saw Omar sitting in the next car.

Mohammed sat where he could still see if Omar was getting off. He kept his hat down and his newspaper up.

Omar took the same trains into Queens that he'd taken the day before. The light rain became a little heavier as the elevated train descended underground into the dark tunnel. The train stopped at the last stop, Main Street, Flushing.

The doors opened and everyone got out.

Mohammed hoped Omar didn't make him again as he stepped out of the train. He stayed far behind Omar this time while following the crowd up the stairs to the sidewalk above.

Mohammed stepped to the side and stood facing a store window. Omar looked around before opening a small umbrella and heading south on Main Street.

With his large umbrella blocking the rain and at the same time hiding his face, Mohammed stayed at least two blocks back as he followed Omar down the busy sidewalk for about fifteen minutes to a less populated intersection with a few Afghani stores and restaurants.

Omar turned the corner.

Mohammed hurried to the corner, but he didn't turn, he just watched. He could still see Omar from three blocks away. Mohammed waited and watched as Omar continued down the quiet residential street then into a small building.

After waiting thirty seconds, Mohammed turned the corner and followed Omar's steps. The two-story wood houses with cross-gabled roofs appeared much older than the houses he'd seen in Staten Island, and they had less space between them. The next few blocks consisted of more houses.

Mohammed stopped at the building that Omar had entered, a mosque. He thought it was funny that the two-story beige stucco-faced Mosque would be sitting directly across the street from a two-story beige stucco-faced Christian church.

Complete with an arched entrance, a dome, and a tower, the modern mosque had been designed in the traditional style. The church across the street was a rectangular building with a tower, a steeple, and a cross. It looked as if both buildings had the same designer and the same builder.

Mohammed entered the mosque and slipped off his hat and shoes. He looked around, but didn't see Omar anywhere. He noticed a fire exit on the opposite wall and realized Omar may have slipped away. He knew this place wasn't random. Omar had to have been here before, or he wouldn't know where to find it.

Mohammed approached an old man who was filling the washbasins with fresh water. He raised his right hand to his forehead and said, "As-Salamu Alaykum."

Also raising his right hand to his forehead, the old man said, "As-Salamu Alaykum."

Mohammed began to wash his hands and forearms. He wasn't sure where the man was from, so he spoke English. "I am late in meeting a friend. Maybe you know him. His name is Omar."

"I just saw him." The old man looked around. "You must have just missed him."

"I see."

The old man wiped his hands with a towel and said, "You

could probably find Omar at the youth center on Sanford."

"Is that near Main Street?"

"It's a few blocks after Kissena."

Mohammed wanted to get more information, but didn't want to make the old man suspicious. He thanked the man then went to pray on the checkered carpet.

After a few minutes of prayer on his hands and knees, Mohammed put his shoes and hat back on and left the building.

It was still raining outside, not as heavy, but steady. Before stepping all the way out, Mohammed looked around, ready to open his umbrella.

A black sedan passed right in front of the mosque. Mohammed stepped back, under the arched doorway. The license plate number on the car was 2211.

The sedan continued north toward Main Street. Mohammed wondered if they had followed him here. Then he wondered why they didn't just arrest him if they already knew where he was. Maybe they were just following him to see where he went. Maybe they were after Omar and the real terrorists.

Mohammed left the mosque with his umbrella overhead and hurried back toward Main Street. He stopped at a Shish-Kebab restaurant he'd seen on his way to the mosque. He needed something to eat and hoped someone there could give him exact directions to the youth center.

Inside, the Shish-Kebab restaurant looked like it used to be a pizzeria. Pictures of the Mediterranean hung on the walls along with a Turkish flag.

Mohammed approached the tall Turkish girl at the register and ordered two chicken kebabs, a small order of rice, and a can of Coke.

After writing the order on a paper ticket and giving it to the short Mexican man in the kitchen, she returned to the register.

Mohammed asked for directions to the youth center. She wasn't sure about the center, but she told him how to get to Kissena and Sanford.

CHAPTER 56—WEDNESDAY 1:45PM

Andrew's mind kept drifting. The numbers on the screen blurred together. He couldn't tell what he was looking at anymore. He had to stop. He closed his eyes for a minute and rubbed his temples.

He decided to call Agent Grant and tell him what he discovered about Omar Kadir. He didn't care about the consequences. Even if Agent Grant fired him, he would just go back to San Diego. He picked up his Motorola and dialed. The phone went to voicemail. Andrew spoke, "This is Agent Miller. I just came across some interesting—"

A beeping sound interrupted his message. He checked his phone. It was Agent Grant calling. He ended the message and switched over. "Miller here."

"Agent Miller. What can I help you with?"

"I was just leaving you a voice mail. I found something interesting. I looked up the building where Mohammed Ali works and discovered a man named Omar Kadir. This guy really fits the profile of a terrorist."

Agent Grant asked, "Have you finished your primary case?"

"No, sir." Andrew decided honesty was the best policy. "That case had me falling asleep, sir. I just needed something to keep my mind working, so I looked up the 911 call from Mohamed Ali. I'm sorry, sir. I'll dock myself for the time I spent off my case."

"You will do no such thing, Agent Miller. You have proved to be quite the investigator. I could use more of your help on this case, if you do not mind giving up your primary case."

"I don't mind at all, sir. I'm anxious to get out there with you."

"I need you to meet me in Queens at 3:15PM. I will text you the address now."

"Yes, sir. Thank you, sir" Andrew listened for a minute but didn't hear anything. Agent Grant had already hung up.

Just as Andrew terminated the call a text message came through, an address in Queens.

CHAPTER 57—WEDNESDAY 2:00PM

The rain began tapping a little harder on Mohammed's umbrella as he hurried down Main Street going the same direction the black sedan had gone. He turned on Kissena, a tree-lined street populated with brick apartment buildings.

Sanford was two blocks away. He turned and followed it for a few blocks until finding a block of stores. All one-story buildings, all connected, a small grocery store, a pharmacy, a car service, and a laundromat. A few stores were empty.

Above the last store was a sign that read Queens Islamic Community Youth Center. There were no windows, only a door with an air conditioner above it. There was no way to see inside without going inside.

Mohammed prayed for guidance then entered the building. It looked like a giant classroom. An old wood desk and chair on the back wall faced row after row of metal foldout chairs. A few young men were sitting in small groups here and there, talking, and some laughing.

Mohammed looked around for Omar or either of the other two men whom he'd seen with Omar on Thursday. He didn't see any of them.

An older man with a black and gray moustache and goatee approached Mohammed with a smile. A red and white checkered scarf covered his head and a spotless white robe covered his body down to his ankles, revealing only the black sandals on his pedicured feet. The man placed his hand over his heart and bowed.

"As-Salamu Alaykum."

"As-Salamu Alaykum." Mohammed looked into the man's faded blue eyes and said, "A friend from work told me I should come here, but I don't see him."

The man spoke with an Arabic accent, "I am Hesam."

"I am Mohammed, Mohammed Ali."

Hesam smiled. "You can wait here for your friend if you like."

"I have to pick up my cousin in an hour." Mohammed lied again, but hoped God would forgive him under the circumstances.

Hesam handed Mohammed a business card with the name and phone number of the youth center. The address wasn't there. "You are welcome anytime, son."

"Thank you." Mohammed looked around. "I am very sorry, but may I use your bathroom?"

"Of course." Hesam pointed to a door on the side wall. "Those stairs will take you down to the bathroom."

"Thank you." Mohammed went down the stairs to the bathroom in the basement, wondering if he should wait for Omar. He didn't want to wait too long after telling Hesam he had to pick up his cousin.

After finishing in the bathroom, Mohammed headed back up the stairs. He thought about returning tomorrow and realized that tomorrow was already Thanksgiving.

Upon reaching the top of the stairs, he saw Hesam talking with Omar and two other men, the same three men whom he'd been searching for all this time. The same three men who were talking about explosives and Jihad on Thursday afternoon.

Mohammed turned to the side, trying to act natural, standing against the wall by the door. He took out the iPhone Tony had given him. He turned it on then quickly checked that the ringer was still on mute. Lady Gaga would not do well in a place like this. He set it up to take photos before holding it up to his ear.

He snapped a picture while pretending to talk to someone. With the phone in his trembling hands, he turned around and pretended to dial another number while looking at the picture. It was a little dark, but he could see their faces.

Mohammed was ready to walk away when he decided he could get another picture with better lighting if he was closer to the front door. He set the phone to picture mode again and placed it against his ear as adrenaline filled his veins and his heartbeat increased.

Pretending to speak with his cousin whom he said he was picking up, he continued his fake conversation while passing the men, then stopped at the front door. He turned his head slightly and snapped another picture before reaching for the door.

Mohammed didn't check the picture this time. He decided to get out while he was ahead. He hurried outside and opened his umbrella. The rain was coming down heavier now.

Trying to keep the umbrella steady in the rain and wind, Mohammed dashed down the sidewalk to the small grocery store he'd seen on his way.

Standing under the awning in front of the store, he stomped some of the water off his shoes and shook out his umbrella after closing it. His suit was wrinkled, twisted, and wet from the knees down.

Mohammed froze when he saw the black sedan pass right in front of him and park up the block from the youth center. If they were there for the real terrorists then he would be off the hook, or maybe not. Mohammed had spent four years in the Pakistani army and no one had ever shot at him until a few days ago. He still had a feeling something wasn't right about the situation, so he decided to stay out of sight and have faith in God to guide and protect him.

He slipped into the small, half-empty grocery store and bought two bananas. The thick shapely Dominican woman behind the counter gave Mohammed a sensual smile that made him feel uncomfortable.

Mohammed smiled back. "I am waiting for a friend. He should be here any minute. Do you mind if I stay inside and wait?"

The woman smiled and flipped her thick curly hair to the side. "Not at all, Lindo. I wouldn't want you to get all dripping wet."

Pretending not to notice the way she was gawking at him, Mohammed said, "Thank you." Women never looked at him like that when he had his beard.

He proceeded to eat the first banana while glancing outside at the downpour. He saw the sedan still parked ahead.

While eating the second banana, Mohammed saw Hesam leave the youth center, running across the street with an umbrella overhead trying to shield himself from the rain. Hesam opened the passenger door of the sedan and climbed in while closing his umbrella.

Mohammed wondered why Hesam would be getting into Agent Grant's car. He decided to follow them and find out what was really going on. He knew it was dangerous, but he had no other choice. He had to prove his innocence.

He darted out of the grocery store without saying goodbye and raced to the car service next door. He stumbled through the door and said, "I need a car, quick!"

The old Ecuadorian man behind the desk asked with a heavy accent, "Where are you going, sir?"

"I . . ." Mohammed didn't know where he was going. He couldn't say follow that car. The first thing that came to his mind was the glass skyscraper across the street from his union hall. "Court Square." He peeked out the window to make sure the sedan was still there.

The old man turned to a younger, fatter Ecuadorian man who was eating a pork sandwich. "Take him to court square."

The driver grunted while forcing the rest of his sandwich into his mouth and washing it down with a Coke.

Mohammed followed him outside to an old Lincoln Town Car and got into the back seat, trying not to inhale the smell of pork that exuded from the fat man's pores.

Still parked across the street, the sedan's engine was running and the brake lights were on. Mohammed glared at the number 2211 on the license plate. He refused to give up without a fight.

The cab driver finished the rest of his soda, burped, then started the car. The windshield wipers swept away the rain as the driver stepped on the brake and grabbed the gearshift.

Mohammed said, "Wait, not yet."

"Not yet? I don't get paid to wait."

"I'll pay—" Mohammed noticed the sedan's brake lights go out. The sedan pulled out of its parking spot and moved forward. "Follow that black car."

"What? I thought you wanted to go to Court Square?"

"Please, my friend." Mohammed handed him two twenty-dollar bills. "Just follow that car."

The driver pocketed the money then pulled out of his spot and followed the sedan.

Mohammed said, "Not too close. Stay a block or two back."

They followed the sedan back to Main Street then south to the Expressway. They headed up the ramp and continued south toward JFK Airport. Mohammed fondled the switchblade in his pocket and wondered if he really had the guts to use it. He didn't want to kill anyone, but he thought he might stab someone in the arm or the leg, but only if he was backed into a corner and it meant life or death.

After about fifteen minutes, the driver looked in his rearview mirror at Mohammed and said, "How far do you expect me to go for forty dollars?"

Mohammed handed him another twenty.

They followed the sedan onto another Expressway. Traffic wasn't bad yet. It only took another ten minutes to reach Liberty Avenue, which they then followed to Sutphin Boulevard.

The area consisted of gas stations, auto shops, warehouses, and a few stores and delis.

The sedan turned the corner, passed a fenced-off empty lot, then slowed to a stop. They were getting ready to turn into a driveway.

Mohammed told the taxi driver to stop across the street. The rain outside had lightened up to a moderate but steady downpour.

The sedan pulled into the driveway of a one-story red brick warehouse with a steel personnel door and a big rolling steel garage door. The garage door rolled open automatically. The sedan entered the building.

Mohammed snapped as many pictures as he could from inside the taxi, but the quality was terrible. He opened the door and then opened his umbrella above so he could take a few more shots from outside. The pictures were still not perfect, but better. He didn't get any clear shots of the sedan's license plate, but he already had the plate number. He got a few shots of the building as the garage door closed behind the sedan. Mohammed closed his umbrella and got back into the car, closing the door behind him and hoping the pictures were clear.

The driver turned and asked, "How long do you want to stay here?"

"Only a few more minutes, my friend. Please."

Mohammed took the phone out of picture mode. Just as he looked down, ready to check the pictures and send them to Tony, the car door opened.

Before he had a chance to turn and look, someone grabbed Mohammed and pulled him out of the back seat as the driver yelled.

A white man wearing a black suit threw Mohammed against the car and pointed a pistol at his head. "Hands in the air!"

Mohammed slipped the iPhone into his front jacket pocket then put his hands up.

CHAPTER 58—WEDNESDAY 3:13PM

Less than a block from the warehouse on Sutphin Boulevard, standing next to the cab, Andrew Miller had his gun pointed at Mohammed and Mohammed had his hands in the air.

The rain lightened up, but remained steady.

Andrew knew what Mohammed looked like from the pictures in his immigration files. Although he didn't personally believe Mohammed was a terrorist, he still knew he had to be careful. Agent Grant treated Mohammed as a suspect, so Andrew decided to do the same, just in case.

With his left hand, Andrew wiped the water from his forehead and glanced at the TLC license posted inside the car. He pointed at Mohammed and asked the driver, "How do you know this man?"

"He's my fare. I only see him for the first time today."

Andrew memorized the license number and the driver's name while keeping his gun pointed at Mohammed.

Andrew believed what the fat Ecuadorian said, so he decided to let him go. "I'm a federal agent, and I know who you are. Now, get out of here."

"Yes, sir. I'm going, sir." The driver slammed on the gas pedal and skidded down the block and around the corner with the back door still open.

Andrew turned around to face Mohammed. He heard the sound of wood cracking and felt a sharp pain behind his eyes. Everything around him started to spin.

CHAPTER 59—WEDNESDAY 3:16PM

Mohammed had taken the umbrella from the back seat and kept it at his side while the man who said he was a federal agent was looking at the cab driver's license. He had thought about using the switchblade, but just couldn't stand the idea of penetrating someone's flesh.

Just as the taxi had taken off with its door still open, Mohammed spun around and cracked the man in the side of the head with the wooden umbrella handle.

The man stepped back, almost losing his balance.

Mohammed hoped the man would fall, but he didn't.

The man just kept staggering and trying to aim his gun at Mohammed.

Mohammed gave him another smack to the head, a little harder. The metal umbrella shaft bent like a boomerang as blood squirted everywhere. The man's legs wobbled, his eyes rolled back in his head, but he still did not fall.

Tears streamed down Mohammed's face mixing with the rain. He clenched the twisted umbrella in his trembling hands. He didn't want to hit him again, but he had no choice, the man wasn't going down. As he struck the man again on the side of the head, hard, the man finally went down.

Mohammed's stomach dropped when he heard the thud of the man's head against the sidewalk. He froze, watching as the rain washed blood down the sidewalk and into the gutter. He hoped he didn't kill him. Mohammed's entire body trembled as tears continued down his face.

A truck blew its loud horn as it passed on the street. Mohammed jumped. His skin tingled as a chill ripped through his spine. He turned around and bolted down the sidewalk still clenching the twisted umbrella.

He raced toward an area on Sutphin Boulevard populated with houses and a few stores. He knew he shouldn't turn back, but he had to know if the man was alive. Mohammed slowed down and turned his head. He could barely see the man's arm moving, trying to grab something to hold onto. He was happy he didn't kill him and confident he wouldn't catch up with him. He wondered if stabbing in in the leg would have been more efficient, and more humane.

Mohammed ran toward the stores and into the driveway of a gas station on the corner. Without slowing down, he climbed a fence into a grassy field. He raced through the muddy field as his rib cage ached. At the other side, he found a hole in the fence and climbed through it. The broken fence sliced through the back of his jacket and shirt, leaving a burning gash on his skin. He cringed from the pain, but kept moving forward.

Mohammed found himself across the street from a high school that had just gotten out. Boys and girls were playing, yelling, fighting, and kissing. Two boys pretended to swordfight with their closed umbrellas while a couple other boys with rubber boots jumped in and out of puddles.

He crossed the street, and even though he knew he could never blend with the crowd, he hoped to stay out of sight behind the few kids who had their umbrellas open.

Staying as close to the building as possible, Mohammed continued down the block with the crowd of noisy kids. He entered a park behind them, then, when he knew he was out of sight from anyone on the street, he broke away from the crowd. He thought about getting out of the neighborhood, but decided it would be best to send the pictures to Tony right away, just in case something else unexpected came along.

On the far side of the park, Mohammed found a secluded bench under a tree. He managed to get his twisted umbrella partially open. The top was oval-shaped and lopsided, but one part of the edge was still able to repel water. With one hand holding the umbrella overhead, Mohammed used his other hand to send the pictures he'd saved on the phone. One by one, he sent all the pictures from the youth center and the warehouse to Tony. It took a while for each picture to upload and send.

After all the picture messages, Mohammed sent Tony a text message with the address of the youth center. Just as he prepared to type another text message, the address of the warehouse, he heard something, a gun racking and a bullet entering the chamber.

He turned around and saw the man in the black suit, his angry bruised bloody face, and the barrel of his gun.

"Drop everything and put your hands in the air!"

Mohammed dropped his umbrella onto the ground, put the phone on the table, stood, and put his hands in the air.

The man took one step forward and smashed Mohammed's face with the butt of his gun.

CHAPTER 60—WEDNESDAY 3:34PM

After the funeral, Diane had gone straight home. Some of the cops from her precinct wanted her to join them for lunch, but she just was not in the mood.

She had decided to go home and get caught up on some house cleaning. After finishing with the living room and kitchen, she was ready to tackle the bathroom when her phone rang and vibrated across the coffee table.

She checked the screen. It was Tony. She answered it, "Hey, Tony."

"Hey, sis. Sorry to bother you again."

Diane said, "Is this about that Mohammed guy again? You're gonna get both of us in trouble, Tony. Both of our phones are tapped."

"Come on. What are you talking about?"

"A federal agent named Agent Grant paid me a visit at the precinct. He asked if I knew where your friend was. He said your friend is a terrorist and he thinks you're helping him."

"There's no way Mo is a terrorist."

Diane lit a cigarette and sat down. "I don't believe it either."

Tony sounded surprised. "You don't?"

"No, I don't. Something's going on. I called Jack. I'm waiting for him to get back to me with some info."

Tony asked, "So, how did Jack sound?"

"What do you mean, how did he sound? He sounded the same as always."

"Did he sound like he was happy to hear from you?"

"I don't know. Listen, I'll call Jack again then I'll call you. Alright?"

Tony said, "Maybe you should invite him over for Thanksgiving, if he's not going back to Pittsburg, you know."

"I have to go, Tony. I'll call you later."

She was just about to get started on the bathroom when she decided she should call Jack before getting bleach on her hands. She dialed his number.

It rang once then he picked up. "Hello, Diane . . . I was just about to call you. I found some interesting facts about your Agent Grant."

Diane got a pen and a notepad and sat at the table. "What do you got?"

"Five years ago, when he was still with the CIA, his fingerprints and his partner's fingerprints were found at a murder scene, the murder of another CIA agent in DC. Someone stabbed him through the eye with a letter opener. The local police began the investigation and the Pentagon stopped it. A few months later, the head of Homeland Security appointed Agent Grant as chief of the newly formed Domestic Counter Terrorism Agency, the DCTA. They are technically part of Homeland Security, but operate independently. His former partner from the CIA is now a security consultant for an energy company based in Indonesia."

Diane's call waiting buzzed, but she didn't check it, she wanted to verify what she was hearing from Jack first. "So, instead of being investigated for murder, they were offered better jobs?"

"That's the way it appears."

Diane asked, "And what about my brother's friend, Mohammed?"

"Nothing. He checks out clean. But, of course, that doesn't mean anything."

"Of course. Thank you, Jack."

The call waiting buzzed again.

"Anytime, and don't forget next week."

"Next week?" It took a moment to remember she said she might have dinner with him. "Oh, next week. Dinner, right? I'll call you."

"Okay, bye for now."

"Bye, Jack."

She hung up the phone and saw that she just missed a call from Tony. Just as she was about to call him back, a text and a picture message came in.

She read the text message: Hey sis, Mo just sent me these pictures of the terrorists.

The phone vibrated again with another picture message.

Diane studied the first picture. It was three young bearded Muslims talking with an older Muslim man in what appeared to be some sort of classroom. The phone vibrated again. She looked at another picture; the same three men with the older man again, in the same place.

While opening the third picture, the phone vibrated again. The third picture was the older man getting into a black sedan. Rain obscured the picture, but not so bad that Photoshop couldn't clear it up.

The fourth photo was of the front of a red brick warehouse.

Diane forwarded the pictures to Jack then wondered if Mohammed could have been telling the truth. He did say there were three terrorists. Could those three men really be planning a terror attack? They certainly looked the part, but then so did Mohammed. And who was the older man? Maybe the three men were undercover agents and Mohammed was the real terrorist. Maybe the old man was the real terrorist. The possibilities were endless.

Diane picked up her pack of cigarettes and coughed. She didn't have one. She opened a bottle of water from the refrigerator and took a sip when her Blackberry rang. It was Jack.

She answered, "Hey, Jack. I guess you got the pictures."

"Yes, and who exactly am I looking at?"

"I don't know. Tony just forwarded me those pictures. He said his friend Mohammed took them and sent them to him. I believe the three young men are the guys Mohammed accused of being terrorists. I have no idea who the older man is."

"I'll find out what I can and call you back."

CHAPTER 61—WEDNESDAY 4:01PM

The rain continued outside as Andrew sat in the driver's seat of the SUV, parked in the driveway in front of the warehouse in Queens. His head was throbbing so badly, he felt as if he would have an aneurism at any moment.

Mohammed sat unconscious in the passenger seat with his hands cuffed in front of him.

Andrew considered going to the pharmacy to get something for the pain, but instead he decided to call Agent Grant. The phone went straight to voicemail. He left a message. "This is Agent Miller. I have apprehended Mr. Mohammed Ali—"

A beep interrupted him. He looked at the screen and saw that Agent Grant was calling him on the other line.

He cut the message short and switched over. "Agent Grant, this is Agent Miller."

"Yes, Agent Miller. What is it?"

"I have apprehended Mr. Mohammed Ali."

"Where are you?"

"At the warehouse you told me to come to in Queens."

"I am on my way." Agent Grant didn't say anything else. He just terminated the call.

Andrew checked his phone to make sure Agent Grant wasn't still on the line then hung it up and put it away.

He pulled up the pictures on Mohammed's iPhone, pictures of high school girls acting foolish. He scrolled through them quickly, wondering who these girls were and if Mohammed was a pedophile. He slowed down when he saw pictures of Agent Grant's car Parked on Seventh Avenue in Manhattan. He stopped scrolling and studied the picture of an old Arab man with Omar and two young bearded men. He knew exactly who Omar was, and he was pretty sure he knew who the old man was also.

Tires screeched down the street. Andrew checked his rear view mirror and saw Agent Grant's black sedan speeding toward him. How did he get here so fast? He must have been already on his way here.

The car stopped and Agent Grant leaped out. Andrew had never seen his boss act this way. Agent Grant hurried to the SUV and approached the window.

Andrew rolled the window down. Rain came into the car.

Agent Grant peered in at Mohammed and said, "Take him inside." He pushed a button on a remote control and the garage door rolled open.

Andrew said "But, sir, shouldn't we take him to—"

"We do not have time. We must question him now. They are planning to bomb the Thanksgiving Day parade."

Andrew realized the urgency. The parade was tomorrow morning. There was no time for paperwork or formalities. He started the engine and pulled the SUV into the warehouse.

Agent Grant entered the building and pressed the remote control closing the garage door behind him. On the far side of the building, he switched on one fluorescent light even though there were at least a dozen of them hanging from the ceiling.

Andrew got out of the car and circled to the passenger side to get Mohammed.

Agent Grant turned on a single light bulb hanging above a wood chair just a few feet from the SUV. "Bring him here."

Andrew lugged Mohammed over and placed him on the chair.

A few boxes and wood crates sat against the far wall and there were three closed doors on the back wall. Cobwebs and dust filled the corners.

Agent Grant took a rope from a box and tied Mohammed to the chair. He tied a piece of cloth around Mohammed's mouth and said, "I see he put up a fight."

That statement made the throbbing in Andrew's head worse. But he had more important things to worry about.

Andrew scrolled through the pictures on Mohammed's

iPhone. He skipped the high school pictures then found the picture of Omar with Hesam and other two men and said, "This is the man I called you about, Omar Kadir." Andrew showed Agent Grant the picture.

While tightening his knots, Agent Grant glanced at Andrew, but didn't say anything. That's when Andrew realized Agent Grant already knew about Omar. He hoped Agent Grant was hiding evidence for a good reason, maybe to protect the life of an undercover agent. Andrew asked, "Is this man working for you?"

"In a manner of speaking."

Andrew considered the fact that maybe Agent Grant didn't want to say too much in front of Mohammed, so he asked, "Can I speak with you in private, sir?"

Agent Grant said, "You may speak freely in front of Mr. Ali, Agent Miller."

"Why? Is he working for you?"

"He is unconscious, Agent Miller."

"Maybe he could still hear us." Andrew pushed Mohammed's shoulder, shaking him, waiting for a reaction, but there was none.

Agent Grant took his gold cigarette case out of his jacket pocket, held up a cigarette, stared at it for a moment, then put the cigarette back in the case. He slipped the gold case back into his jacket pocket and turned his attention toward Andrew.

Andrew didn't let his boss' eccentric behavior distract him. He pointed at Hesam's picture on the iPhone and said, "I remember seeing this man on one of our watch lists. His name is Hesam, aka, The Sword." He scrolled to the next picture. "Here he is again with Omar Kadir and the same two other men." He scrolled to the next picture, Hesam getting into Agent Grant's car. "And then, here he is with you . . . getting into your car. Is there something I should know?"

CHAPTER 62—WEDNESDAY 4:21PM

Mohammed woke up tied to a wood chair with his mouth gagged. The first thing that came to mind was he was in Guantanamo Bay. The room was dark except for a small amount of light coming from a single bulb dangling above his head. He saw another light hanging from the ceiling against the far wall, a long fluorescent tube light.

When his eyes began to adjust, he recognized the two men in front of him, Agent Grant, and the man in the black suit. Behind them, a black SUV blocked his view of everything else in the warehouse.

He tried to move, trying to force his hands and feet loose. He tried harder and harder as various torture methods ran through his mind.

After finally accepting that he could not break free, Mohammed stopped moving and tried to slow his heavy breathing, which was even more exhausting because he had to breathe through his nose.

Agent Grant said, "You have proved quite the challenge, Mr. Ali. Thank God Agent Miller found you when he did." He removed Mohammed's gag.

Mohammed asked Andrew, "If you already know who the terrorists are, why do you hunt me like an animal?"

Andrew turned to Agent Grant and said, "Maybe you should ask my superior that question."

Agent Grant put his arm around Andrew's shoulder. "Do you

remember your first day on the job? I asked if you were willing to do whatever it took to protect America."

Andrew glared at Agent Grant.

Agent Grant continued, "You said yes. You said you were willing to do whatever is necessary to protect America. Now that time has come, Agent Miller. Threats to our country come in various forms."

Andrew pulled away from Agent Grant and said, "What the hell are you talking about? Are those men terrorists or not?"

"Yes. They are. We need this attack to take place to convince the people and the President to invade Iran."

"Iran? What do they have to do with this? I thought those men were Afghani and Pakistani?"

Agent Grant chuckled, then said, "The American public does not know the difference between an Arab and an Indian, not to mention an Iranian." He pointed at Mohammed and said, "As long as they are brown and Muslim, they are the enemy."

Mohammed said, "Allah will punish you—"

Agent Grant interrupted Mohammed's sentence by tying the cloth back around his mouth.

Mohammed tried to speak through the gag, but it was useless.

Andrew shook his head. "This is crazy. You can't seriously consider letting some group of fanatics kill innocent people."

Agent Grant reached for his gun from inside his jacket. "My associates would be extremely unhappy if our plan did not culminate." He took out his pistol and wiped a dull spot with his finger.

"Put your gun down!" yelled Andrew while taking a step back and reaching into his jacket for his own gun.

Mohammed couldn't believe this was happening. He wondered if it might be a dream.

Agent Grant clicked the safety off before lowering his gun.

Andrew released his safety and aimed at Agent Grant. He yelled louder, "Drop the gun, now!"

Mohammed tried again to break free of his ropes, but even if he was at his best, he still could never break free. Whoever tied those knots knew what they were doing.

Agent Grant didn't seem scared of the gun pointed at him. He spoke in a calm voice. "As you know, Agent Miller, the American economy has been deteriorating rapidly. China and Russia may be our allies now, but we still cannot give them the upper hand."

Andrew said, "Put the gun down or I will shoot!"

Agent Grant said, "Please, Agent Miller, listen to what I have to say, then, if you still wish to shoot me, by all means, do as you wish."

Andrew kept his gun pointed at Agent Grant.

Mohammed knew it was wrong, but he wanted Andrew to shoot Agent Grant.

Agent Grant said, "I assure you, Agent Miller, I wish this type of action were not necessary, but as you must know, Iran has always been a pain in America's ass, and to speak frankly, we need their oil."

Mohammed couldn't believe what he was hearing. He knew Agent Miller was also surprised

Agent Grant continued. "If we cannot provide the American people with affordable fuel sources then the people cannot go to work. If the people cannot go to work . . . well, must I give you a lesson in economics? In addition, do not forget that our military also runs on fossil fuel, the same military that protects our freedom and our way of life. The same military that you so proudly served in, Agent Miller. You seem like an intelligent and reasonable man. Please do not make this more difficult than necessary."

Still pointing his gun at Agent Grant, Andrew said, "Reasonable? I will not stand by while innocent Americans are murdered. Fuck this! I didn't sign up for this shit!"

"This is your last chance, son. Are you with us or are you against us?"

While still aiming at Agent Grant, Andrew racked his gun. The bullet popped into the chamber. "I'm against you." Andrew kept his finger ready to pull the trigger while his eyes stayed trained on Agent Grant's gun.

With his gun still pointed at the floor, Agent Grant said, "I am sorry you feel that way."

Mohammed waited for Agent Grant to make a move. He felt like he was watching a duel in an old western movie. The two agents just stood there, staring at each other.

Out of the corner of his eye, Mohammed saw a light flicker near the back of the building. He could only turn his head a few inches, but he could move his eyes. He saw something coming from behind the SUV, behind Andrew, something coming closer.

He tried to focus in on it. He knew Agent Grant saw it, too, because he was facing in that direction.

Agent Grant stepped back, away from Andrew.

Andrew yelled, "Don't move!"

Agent Grant took another step back. Mohammed thought Andrew was going to fire, but he didn't. The movement in the shadows got closer.

Mohammed tried yelling through the gag when he realized what he was seeing.

Hesam snuck up behind Andrew.

Mohammed shook the entire chair while trying to get up and warn the young agent, but his muffled words were in vain.

Just as Andrew glanced over at Mohammed, Hesam stuck the tip of a long sword into the back of Andrew's neck.

Mohammed knew Hesam hit the spine when Andrew's body stiffened.

Agent Grant stepped back farther, away from the splattering blood.

With both hands on the handle, Hesam pushed the metal blade deeper into Andrew's neck. Andrew choked on the cold steel blade while gasping for air.

Mohammed's stomach twisted as Hesam pushed the blade in even deeper. Andrew choked on his own blood, his hands and feet flailing around. Mohammed watched as Hesam mustered up enough strength to force the blade all the way through, inch by inch, until finally penetrating the front of Andrew's throat. Blood shot out from the front and the back at the same time. Hesam released his grip.

Andrew's convulsing body dropped to the blood saturated concrete floor with the sword sticking out of his neck.

Hesam bent down and grabbed the sword handle. He twisted the blade before ripping it out of Andrew's neck.

Mohammed lost control of his bladder. Urine streamed down his leg. But he held back his vomit. He knew he would choke on it and die. He closed his eyes and tried to keep his mind off what he just saw. He heard the blade of the sword strike something soft. It sounded like flesh, again, and again.

Someone grabbed Mohammed from the back of the neck. It was Agent Grant. "Open your eyes."

Mohammed kept his eyes closed tight. Something struck

Mohammed on the temple. A throbbing pain spread across his face.

Agent Grant said, "Open your eyes or I will pluck them out."

Mohammed opened his eyes and saw Agent Andrew Miller's severed head three feet from his bloody body.

He couldn't hold it. Mohammed threw up. He tasted the vomit in his mouth while breathing heavy through his nose. The smell made him gag again. More vomit came up through his esophagus and into his mouth where it stayed.

There was too much fluid in his mouth. He tried desperately to break free of the ropes holding him to the chair.

As the vomit went back down his throat and he began to choke, Mohammed tipped the chair over, still bouncing around, trying to break free. His face turned red, his eyes rolled back in his head. Everything started to fade as he suffocated. He never thought he would die like this. He finally gave up fighting and made his peace with God.

Mohammed felt something cold and hard touch the side of his face. He opened his eyes.

Hesam used a knife to cut Mohammed's gag. Part of the blade sliced his flesh at the same time.

Mohammed was still choking. Hesam kicked him in the back. All the vomit spewed out of Mohammed's mouth as he coughed and spit uncontrollably. Hesam grabbed the chair and picked it up, placing it back on its legs.

Vomit and saliva dripped from Mohammed's mouth, mixing with the blood from his face. He gasped for air, occasionally coughing until his heart rate returned to a semi-normal state.

Agent Grant bent down and looked in Mohammed's face. "Are you finished?"

Mohammed spit in Agent Grant's face.

Agent Grant took an embroidered handkerchief from his outer jacket pocket and used it to wipe the vomit-flavored saliva from his face. He then slipped a leather glove over his right hand and gave Mohammed a hard shot to the face.

Mohammed's head jerked, everything started spinning. He felt the skin around his eye swelling up. "Allah will never let you get away with this!"

"Fuck you and Allah." Agent Grant gave Mohammed another hard shot to the face then he turned to Hesam and said, "Set it for midnight."

Mohammed turned his head to the side just enough to see Hesam out of the corner of his eye. He was about ten feet away, connecting a circuit board and wires to four metal canisters tied together. Mohammed heard something beep twice then Hesam covered the contraption with an upside-down empty cardboard box.

Agent Grant said, "You are going to be famous, Mr. Ali. Dead, but famous."

Hesam chuckled while rummaging through some stuff in another cardboard box.

"Allah will know my soul after death."

Agent Grant said, "That is perfect, I will make sure the newspaper people print that quote. You see Mr. Ali, you are going to be the fourth terrorist, the one who accidentally blew himself up."

Hesam approached Mohammed with a short piece of rope.

Mohammed struggled as Hesam tied the rope around his mouth. Mohammed stopped moving, trying to breathe, still surrounded by the stench of his own vomit.

Hesam stood next to Agent Grant.

With his leather gloves on, Agent Grant took Andrew's gun from the floor.

Mohammed closed his eyes and waited for death. He heard two gunshots. He jumped in his seat, but didn't feel anything, so he opened his eyes.

Agent Grant had fired two shots into Andrew's headless corpse. He then took the clip out of the gun, placed the gun handle in Mohammed's hand, and squeezed his fingers down on the handle and the trigger, making an impression of Mohammed's fingerprints. "My grandfather always said, leave no stone unturned."

Agent Grant put the clip back into the gun, threw it onto the floor out of Mohammed's reach, then strolled out the door.

Hesam turned off the lights and followed Agent Grant outside.

The first thing that came to Mohammed's mind was the switchblade. He could cut himself loose if he could only reach into his pocket and get it. He wasn't sure if he still had it. Chances are one of the agents took it away from him. It didn't matter; even if he did have it, he couldn't get to it anyway.

Surrounded by darkness and despair, Mohammed asked God to cleanse his soul before death then he closed his eyes and waited for it to come.

CHAPTER 63—WEDNESDAY 5:44PM

Diane would have had dinner with her parents downstairs, but Wednesday was their card game. Three old couples met every week, rotating houses where they played.

She decided to go for a quick workout and eat something later. This was her first workout all week. Her ankle and her arm were feeling better, but she knew she still had to take it easy.

Wearing a tight pair of black spandex pants and a loose white T-shirt that covered her butt, Diane tied her hair into a tight ponytail, threw on her pink Yankees baseball cap and white New Balance sneakers, and grabbed her keys on the way out the door.

She glanced down at the fresh gauze on her arm while going down the steps. A tiny spot of blood dried up in the center, but the gauze was still tight, so she continued on her way.

Outside, the rain was gone and so was the sun. The cool night air felt crisp and energizing as Diane headed to the end of the block where she had parked her car. The streets and sidewalks were still saturated, and a heavy wind blew in from the northwest.

She got into her car and drove along a quiet residential avenue for about thirty blocks to a large fitness gym that used to be a warehouse on Bath Avenue.

She circled in her car for another fifteen minutes while searching for a parking spot and wishing there was a gym closer to her house.

Once inside, the first thing Diane noticed was her face in the gym mirrors. Although the scabs were healing well, the bright lights made it look worse.

She cranked out twenty slow minutes on the Stairmaster while thinking about what she had said to Jack. She didn't want to lie. She knew she had to have dinner with him now.

After her cardio, she entered the weight room. Wednesday was her scheduled leg workout, but she felt a little pressure on her ankle from the Stairmaster, so she decided to skip legs and just do a little abs. She did some leg raises and some crunches then spent about fifteen minutes punching the heavy bag while her mind reviewed everything that had happened in the past week. She let everything out.

While taking her bag from the locker, she checked her phone and noticed a missed call from Tony. She couldn't call him back. She didn't have enough signal in the gym. There was nothing new to tell him anyway, so she decided to call him back from the house.

After driving home and finally finding a parking spot, Diane went straight upstairs to her apartment and called Tony. Tony's phone went to voicemail. Diane left a message. "Hey, Tony . . ." Diane heard a beep on her phone. She checked the screen. It was Tony calling. "That's you calling me now."

She pressed switch and Tony came on the line. "Hey, I was just leaving you a message."

"Sorry, I was in the bathroom. You hear anything about Mo? Is the FBI going after those three guys or what?"

Diane replied, "I don't know. I'm waiting for Jack to call me. I just came from the gym and I need a shower."

Tony spoke in a childish voice, "Ooh, stinky."

Diane chuckled. "I'll call you in a little while."

Tiger meowed jut as Diane ended the call. "Don't even think about eating again. I'm taking you to the gym with me the next time I go."

Tiger meowed again as Diane undressed in her bedroom and headed to the bathroom.

After examining her body in the mirror, taking a shower, and blow-drying her hair, Diane threw on a pair of cotton shorts and a tank top and called Jack. Jack's phone went to voicemail, but she didn't leave a message. She called Tony.

Tony answered, "Hey."

"Hey, he hasn't called me back yet. This might have to wait for tomorrow."

"I don't think Mo's gonna make it that long. I've been trying to call him. At first the phone rang, but after a few more tries, the phone went straight to voicemail."

"Maybe the battery is dead."

"It can't be. The phone was fully charged, and Mo had it turned off until he sent me those pictures."

Diane couldn't figure out why Tony was so concerned with what happened to some Pakistani immigrant who may or may not be a terrorist. She had to ask, "Why do you even care, Tony?"

"What do you mean?"

"How many guys have you worked with in the past twenty years? Why do you care so much about what happens to this one?"

"Because he's innocent, and the whole world is against him. You know I always root for the underdog."

Diane said, "Just because you like the Mets doesn't mean that this guy is innocent."

"Mo is not a terrorist, and I'm not going to just sit on my ass while the government takes him to some concentration camp and slices his nipples off."

"That's disgusting. I think you've been watching too many movies."

Tony said, "I can see the address in the picture of that youth center. I'm sure we can find it on Google. Come with me."

Diane said, "And what are you gonna do, Tony? Listen, stay at home with your family. You can't get involved."

"I'm already involved."

Diane knew how stubborn her brother could be, just as stubborn as she was. They both had the same hardheaded Calabrese blood. "Wait until Jack calls me, and if you still haven't heard from Mohammed, I'll go to the youth center. You can't get directly involved in this thing, Tony. Please."

Tony said, "I can't let my little sister go down there alone."

"Are you kidding me? Haven't you been reading the papers? I'm plenty qualified for the situation. Just let me handle it."

"Why don't you take Jack with you?"

Diane said, "I'll call you back in a little while, Tony."

She didn't want to keep bothering Jack, so she sat on the sofa next to Tiger, closed her eyes, and waited for him to call her.

Just as she began to drift off, the phone rang. It was Jack. She answered it.

"Hello, Diane. Sorry I didn't return your call earlier. I was in a meeting."

"That's alright. I know you're busy."

"I did get some interesting information on one of the men in the pictures. I have the file with me. If you like, I could drop it off. I'm downtown on State Street now. I can be there in twenty minutes."

"Uh . . ." Diane didn't know what to say. What if people saw him and thought they were back together? What if he tried to kiss her? What if she let him?

Jack asked, "Diane, are you there?"

"Yeah. I'm here." She tried to clear her head of schoolgirl thoughts and act like a professional. "So, you want to drop it off?"

"Unless you'd like to pick it up at my office tomorrow morning."

Diane said, "I'd rather get it tonight, but you don't have to come all the way out here."

"I don't mind. I'm hungry anyway. Maybe we could get a bite to eat while I'm there."

"I don't know if that's such a good idea."

"It's up to you. I'll bring the folder by then you decide if you're hungry."

After hanging up the phone, Diane looked down at Tiger, who was purring in his sleep. She began to caress Tiger's back while thinking about what to do when Jack came over.

She wondered if she should invite Jack up for coffee. It would be rude to meet him at his car. Maybe he wouldn't be able to find a parking spot and she'd have no choice but to meet him downstairs. Although she was hungry, she wasn't sure if going out to eat with Jack would be such a good idea.

Diane still loved Jack, but she wouldn't give in to pressure. She had broken up with him because of pressure. Jack wanted her to move in with him, to his apartment in Manhattan. He said it was the next step in their relationship. Diane didn't want to take another step. She wanted to keep things the way they were. She liked the fact that she lived close to her parents and she liked the fact that after a few days at Jack's place, she had a place of her own to go home to. She knew she'd been a rough on him, and she knew he didn't deserve it, but she wasn't sorry. He was persistent, and she knew she wouldn't be able to change his mind. Both had been married and divorced before, and it just didn't seem logical to make the same mistake again. Diane had decided to break off the relationship. She felt bad, and she missed him, but she knew it was for the best.

Still purring, Tiger woke up and licked his lips. He looked up at Diane and meowed.

Diane smiled. "You are a lazy glutton, but I love you." She kissed him on the top of the head. Tiger meowed. Diane stood and Tiger followed her into the kitchen. She opened a can of tuna and put it in a clean bowl. She rinsed out Tiger's water bowl and gave him some fresh water. Tiger ate with his tail in the air. Diane wished she could enjoy that type of serenity, for even just one day.

She called Tony back and told him that Jack was on his way over. She told him again to stay home and let her handle things. She didn't want anything to do with Mohammed, Agent Grant, or any of this, but she knew if she didn't get involved, Tony might get himself into trouble trying to help his friend.

After changing into a pair of jeans, a thin tight sweater, and a pair of Uggs, Diane looked at her long silky black hair in the bathroom mirror and decided not to tie it into a ponytail. She didn't want Jack to think she was trying, but she did decide to apply a thin coat of lipstick.

Tiger pranced into the bathroom and meowed.

Diane turned around and said, "I know what you're thinking."

Tiger meowed again.

Diane's phone rang. It was Jack. She answered it, "Hi, Jack."

"Hello, Diane. I'm double parked in front of your house."

"I'll be right down." Although she was relieved he was not coming up, she also felt a bit of disappointment at the same time.

After hanging up, she put on her black leather jacket, checked her hair one more time, and went outside. She zipped her jacket when a gust of wind came through.

While approaching Jack's blue four-door Lincoln Hybrid, Diane noticed someone sitting in the passenger seat next to Jack.

Jack smiled when he saw Diane. "Hello, Diane."

"Hi, Jack." Diane peered into the car and saw a petite young woman in a ponytail dressed in business attire.

Jack said, "This is Justine Campbell. We work together. I'm taking her to Queens."

Diane gave the best fake smile she could mutter. "Nice to

meet you." Diane wondered if Jack did this on purpose. Did he bring this girl here to try and make her jealous? She lit a cigarette and took a deep drag.

Jack handed Diane a 9"x12" yellow envelope and said, "A friend in counter terrorism gave me this. It seems the old Arab in the pictures is a man nicknamed Hesam. Some call him The Sword. He's been around for quite some time. He fought alongside Osama Bin Laden in Afghanistan against the Russians. He's a citizen of Saudi Arabia, but he seems to have many powerful friends in Syria, Pakistan, England, and America. He has always been under suspicion, but there's never been any evidence linking him to any terrorist activity."

Diane asked, "And who are the three young men?"

Jack said, "I don't know. There was no face recognition in the FBI database. I have a friend at immigration who's checking it out."

Diane said, "Tony called and said he lost contact with Mohammed just before 4PM."

Jack said, "Justine and I are going for a quick bite. Come with us. Between the three of us, I'm sure we could come up with something."

Diane finished her cigarette and stomped it out in the street. She was hungry, and she didn't want to be rude or appear jealous, so she said, "alright, let's go."

She climbed into the back seat and Jack took off down the block. Other than a few restaurants and small grocery stores, most of the stores along Bay Parkway had already closed. They turned left under the elevated train on 86th Street and followed it past more closed stores until reaching the beginning of Avenue U.

After a few quiet blocks, they parked in a small parking lot next door to Spumoni Gardens, a pizzeria and restaurant with tables outside. It was too cold to eat outside, although a few high school kids were out there smoking cigarettes, drinking sodas, and being loud.

Inside, Jack ordered two regular slices, Justine ordered one regular slice, and Diane ordered a square with pepperoni.

They only waited a few minutes for the pizza to come out of the oven.

Justine looked down at her pizza and said to Jack, "I thought you were joking when you said they put the sauce on top of the cheese."

Jack said, "I joke not."

Justine laughed and tapped him on the arm.

Diane thought Justine was laughing just a little too much. "I'm going to get a table."

She carried her pizza down the aisle and sat at an empty table. She forgot how good Jack looked in a suit, and today he was wearing her favorite, navy blue. His tall muscular physique filled it out in all the right places. She tried to keep her mind off Jack and on the problem at hand.

Justine sat next to Diane while Jack sat across from them. Diane felt a little uncomfortable. Not that she wanted to sit with Jack, but she would have liked to sit alone on her side.

At five-foot-three, Justine was two inches taller than Diane and about ten pounds lighter. Justine had dark skin and Asian features. She took a pair of reading glasses from her pocket and put them on.

Diane turned to Justine and asked, "So, you live in Queens. How's that?"

"Queens is nice. My husband and I live in Bayside. I usually take the train home from the city, but because we were in Brooklyn today, Agent Sullivan offered to give me a ride home."

"That was very nice of Agent Sullivan." Diane bit into her pizza while pretending to smile.

Jack said, "So, you look great, Diane."

"Thanks. You, too." She glanced at his face, but tried not to stare at his mesmerizing blue eyes or his hard jawline or his round shoulders. "So, what have you been up to?"

Justine quietly took small bites of her pizza and looked around at the other customers while Jack and Diane exchanged pleasantries.

"Busy, with work. And still teaching my class on Saturdays." Jack took a sip from his soda. "How are your parents?"

"They're fine." Diane sipped her soda then took another bite.

All three sat quietly eating their pizza.

Justine was the first to break the silence. "I've always wanted to meet you, Detective Lasalvo. I remember reading about that big sting that you and Agent Sullivan worked on. In one day, you guys brought down seven members of the Luchese family for selling heroin in The Bronx. I had just joined the FBI at the time, and it was inspirational."

Jack said, "I can't believe it's been four years already."

Diane said, "More like three and a half."

Jack sipped his soda and said, "It feels like time goes faster as we get older."

Justine said, "I know. I can't believe I'm going to hit the big three-oh this year."

Diane could have killed Justine at that moment. She wished she could go back to the big three-oh. She would do almost anything to go back to the big three-oh. She couldn't believe she was already coming up on the big four-oh. Diane took a small sip from her soda and said, "Age is only a number."

Justine took another tiny bite of her pizza, which was still only half-finished. "I guess you're right. Agent Sullivan is older than both of us, and he's in incredible shape."

Jack smiled. "Not incredible."

Justine argued, "Yes, incredible."

Jack chuckled.

Diane knew he was enjoying every second of flattery, and she couldn't stand it. She didn't know why, but she wanted to burst his bubble. "He does look pretty good . . . for his age."

Jack turned halfway toward Diane and said, "Thanks, Diane."

Diane's phone rang. It was Tony. "Hey, Tony. I'm here with Jack. We're at Spumoni Gardens."

"I love that place," replied Tony

Diane said, "I know."

"So what did you find out?"

Diane said, "The man in the pictures is a dangerous man. Nobody has been able to identify the other three men. We can't make out the address in the picture of the warehouse and that's the last place he was."

Tony said, "But we have the address for the youth center. Let's go there and ask some questions, that's all."

Diane said, "I'll go there and ask some questions. You stay home. I'm only doing this so you won't."

Tony didn't answer.

Diane said, "Tony, promise you'll let me handle this." She waited for his reply.

"Okay, but if you need me . . ."

"If I need you, I'll call you."

"Be careful, sis."

"I will." She hung up the phone and said, "My brother."

Jack interrupted, "The parade. Seventh Avenue. It would be the perfect place for a bomb."

Diane knew exactly what Jack was thinking, a terror attack on the Thanksgiving Day parade tomorrow morning.

Justine said, "Oh my God, you're right."

Jack said, "After I drop you and Justine off, I'll go to that youth center and find out what I can."

"I told my brother I would go."

"You don't need to go," replied Jack.

Justine said, "I'm going, too."

Jack said, "Nobody is going with me."

CHAPTER 64—WEDNESDAY 9:00PM

Still tied to the chair and gagged, Mohammed sat in the darkness, his mouth dry from dehydration, his body aching from the beating he took and from being tied to the chair for all these hours. The only thing he heard was the faint sound of cars passing on the street outside and the occasional gust of wind against the steel garage door.

He'd prayed at least a hundred times in the past few hours, and he wasn't about to stop. He was going to die here, alone, and for the rest of history people would think he was a terrorist. Mohammed cried.

Something moved. Mohammed slowed his crying and listened. It moved again, this time closer. It sounded like a rat or a mouse. Mohammed cringed at the thought of rats eating him alive. He hoped the rodents would at least wait until he was dead before feasting on his flesh.

A shiver ran up his spine as he heard it move closer. He felt something on his leg. He tried to shake it off then realized it was his imagination. He felt rats all over his body. They weren't really there, but he was beginning to lose his sanity.

Mohammed tried with the last of his strength to break free of his ropes. He struggled and shook the chair. The chair tipped over. Lying on his side, he struggled harder as he heard small claws against the concrete floor getting closer.

CHAPTER 65—WEDNESDAY 9:12PM

While getting back into Jack's car, Justine tried to give Diane the front seat but Diane wouldn't take it. She sat in the back, behind Justine.

Jack typed the address of the youth center into his GPS, then headed to the Belt Parkway, then into Queens. Just before JFK airport, they took the Van Wyck Expressway north then followed the streets to the youth center.

The residential neighborhood was dark and quiet. Jack slowed down while passing a row of stores, which had all closed except for the car service.

He slowed down a little more while passing the youth center. Although the sign on the door read closed, the lights were still on inside.

Jack double-parked alongside a row of cars in front of the building. He shifted into park, but left the engine running.

Diane opened her door.

Jack turned to Diane and said, "I should go alone."

"Why? Because you're a man?"

Jack didn't answer. He glanced at Justine, but she wasn't saying anything. The heavy wind outside whipped some leaves into the air. He opened his door and glanced over at Diane. "You coming?"

They both stepped out of the car and advanced toward the youth center. Just as they approached the entrance, the lights inside turned off.

Diane realized she didn't have her gun with her. She wasn't planning on going anywhere except to have a slice of pizza at Spumoni Gardens. Maybe she should have listened to Jack and stayed in the car. She whispered, "I don't have my gun."

With his hand, Jack tapped on a steel bulge in his jacket. She should have known. Jack grew up with guns, and he would never leave home without his favorite, a 10mm Glock.

She felt a little better, but she still wished she had her own firearm.

Jack knocked on the door. They waited but didn't hear anyone inside. They waited a few more minutes and still didn't hear anything. Jack knocked again, this time louder. Still, no answer.

Diane motioned with her head for them to go back to the car.

They went back to the car and got inside.

Justine said, "Someone's in there."

"We know," said Diane, "But they obviously don't wanna answer the door. Maybe they think we're Jehovah's Witnesses."

Jack chuckled.

Justine didn't.

After waiting quietly and watching the building for a few minutes, Jack said, "They're never coming out as long as we're here."

Diane said, "Let's drive around and look for the warehouse then come back around to see if the lights are back on. If we don't find anything in an hour, we forget the whole thing and go home."

Justine asked, "And what about the parade tomorrow?"

Diane said, "That's only a theory right now." She shot a glance at Jack then turned back to Justine. "You don't have to stay if you don't want to. How far is Bayside from here?"

No one said a word for at least fifteen minutes while they sat in the car and watched the youth center. No one went into the building and no one came out.

Diane said, "They could stay in there all night, and I'm getting tired. Let's go around and look for the warehouse so I can at least call my brother back and tell him we tried. As far as the parade tomorrow, I'll call my captain and tell him what I know. You call your friends at the bureau. That's pretty much the best we could hope do."

Jack started the car. He studied the picture of the warehouse on his phone then handed the phone to Justine. "That's the building."

They drove up and down every block in the neighborhood. Houses and apartment buildings occupied most of the streets. The avenues were lined with stores, most of them closed. They only found a few blocks of warehouses, and none matched the one in the picture.

Justine said, "Are you sure it's around here?"

"No, I'm not," snapped Diane. "I don't even know if it's in Queens. This is a waste of time." She pulled a black scrunchy out of her jacket pocket and tied her hair into a tight ponytail.

Jack asked, "So, what do you want to do?"

Diane answered, "Drop Justine off then take me home."

Just as they entered the highway, Diane's phone rang. She was expecting Tony, but it was her partner. She answered, "Hey, Garcia. What's up?"

"Some guy named Agent Grant from Homeland Security came to see me at my house, said he was looking for you. I told him you were at home. Are you?"

"No, I'm not home right now. I'm in Queens."

There was silence on the line for a moment. Diane checked her phone. The signal was fine. "Garcia, you there?"

"I'm here. Listen, he gave me an envelope, said it's important that you get it tonight."

Diane was physically and mentally exhausted. What could possibly be in the envelope? She was in no mood to go to the Bronx now. All she wanted was to go home and crawl into bed with Tiger. She asked Garcia, "What's in it?"

"I don't know. It's sealed."

"So, open it."

"He told me not to. He said to give it to you, and only you could open it. It's a federal offense if I open it."

"Oh, get real, Garcia! Just open the envelope!"

"I'm sorry, Diane, I can't open it. I'll bring it to you in Queens. Where are you?"

She took a deep breath and tried not to be a bitch. "We just left Flushing, on our way to Bayside. But you don't have to come to Queens. I'll—"

Garcia interrupted, "Meet me at the Dunkin' Donuts on the corner of Sutphin Boulevard and Liberty Avenue."

Diane refrained from any of the obvious fat jokes she could

have used, she just wasn't in the mood. "Alright, I'll be waiting there."

She told Jack and Justine what the call was about. Justine insisted on going with them. Diane finally agreed. They took the highway to Liberty Avenue then followed it to Sutphin Boulevard.

Jack parked in front of the Dunkin' Donuts and they all went inside. Diane and Jack both ordered coffee. Justine ordered tea. They sat at a small table against the wall.

After a few minutes, Diane noticed Jack squinting while bringing his face closer to the window. She peered out the window at the dark quiet intersection, but didn't see anyone or anything.

Diane asked Jack, "What are you looking at?"

On his phone, Jack scrolled to the picture of the warehouse. He checked the picture then looked outside again. "Look."

Diane and Justine both peered out the window.

Jack said, "Down Sutphin Boulevard, after that empty lot."

Diane saw it. It was hard to see at night, but it did look a lot like the warehouse from the picture. "I see it." She stood, threw her almost empty coffee cup into the garbage, and hurried to the door.

Jack and Justine followed her outside.

They crossed Liberty Avenue.

On the other side, Diane raced down Sutphin Boulevard to the red brick warehouse.

Jack and Justine both came up behind her and approached the door next to the rolling steel gate. The only thing they heard was an occasional car or truck passing.

Diane banged on the door, but there was no response. She waited while Jack and Justine stepped toward the gate.

Jack said, "You think there's someone in there?"

"Probably not. But I'd like to be sure."

Jack asked, "So, what next?"

Diane looked up the dimly lit block at more warehouses and loft buildings. "I have no idea. All I know is that Tony said his friend sent him those pictures then disappeared. Tony tried texting him and calling him, but the phone goes straight to voicemail. So your guess is as good as mine. Maybe we should just call it in and let someone else take care of it."

Justine checked the lock on the rolling door, which was inside a metal shield. She said, "The gate is unlocked."

Jack and Diane both turned to her at the same time and said, "What?"

"The gate is unlocked." Justine pulled the open lock out of its sleeve and showed them.

Diane looked at Jack. Jack must have understood her look, because he took his gun out and held it close to his side, pointing down.

Justine said, "What's the matter?"

Diane whispered, "It could be a trap."

Justine dropped the lock onto the ground and took her gun out. She clicked off the safety and held it down at her side.

Diane noticed that Justine's hand wasn't completely steady. She would have felt much more comfortable if she had the gun instead of Justine. Diane whispered to Jack, "I'll open it. You cover me."

Jack nodded. He quietly motioned for Justine to stand on the other side of the gate.

Jack and Justine stood on both sides with their guns drawn. Diane held her breath while squatting to grab a flat piece of steel at the bottom of the gate. She pulled it up and jumped to the side. The heavy steel gate sounded like thunder in the quiet neighborhood as it rolled up along its tracks and disappeared above.

Jack and Justine entered the building ready to shoot. Diane waited a few seconds then followed them in. She felt helpless, wishing she at least had a baseball bat or something.

The room was cold and dark and stunk of feces, vomit, urine, and who knows what else.

Diane held her breath and stayed close behind Jack.

While Jack peeked into the dark windows of the SUV, Diane walked around to the other side and found Mohammed unconscious, tied to a chair, the chair tipped over on the ground. Next to his face was a bloody rat torn in half. Diane saw human teeth marks on the dead rat. She tried to stop her mind from visualizing what happened. Blood covered Mohammed's face, and his clothes were saturated with vomit. Diane wanted to check his pulse, but didn't want to touch him.

She heard Justine a few feet away, gagging, then vomiting. With just the light coming in from the street, Diane couldn't see what Justine was looking at. She took the flashlight from Justine,

JIHAD ON 34TH STREET

which was pointed down at the floor, and while Justine caught her breath, Diane shined the light ahead. She also wanted to gag when she saw a headless corpse on the blood-streaked concrete. She kept her composure, but didn't get any closer to the body. What the hell happened here?

Diane turned away from one disgusting sight just to see another, the man's head, a few feet away from his body, his mouth and eyes still open. It took even more effort to hold down her pizza this time, especially with that disgusting stench floating around. She lifted the front of her shirt to cover her nose and mouth. The Dolce and Gabbana perfume she'd sprayed on before leaving the house was a welcome aroma. She closed her eyes for a moment, trying to clear the images from her mind.

Jack said, "He's alive."

Diane opened her eyes and turned around.

Jack untied Mohammed's ropes and tried to lift him.

Diane's phone rang. It was Tony. She pulled the shirt away from her face and tried to ignore the stink.

Tony sounded like he'd been sleeping when he asked, "Any news?"

Diane said, "We found him. He's alive, but he needs to go to a hospital. Go back to bed, Tony, there's nothing you can do for him now. Anyway, he's safe. I'll take care of him. I'll call you in the morning."

"I knew you would find him. I'm going back to bed."

Diane hung up and felt a feeling of relief. She put her phone into its case and approached Jack as he tried holding Mohammed up, leaning his limp body against the SUV.

Justine left the building and continued down the sidewalk toward the corner.

Jack said, "Justine needed some fresh air, so I sent her to the store for water."

Mohammed began to wake up. His eyes opened slowly.

Diane said, "You're alright now. I'm Diane Lasalvo, Tony's sister. I'm here to help."

Mohammed's eyes opened wide. "There is a bomb." He tried to point, but he seemed too weak to lift his arm. "Under that box. Please."

Diane noticed the upside-down cardboard box Mohammed was looking at. She turned around and advanced toward it. After a moment of hesitation, she gently lifted the box and found four metal canisters tied together and wired to a small circuit board.

Mohammed stumbled while trying to stand, holding onto the SUV to keep his balance. "They set it for midnight."

Jack grabbed Mohammed to help hold him up then he checked his watch and said, "It's 11:54. Let's move. On the double."

Diane and Jack helped Mohammed stagger toward the door.

Diane was pleasantly surprised when she saw Detective Garcia enter the building with his gun drawn. "Garcia. Just in time. Help us out."

Garcia racked his gun and pointed it at Mohammed. "Drop the Arab, Diane."

Mohammed pleaded, "Please no! Please do not let him kill me!"

"Relax. He's not gonna kill you." Diane turned to her partner and asked, "Garcia, what are you doing?" She noticed a large manila envelope in Garcia's other hand.

Garcia said, "Drop the Arab and put your fucking hands in the air!"

He was trembling, and his eyes were moist. Diane had never seen him shook up before, not even in the face of danger. She wanted to find out what was going on, but there wasn't time, so she decided to tell him about the bomb and talk to him later. "Garcia, there's a bo—"

Garcia fired a bullet into the ceiling and yelled, "Drop the fucking Arab now!" The sound of the shot echoed throughout the warehouse and off the buildings across the street.

CHAPTER 66—WEDNESDAY 11:55PM

Diane, Jack, and Mohammed stood with their hands in the air.

Diane said, "There's a bomb." She glanced up at her watch. The second hand was already halfway around. She turned to Garcia and asked, "What's going on, Garcia? Are you with them, too?"

"With who? I'm not with anyone. Agent Grant told me all about you, Diane. How you and your brother are helping this terrorist. I didn't want to believe it. But now I see the truth with my own eyes. How could you?"

Diane pleaded with him, "You know me, Garcia."

"I thought I did." Garcia glared at Mohammed who was struggling to keep his hands above his head and asked, "Why are you helping this Arab bastard?"

Jack said, "He's Pakistani."

"I don't care what fucking country he's from, he's a terrorist!"

Mohammed said, "I am not a terrorist!"

Diane said, "He works with Tony on the scaffold. He's not a terrorist."

"They're all terrorists!" Garcia racked his gun as tears rolled down his fat face. "These mother fuckers killed my brother!"

Jack said, "You can't blame a whole race or religion for a group of bad apples."

Garcia pointed his gun at Jack. "Shut the fuck up already, Poindexter!"

Diane said, "You know I lost friends on 911, too, Garcia. I know how you feel."

"You didn't lose a brother. And if you knew how I felt, you'd let me kill this Arab bastard right now."

Jack said, "If we don't leave now, we'll all be killed by that bomb over there."

Garcia glanced out the corner of his eye at the bomb. Diane wished the bomb had a timer like in the movies, then Garcia might believe her.

Diane could still see her watch, 11:58, and counting. "We have less than two minutes. We gotta get out of here, Garcia."

Sweat poured from Garcia's head and down onto his face. He wiped the sweat from his eyes using his left hand while his right hand kept his gun on Mohammed. He told Diane, "You and Poindexter can go, but the terrorist stays. He can die with his own bomb. Like the Lord said, if you live by the sword, you die by the sword."

Diane tried to distract Garcia when she saw Justine creeping up behind him with her gun drawn. Diane said, "The Lord doesn't want you to kill an innocent man, and that's what he is, innocent."

Garcia said, "Again with this innocent shit."

From behind Garcia, Justine said, "Drop your gun!"

Just as Garcia turned his head to look at Justine, Jack dropped and grabbed his gun from the ground. He shot Garcia in the foot. Garcia fired a stray bullet into the air as he lost his balance and fell backward.

Justine grabbed Garcia's gun while Mohammed limped outside.

Jack and Diane struggled to lift Garcia.

Diane glanced at her watch and saw that they had less than thirty seconds, 29 . . . 28 . . . 27 . . . "Hurry!"

With Garcia on his feet, Jack and Diane each got under one arm and helped him out of the building and up the block. Diane knew Jack had most of the weight on his side, but she still gave all her strength to help hold Garcia up. Garcia didn't use his good foot to help. It hung there, dragging along the sidewalk as Jack and Diane heaved him away from the building with only a few seconds left.

Just as they were passing the empty lot on the corner, ready to cross the intersection, the building exploded. The Earth shook. The force knocked everyone down. Car alarms blared up and down the street as dogs barked and howled. The heat and light from the inferno illuminated the entire neighborhood.

Diane's ears were ringing, and everything looked blurry. It took a few minutes for her head to stop spinning and for her eyes to focus. She welcomed the smell of smoke as opposed to that smell inside the warehouse.

Still on the ground, she checked to see if everyone was alright. Garcia lay on his back with his eyes closed, but he was breathing. Already on his knees, Jack struggled to his feet. Justine stayed down, just lifting her head and looking around. Everyone seemed fine, but someone was missing.

Before getting up, Diane asked, "Where's Mohammed?"

Garcia opened his eyes.

Sirens in the distance got closer as enormous clouds of smoke and dust drifted up into the cold night air.

Jack helped Justine to her feet while Diane knelt next to Garcia. He turned his head away from her. She placed her hand on his shoulder. He pushed her hand away.

The fire department showed up first with two trucks, then a police car, then another police car.

Firemen yelled and scrambled while unrolling their hoses and connecting to nearby fire hydrants. Two gushing streams of water quickly brought the flames down to a manageable level. Debris smoldered in the empty lot next door while the brick building on the opposite side of the warehouse was stained black, but undamaged.

Diane stood when she saw an ambulance approaching. She waved her hands in the air. "There's an injured officer here!"

The paramedics got out of the ambulance with a stretcher. Jack and Diane helped with the weight as they heaved Garcia onto the stretcher.

She tried one last time to get his attention. "Garcia." He turned his face away from her again. It broke her heart.

More fire trucks, police cars, and ambulances arrived. Diane picked up the manila envelope from the floor and opened it. It contained three 8x10 photographs, one of herself, one of her brother, and one picture of Mohammed with his beard. She slipped the pictures back into the envelope. What was this supposed to be about? Some kind of threat?

Two uniformed officers approached. Jack and Justine showed their FBI badges. Diane had nothing to show. While glancing at the names on their badges, she gave them her driver's license and told them her NYPD badge number.

Officer Kowalski called in Diane's badge number while Officer Castro took out a notepad and a pen.

Diane said, "The man in the ambulance is my partner, Detective Garcia."

"Were you working on a case?"

"No. It's our night off."

Castro looked confused. Jack and Justine stayed silent.

Diane said, "And there's a decapitated body in the warehouse. It was there before the bomb blew."

Officer Castro looked confused again, then hesitated before calling in the information on his radio.

A young, West Indian female paramedic approached and asked with a light Caribbean accent, "Were any of you injured?"

Jack said, "I'm fine." He turned to Diane and Justine.

"Justine said, "I'm fine, too."

Diane said, "I think I need some fresh gauze."

The young paramedic looked Diane up and down.

Diane winced while taking off her now scratched up leather jacket. "It didn't happen now. But it's killing me." She winced again while pulling her arm out of the sleeve. The old gauze on her arm was saturated with fresh blood and crusted with dry blood.

The paramedic said, "Let's get that cleaned up." She led Diane to her ambulance parked around the corner.

Jack and Justine stayed near the police cars with Castro and Kowalski.

Other cops kept spectators from getting too close while the firemen finished extinguishing the fire. Black soot and smoke covered the entire area.

The paramedic cleaned Diane's wound and wrapped it with fresh gauze. Diane watched an unmarked police car speed to the scene. A young Asian man in a black suit got out of the driver's seat. An older black woman in an olive green pants suit stepped out of the passenger side. She knew they were cops.

Diane thanked the paramedic, threw her jacket on, and intercepted the man and woman on their way toward Jack and Justine. She held out her hand and said, "Detective Lasalvo, 46th Precinct."

The woman shook Diane's hand. "I'm Detective Fletcher and

this is Detective Chang." Fletcher continued talking while Diane shook Chang's hand. "We were on another case when we got this call. Let me just make sure I heard correctly. There's an officer down, shot in the foot, and . . . a decapitated body? And all this was before a bomb exploded?"

"Correct."

"Busy day, huh?"

Diane nodded.

"Okay, now that we got that straight." Fletcher stopped talking when Jack and Justine approached with their FBI credentials out. Fletcher glanced over at her partner.

Jack said, "I'm Agent Sullivan. Detective Lasalvo was helping me with a lead on a terrorist case. I shot Detective Garcia in the foot."

Fletcher asked, "And why exactly did you find it necessary to shoot an NYPD detective in the foot, Mr. FBI man?"

The Asian detective just stayed quiet and grinned while watching his partner grill Jack.

Justine said, "He thought we were helping a terrorist."

Fletcher glanced over at her partner who was still smiling.

Jack interjected. "Diane was helping me with a case. I asked her to keep it quiet. When her partner found out, he thought she was helping a terrorist. It's a long story."

Diane was surprised that Jack just lied for her. He never lied. Every part of his being was against lying.

"And the bomb?" asked Fletcher. "That sounds kind of . . . terroristy, if you ask me."

Jack answered, "The real terrorists planted the bomb. That's who we were after. The man we were helping was the one who discovered the plot. We came here to save him."

"And where is this man now?"

Diane answered, "He disappeared."

Fletcher looked at Diane and said. "Well, Honey. I'm homicide. So the body without a head . . . that's my business. But I'll let Internal Affairs deal with you and your friends. Sounds like a hell of a lot of paperwork." She turned to her partner and said, "Call the Captain, let him know what's happening, then stay with these three. I'm going to talk to those hunky fire fighters about that headless man in there."

Fletcher walked away while Chang called in his report.

It wasn't long before Internal Affairs arrived, two older Irish men with short cropped blond hair and brown suits, short and stout Malone and tall and thin McCormack. They questioned Diane about Garcia.

Diane said, "I should have told him the truth, but I didn't think he would ever find out. He only lost control because of his brother. His brother was killed on 911."

Malone said, "Personally, I understand that you kept things quiet because Agent Sullivan here asked you to. But you shouldn't have been working on a case with the FBI or anyone else without notifying your captain."

McCormack said, "I'm sorry, Detective, but we're gonna have to take you in." He placed his hand on her wrist.

Diane wanted to pull away, but she didn't try.

Jack raised his voice. "You better take your hand off her right now." He stepped up to McCormack and grabbed his wrist while McCormack still had hold of Diane's wrist.

Diane had never seen Jack this way.

Malone stepped up to Jack, but didn't touch him. "This is an internal matter, sir. I suggest you let go of my partner and not interfere."

Jack overpowered McCormack and pulled his hand off Diane's wrist. Diane's wrist burned from the pressure of McCormack's grip. Jack let go of McCormack. McCormack backed up.

Jack raised his voice again. "This is a matter of national security. And you two assholes will not only have to answer to a federal judge, but you'll have to answer to me!" Jack stepped toward McCormack.

McCormack stepped back. Diane could tell by the look in his face that he was scared. Malone stayed quiet and kept his distance.

Two white men in black suits joined the crowd. They showed their credentials and introduced themselves, Homeland Security.

"Good," said McCormack. "This is your mess now." He turned to his partner and said, "Let's get outa here."

Malone looked at Diane and said, "Don't think this is over, Lasalvo."

The two Internal Affairs detectives headed toward Fletcher and Chang, who were still talking with the firemen.

Diane could tell that Jack was still boiling, so she decided to talk with the Homeland Security agents and give Jack a chance to cool down. "I'm Detective Lasalvo. Do either of you know Agent Grant?"

The younger agent shook his head no.

The older agent asked, "Agent Grant? Is he from Homeland Security?"

Diane said, "Yes. He's with the DCTA."

The older agent said, "I'm sorry, Detective, but I am not familiar with the D, T—"

"DCTA," said Diane. "It's a division of Homeland Security."

The older agent said, "Like I said, I'm not familiar with them. This is the first time I've ever heard of it. But we do have much to discuss. I need you three to make a statement at our office."

Jack interrupted, "We're not going anywhere tonight."

The older agent said, "As an agent of Homeland Security, Agent Sullivan, we are authorized to take into custody anyone we choose. Civilian or otherwise."

"We'll see about that." Jack picked up his cell phone and stepped away while making a call.

The older agent glanced at the younger agent then both of them stepped closer to Jack. Diane and Justine blocked their path.

Diane said, "We've had a long night. Don't make it longer."

The two agents backed up and waited for Jack to finish his phone call, which took about four minutes. The men grew impatient.

The older agent looked down when his phone rang. He answered it and listened for a few minutes. Jack hung up his phone and stood between Diane and Justine.

The older agent hung up his phone and glared at Jack. "It seems I have to let you three go. But don't think I won't find out what really happened here."

Diane, Jack, and Justine turned around, crossed the police line, then crossed the street. They got into Jack's car. Justine sat in the back. Everyone sat in silence as Jack drove.

The highways and streets were almost empty. They traveled quickly to Bayside, a quiet residential neighborhood with large unattached houses, most of them decorated for Thanksgiving.

They dropped Justine off at her house, a well-kept two-story light blue house with a huge blow up turkey on the front lawn. Before getting out of the car, Justine made sure Diane and Jack knew the inflated turkey was her husband's idea.

Jack waited while Justine unlocked her door and entered her house.

Diane got out of the car and lit a cigarette.

Jack opened the window and said, "Come on, you can smoke in the car."

Diane cocked her head. "Really? I thought no one could smoke in your car."

"I'm tired, and I would like to get home."

"So go." Diane took a deep drag and blew it out. "I'll take a cab."

"There's no need to get like that."

"Like what?"

"Please, Diane, just let me take you home."

She threw her half-finished cigarette onto the ground and stepped on it before getting into the front seat next to Jack.

They glanced at each other, but neither spoke. Jack put the car in gear and took off toward the highway. It took about twenty minutes to reach the border of Brooklyn.

Diane thought about Armstrong again. She thought things couldn't get worse after that, but they did, a lot worse. She was happy Jack was with her, and not just because he lied to protect her. Still looking at the cars on the highway ahead, Diane said, "Thanks for what you did back there."

Jack glanced over at her and smiled.

CHAPTER 67—THURSDAY 2:55AM

After fleeing the warehouse, Mohammed had already made it across Liberty Avenue by the time the bomb exploded. He had used some dirty rainwater from a puddle to wash the blood and vomit from his face and tried in vain to straighten out his filthy, torn suit. He then took the train to 42nd Street in Manhattan.

Although he didn't want to use it, he still wished he had the switchblade with him. Agent Miller must have taken it after knocking him out.

He fought to keep that haunting vision out of his head, but it kept coming back, the image of Hesam stabbing Agent Miller through the neck. He could still hear the sound of his throat choking on blood and steel. Mohammed wanted to throw up, he wanted to cry, but he stayed strong and stayed his course. He had to stop the terrorists.

Mohammed cautiously approached the flashing advertisements and rolling newsflashes that illuminated Times Square. Among an army of police, he saw thousands of people camped out on the sidewalks with folding chairs and blankets. Even though the heavy police presence scared him, Mohammed felt safe among the huge crowd of families.

He trekked up Seventh Avenue, stepping over sleeping people's arms and legs sticking out on the sidewalk until reaching the building where he worked. It was the same there as it was everywhere; people camped out on the sidewalks behind blue police barricades.

Mohammed walked back, two blocks down, and sat on the sidewalk next to a sleeping family. He closed his eyes and listened to the thousands of people laughing and chattering.

Coughing, sneezing, and shivering since he got out of the warehouse, Mohammed knew it would take more than a sunny day and a couple pills to cure him this time. He thought about going somewhere for a cup of tea, just as his mother always said, but he needed to sleep.

After a few minutes, he opened his eyes and looked at the sleeping family next to him, wondering how they could sleep in the street with all these strangers making all this noise.

He closed his eyes again and tried to block out everything around him. His body was exhausted, but he had to wait until his mind finally settled down before he could get some sleep. He thought about his plans for tomorrow. How would he catch the terrorists?

CHAPTER 68—THURSDAY 3:26AM

Back in Benson-Hurst, Jack double-parked in front of Diane's house and gazed into her eyes. They had been quiet during most of the trip back from Queens.

Diane tried not to look into his deep blue eyes. She wanted him, but she disregarded her feelings and tried to make light conversation. "That Justine has some crush on you."

"Don't be ridiculous. She's married."

"Of course, married people never have affairs."

Jack chuckled. "Do I sense a bit of jealousy?"

"I don't get jealous," replied Diane, "especially not of some skinny little thing like her." In a sarcastically high voice, Diane said, "Agent Sullivan this . . . Agent Sullivan that . . . Agent Sullivan looks so incredible."

He smiled and said, "You are jealous. Don't worry, you still look good for your age, too."

Diane laughed. "Sorry about that one."

"That's Okay. I can take it." Jack yawned.

Diane checked her watch. "I'm sorry to keep you out all night like this."

"I'm off tomorrow anyway."

"You're not going home for Thanksgiving?"

"I can't this year. I'm working on a big case. I'll just take it easy tomorrow and watch some football." Jack yawned again.

Diane felt bad he had such a long ride back home. She found herself saying something she knew she shouldn't, "You can sleep on the sofa if you want to." As soon as she said it, she wished she could take it back. She waited for his answer, hoping he would say no.

"I should be getting home."

Diane was relieved. She didn't know why she had invited him up, but she was happy that he said no.

Jack said, "I do need to use the bathroom after that long ride, though."

"Oh, alright." She pointed at an empty parking spot up the block. "There's a spot."

Jack parked his car then they both headed down the block to Diane's house.

Her stomach felt like it was twisting inside her as she unlocked and opened the door. Jack followed her up the stairs and into her apartment.

Diane turned on the lights. Tiger meowed and ran to Jack, rubbing on his leg and purring.

Diane said, "I forgot how much he liked you."

"Am I still the only man that he likes?"

Diane knew Jack was fishing for an answer about a new boyfriend, but she didn't pay attention. "Would you like something to drink?"

"Yes, water, please."

She took two glasses from the cabinet and a pitcher of water from the refrigerator.

Jack pointed at the bathroom door. "I . . ."

"Go ahead, you know where everything is."

Jack hurried into the bathroom and closed the door as Diane poured two glasses of water.

After a few minutes, he returned. Diane sat at the kitchen table with an unlit cigarette in her hand. She was going to light it, but decided to wait until Jack left.

Jack took his water and drank it all down at once.

Diane asked, "More?"

"No, thank you."

Diane put her cigarette and lighter next to the ashtray and stood.

Jack took a step toward her, reached out, and lightly touched her fingertips. "I miss you."

"Jack, don't do this . . ."

Before she knew what was happening, Jack took another step closer and kissed her. The tingling in her lips spread throughout her entire body. She thought about pushing him away, but she couldn't. She wrapped her arms around his strong muscular body and gave in.

Their lips separated only briefly while they stumbled into the living room and onto the sofa. She caressed his head as he gently kissed her. He held her body close to his and buried his face in her hair. She inhaled and savored his aroma. Lightly kissing the side of her neck, Diane could hear and feel Jack breathing. She could hear and feel his heart beating.

CHAPTER 69—THURSDAY 8:03AM

Diane didn't remember falling asleep, but when she opened her eyes, the sun was shining through the kitchen window. Still locked in an embrace with Jack on the sofa, and still completely dressed, Diane was happy she didn't do anything she would regret later. She listened to Jack's breathing and enjoyed the feeling of his body next to hers for just a few more minutes before deciding to get up and pretend they never kissed.

While easing herself out of Jack's arms and off the sofa, she glanced over at the clock on the wall and realized there wasn't much time to get to Manhattan and search for Mohammed and the three men whom he said were terrorists.

Diane stood above Jack and woke him up by shaking him. "Jack, it's after eight! We have to go!"

He rubbed his eyes while looking around. "What? I don't even remember falling asleep."

Diane went to the bathroom and took a five-minute shower while Jack waited in the kitchen.

She changed her clothes in the bedroom with the door closed while Jack used the bathroom.

Jack came into the living room and saw Diane putting her gun into a shoulder holster under her jacket and tying her hair up in a ponytail.

He asked, "What are you doing?"

"I'm going to find Mohammed and the terrorists."

"Where?"

"At that building on Seventh Avenue."

"When Mohammed sees how many police and FBI agents are guarding the building, I'm sure he'll disappear, and the terrorists, too. And if they try something somewhere else, they'll never get away with it. Every cop and FBI agent in the street is already on the lookout for them."

"I'm going anyway." Diane attached her badge to her belt and put a fresh cigarette in her mouth.

Jack said, "I'll go with you."

"You don't have to."

"I know."

Diane didn't argue, she just lit her cigarette and puffed on it while heading out the door.

CHAPTER 70—THURSDAY 9:45AM

Mohammed was still asleep on the sidewalk when he heard a child's voice telling him to wake up. He felt someone tap his arm. He opened his eyes.

A little girl with red pigtails and green eyes stood above him, "Hey, wake up, Mister, the parade is on."

The little girl's mother said, "Leave that man alone."

Still tired and congested, Mohammed lifted his head and looked around. Everyone was awake. People pushed their way back and forth to Broadway where the porta-potties were located. Other people shivered in the frosty morning air while sipping coffee, tea, or hot chocolate.

A rumbling sound became louder as spectators cheered and clapped. Mohammed stood and saw a group of cops on motorcycles riding in a diamond formation down Seventh Avenue. Police stood at intervals along the blue wood barricades that separated the sidewalk and the street.

Mohammed turned to the woman next to him and asked, "Excuse me. Could you tell me the time?"

The woman replied, "It's 9:47."

"Thank you, very much." Mohammed turned around and pushed his way through the people, trying to get back to his job, hoping he wasn't too late.

Drums and horns gradually replaced the rumble of the police motorcycles. Mohammed turned his head and saw a huge marching band dressed in red and yellow uniforms marching down Seventh

Avenue. The band started with a traditional march then the music became a little funky.

The crowd yelled and cheered, some of them danced. A giant red and yellow balloon with Macy's written across it followed the marching band. Smaller balloons, yellow stars, surrounded the large round balloon.

Even though the people got out of his way because he once again looked like a bum and he kept sneezing and wiping his runny nose, it still took over ten minutes for Mohammed to travel just one block.

By the time he was close enough to see the building, he saw police and FBI guarding all the entrances. They even had men on most of the rooftops in the area.

He wondered what happened to the terrorists. It didn't seem that they would give up, they were prepared to die, and they believed they would be dying for Allah. Maybe the cops caught them. Maybe the terrorists saw the police and FBI waiting for them and ran away. Maybe they split up. Maybe they were planning to blow the bombs somewhere else along the route. Mohammed's congested head filled with possibilities. He sneezed while looking around at the oblivious, but happy crowd.

Overhead, a giant turkey approached as spectators clapped their hands and took pictures. In front of the turkey, a man and woman wearing giant pilgrim heads waved at the cheering crowd.

Police and news helicopters hovered overhead.

Mohammed scanned the crowd, hoping for a miracle. He thought about how easy it was to change his appearance and considered the fact that Omar and his two accomplices probably did the same thing. Every face he saw seemed suspicious to him, but he kept looking around, examining the people in the crowd one by one, hoping God would help him find and stop the terrorists.

CHAPTER 71—THURSDAY 9:52AM

Jack and Diane stood in the middle of the crowd on 7th Avenue near 47th Street as the giant turkey passed above.

Diane surveyed the army of police and FBI agents guarding the building that Mohammed and Tony worked on. She turned to Jack and said, "I bet they're going to the stage at Herald Square. That's where the most people are."

Jack said, "Don't forget Times Square . . . and Columbus Circle for that matter."

Diane said, "Maybe we should split up. We could cover more ground."

Jack glanced up at the Felix the Cat balloon approaching and said, "We're looking for a needle in a hay stack. We'll never find them, and you keep forgetting that every cop out here knows what they look like."

"And what if they changed their appearance?"

Jack didn't answer.

Diane said, "You enjoy the parade. I'm going to 34th Street."

Jack said, "Okay, I'll go north to Columbus Circle. If I see anything I'll call you."

"Alright." Diane knew she might be wasting time and might never find them, but she had to try. She stepped out of the crowd and hurried down a side street going west toward Broadway where the NYPD had barricades and camera towers set up.

CHAPTER 72—THURSDAY 10:11AM

A big blue Smurf floated in the sky above while Mohammed pushed his way through the crowd on the sidewalk, making his way down Seventh Avenue.

Mohammed knew the parade well, even the new route. He'd watched it on TV every year since moving to the United States. It had become a tradition for him. He'd always wanted to come and see the parade live, but not like this.

He thought about it and decided the best place for a bomb would be either on 42nd Street at Times Square or at the Macy's store on 34th Street where the parade ended. Of course, he knew he could be wrong, but he just didn't have any other choice. He had to trust his instincts and try his best. He thought about the Egyptian Embassy bombing so many years ago and then he thought about how many people would die here today if the terrorists succeeded. He prayed to God for help then headed south on Broadway where it crossed Seventh Avenue and 44th Street.

Broadway was closed to traffic and full of cops. Parade spectators stood in long lines waiting to use the porta-potties.

After two blocks of trying not to look any cops in the eye, Mohammed noticed three men turning the corner on 42rd Street. He didn't really see their faces, and they didn't look like Muslims, but neither did he. What did catch his eye was that they were in a hurry and all three of them had black backpacks.

He turned the corner and hurried down the block to get a better look at the men before they were lost in the masses of people in Times Square.

Just as they entered the crowd, he caught a glimpse of their faces. None had beards anymore, but he clearly recognized the smallest of the three. It was Omar in a gray winter coat, blue jeans, and a black skullcap on his head.

A giant orange and white dachshund floated overhead as the crowd clapped and cheered.

Mohammed's congested head felt like one of the floats in the parade. A sharp pain stabbed at his brain just behind the eyes. He ignored the pain and kept moving forward, pushing his way through the spectators, trying to follow the terrorists.

They were so close just a minute ago, but now they were so far, it was hard to see them.

He kept following the black skullcap when it occasionally popped up and hoped they would not trigger the bomb. He still had his whole life in front of him, a wife, children, grandchildren.

Mohammed prayed to God again for help then began pushing his way through the crowd a little harder. He didn't want to be rude, but it was better than dead.

CHAPTER 73—THURSDAY 10:25AM

A giant Spiderman float soared between the steel and glass skyscrapers above as giant LED screens flashed advertisements throughout Times Square.

Diane sat in a trailer used as a mobile police station parked on Broadway, just south of Times Square. She watched three monitors that provided three different views of the parade from cameras mounted on towers above. The first monitor showed 42nd Street, the second showed Broadway, and the third showed Seventh Avenue. The crowd was dense. She remembered Jack's statement about finding a needle in a haystack.

A young female officer sat next to Diane and looked at the monitors. "Anything?"

"No." Diane stood and grabbed her jacket. "I think I'll try the main viewing area in front of Macy's."

The young officer said, "I'll call you if I see anything, Detective."

"Thanks." Diane put on her jacket and glanced over at the monitors while putting a cigarette into her mouth. She noticed something on the monitor, Mohammed following three men with black backpacks. They were on Seventh Avenue, inching their way through the crowd toward 42nd Street. "That's them!"

The female officer zoomed in on the men's faces and began typing. "It doesn't look like them."

"They shaved their beards. Call for backup." While hurrying out of the mobile station, Diane called Jack on her cell. "Jack, I got them. They're here in Times Square."

Jack sounded surprised when he said, "Really, you found them?"

"I'm going after them."

"Alone? Be careful."

"I will." Diane hung up and put her phone away while entering the crowd of spectators on 42nd Street. She didn't even consider waiting for backup. She reached for her gun then changed her mind. No reason to scare the people.

CHAPTER 74—THURSDAY 10:29AM

The Spiderman float turned down 42nd Street followed by a high school marching band. The crowd cheered for the band as drums and horns echoed throughout the concrete and steel canyon of Times Square.

Mohammed was just behind the three terrorists on Seventh Avenue when Omar turned his head and spotted him.

Omar said something to the other two men then they began to push their way harder through the crowd.

Mohammed had no choice but to do the same. He pushed some people so hard he almost knocked them over. A few times, he thought he was going to get his ass kicked, but he was moving fast enough to avoid a fight.

Just before reaching 42nd Street, Mohammed reached out with his right hand and grabbed one of the terrorist's jackets. It wasn't Omar, but Mohammed was happy it wasn't the big one. He pulled on the fabric enough to make the man stop, but not enough to tear the jacket.

The man grabbed Mohammed's wrist and tried to break free of his grasp.

Before losing his grip, Mohammed latched onto the man's jacket with his other hand. With both hands, he pulled at the same time. The man lost his balance and Mohammed pulled him down to the ground.

A big redneck in the crowd grabbed Mohammed and pulled him off the other man. He cocked his fist back, ready to swing.

Mohammed said, "He has a bomb in his backpack!"

Only a few people heard what Mohammed said over the blaring music of the marching band and the cheering and whistling of the crowd. The redneck dropped Mohammed and turned around. He pushed the terrorist back down on the ground and took his backpack. After opening it and looking inside, the redneck swung his huge fist at the terrorist and broke his nose in one shot. He hit him again. Blood sprayed all over the sidewalk. People tried to get out of the way.

Mohammed quickly disappeared through the crowd while the redneck continued beating the hell out of the terrorist.

When Mohammed was far enough away, he stood on his toes and looked around. Omar and the tall terrorist were gone. He glanced up at the sky and saw a giant SpongeBob floating through Times Square.

CHAPTER 75—THURSDAY 11:11AM

A giant fireman balloon with red suspenders floated above 42nd Street as Diane got to the front of the crowd on Seventh Avenue. She looked around, but didn't see Mohammed. She scanned the crowd across the street and saw two of the men with black backpacks frantically pushing their way through the crowd.

For just a moment, Diane wondered what happened to the other man and how did those two get on the other side of the street? It didn't matter. She had to get them.

She took her badge off her belt and held it in her hand while jumping over the barrier into the street.

A cop approached her and said, "You can't do that."

She showed him her Detective's badge and said, "It's an emergency! Call for help!"

The cop stepped out of her way.

Diane raced across the street in front of an army of cheerleaders swinging pom-poms. A few of the girls lost their rhythm, but only momentarily, then they continued the cheer.

The two terrorists saw Diane crossing the street and tried to push their way farther into the crowd. Omar was small enough to disappear, but the other man was too big and got stuck in the masses.

Diane jumped on top of a wooden police barrier for a better view. While trying to keep her balance on the thin piece of wood, she saw the tall man unzip his backpack. Like a professional wrestler, Diane leaped from the barrier, knocking it over into the street, and landed right on the tall terrorist before he could reach into his backpack. She wrapped her arms around his shoulders and tried to hang onto his back.

People moved out of the way as much as they could.

The terrorist grabbed Diane's wrists and twisted her arms while prying them apart. She thought her arms were going to snap. It didn't matter how much she tried to fight him, he was too strong. He spun around and threw Diane off his back like a piece of lint.

She reached for her gun and pointed it at him. "Stop or I'll shoot!"

The terrorist put his hand in his backpack and said, "Allahu Akbar!"

Diane shot him in the leg.

The already scared people screamed and spread out as the terrorist dropped to the sidewalk. The bomb was out of the backpack, a pushbutton and circuit board wired to four small metal canisters, almost identical to the one that exploded in the warehouse. The spectators tried to scatter when they saw it. The terrorist slithered toward the bomb and grabbed it.

Before he could press the button, Diane fired a single shot into his head. People screamed as blood sprayed onto their clothes, trampling each other to get away.

Diane showed her badge and tried to yell over the sound of the cheerleaders behind her, "I'm a cop! Don't panic!"

People tried to disperse, but the sidewalk was so crowded, they couldn't get anywhere. Diane noticed that the people farther away didn't have any idea what was going on.

Diane's Blackberry rang. She clipped her badge back onto her belt and answered her phone while still holding her gun in the other hand. It was Jack. Even though it was hard to hear over all the noise, she answered the call. "Jack, I just shot one of them."

"You what?"

"He was going for the bomb. I had no choice. The little one is heading east on 42nd Street toward Sixth Avenue."

Jack said, "I'm in Herald Square now."

Diane said, "You go up Sixth Avenue and I'll go down. He's wearing a gray jacket with a black skull cap."

"Got it."

She hung up the phone just as a uniform cop arrived. She

showed her badge and showed the cop the bomb. She told him to call for back up and to guard the bomb with his life.

She turned around and pushed her way through the crowd on 42nd Street.

CHAPTER 76—THURSDAY 11:24AM

After losing the other two men, Mohammed had walked down Broadway to avoid the crowd. By the time he reached 36th Street, he ran right back into the crowd.

A replica of the Statue of Liberty rolled down Sixth Avenue past the main viewing area in front of Macy's on 34th Street. A marching band followed, playing old American anthems. The band stopped in front of Macy's and performed "The Star Spangled Banner" while the spectators stood at attention with their hands covering their hearts.

Mohammed knew he would never spot the terrorists in the crowd, not from down here anyway. He wanted to sneak up the pipe frame scaffold that covered an old 16-story brick building behind him.

He glanced up at the blue steel frames wrapped in black safety netting and noticed four police officers on the second level guarding the metal stairs going up. He knew he would definitely have a better chance of spotting the terrorists from above, but would he have enough time to stop them before detonating their bombs? He had a better chance of stopping them in the street, if he could only find them.

He decided to take a chance and try to make his way up the scaffold, just a few floors up, and hopefully still have time to make his way back down and stop the terrorists.

He pushed his way out of the crowd and slipped down 36th Street. He strolled to the end of the scaffolding and looked around.

Two cops stood at the end of the street on Broadway in front of the wooden police barricade. They were facing Mohammed's direction but were talking and laughing, not paying much attention to anything.

Mohammed's heart began to beat faster as he stepped to the side, out of sight of the two cops, then snuck under the safety netting against the sidewalk. The black safety netting camouflaged him, but it didn't make him invisible. He looked up and saw that the cops on the second floor of the pipe scaffold were far enough away not to notice him.

Without the luxury of stairs, Mohammed scaled the pipe staging little by little by grabbing the small rungs between the supports and squeezing his feet in anywhere he could get them. One hand, one foot, one hand, one foot, all the way up. His hands and feet were sore by the time he reached the fifth floor. He'd planned on stopping at the fourth floor, but decided to go up one more, just to be farther from the cops.

Squeezing his body between the pipes until he was standing on a platform made of wooden planks, trying not to make any noise or vibrations, Mohammed tiptoed on the platform, along the side of the building toward the front.

Before stepping out onto the front platform, Mohammed peeked between the wall and a loose plank below. He looked down to make sure the cops downstairs were still in place. They were.

When he was satisfied no one could see him, he stepped out onto the front platform. He inserted his finger into a small hole in the netting and ripped it open a little more, just enough to see outside. The Empire State Building stood majestically in the background behind the old brick and stone buildings that dominated the neighborhood. The cold crisp air and clear sunny sky made this a perfect day for the parade.

Mohammed looked down. The entire area was packed full of hundreds of people watching The Rockettes perform in front of the Macy's store entrance, thirty women kicking their long legs into the air while big band music echoed off the buildings above.

Mohammed examined all the spectators on the ground, but didn't see anyone who resembled the terrorists. He looked across Sixth Avenue, but didn't see anyone suspicious there either. He wondered what happened. Were they caught? Did they go somewhere else?

Mohammed knew he couldn't see the sidewalk in front of him without leaning over, but he was scared the police might see him if he did.

He noticed the time on a clock that sat atop a stone tower across the street. It was 11:36. The parade would be ending at 12:00. Mohammed knew this was his last chance. He grabbed the netting and ripped the hole open, making it bigger. He took a deep breath and stuck his head out.

Looking straight down at the crowd on the sidewalk, he noticed one man moving. A small man with a black backpack, inching his way past 38th Street, pushing his way through the spectators, moving toward 37th Street, it was Omar.

Mohammed scanned the area, searching for the tall terrorist, but didn't see him anywhere. He had to concentrate on one thing at a time. He had to get Omar while he still could.

He pulled his head back in and snuck back to the side of the building. His hands and feet were sore from climbing up the first five floors, and he knew he didn't have the time or the strength to climb back down.

The ten-story building next door had a fire escape going down the side, but it was six feet away. He could never reach it, and he didn't feel up to jumping. Mohammed knew the cops would spot him if he used the scaffold stairs. He had to climb back down the pipes. He was running out of time.

With all his strength, he grabbed a pipe and prepared to step down to the next rung.

Someone yelled, "Hey, you! Stop!"

Mohammed looked down. One of the cops on the second floor platform saw him and was on his way up the shaky metal stairs.

Mohammed lunged for the stairs. He stomped his way up the metal steps to the tenth floor, shaking the hanging staircase as much as possible, trying slow down the cop below, hoping the cop was scared of heights.

He raced across a platform to the opposite side of the building and began climbing down the pipe frame scaffold. It was his only way down. The cops had the second staircase blocked from the bottom, and they would soon be on their way up.

All the way down, his hands and feet ached as he climbed with the last of his strength until reaching the fifth floor.

He tore a hole in the safety netting from top to bottom at the seam then peeked out before climbing out of the scaffolding and onto the wooden water tower on the roof of the four-story building next door.

Santa's sleigh was still about ten blocks away as it floated above Sixth Avenue toward 34th Street. Christmas music filled the air in the streets below.

Mohammed tried to balance his sore feet on the sloped roof of the water tower while reaching for the ladder on the side.

The roar of a helicopter in the distance got closer. Mohammed didn't know if it was for him, but he wasn't taking any chances. He unlatched and opened the hatch door on the roof of the water tower and climbed in, closing the hatch behind him.

His clothes absorbed the water and increased in weight as he held onto the metal ladder on the wall. Only his head stood above the water level.

While waiting for his eyes to adjust to the dark, he listened to the chopper overhead, it sounded like it was circling. After a few minutes, the sound faded away then disappeared.

Mohammed slowly opened the hatch and peeked outside. The coast was clear. He still heard Christmas music in the distance.

Shivering in his wet, heavy clothes, Mohammed sneezed about ten times while climbing down the water tower ladder then onto the huge steel I-beams that supported it. While balancing himself on the beam and making his way to the end, he thought about squeezing some of the water out of his jacket, but knew he didn't have time.

He jumped down onto the black rubber roof below and shimmied his way under more steel I-beams that supported two huge rectangular air conditioner units.

After reaching the front of the building, Mohammed peeked over and saw the parade in the street below. There was no way down. It was a straight drop.

The building next door had a suspended scaffold hanging on the front of it, but the building was two stories higher than the roof he was standing on.

Mohammed ducked under one of the air conditioning units as he heard the helicopter circle back around again.

While waiting for it to pass, his flesh stung from the cold air as it welded his wet clothes to his body.

The chopper finally passed. Mohammed snuck out of his hiding place.

He hurried to the building next door. His only option was to climb an electrical pipe on the side of the building that may or may not handle his weight. He didn't have any choice. The parade was ending and Omar was still out there with a bomb.

Mohammed grabbed the pipe and shimmied his way up. He used his feet on the wall to help him climb and to help reduce the weight on the pipe.

Halfway up, the pipe began to bend. He pedaled his feet against the wall and pulled himself up faster as the metal coupling below gave way.

The pipe separated from the wall just as Mohammed was at the top. He reached out and grabbed the parapet wall above. He didn't think he had any strength left, but knew he had to get over that wall. His face turned red and his eyes bulged as he pulled himself up and over the wall, onto the roof next door.

Mohammed heard the helicopter coming back. He knew this was his last chance. He raced to the scaffold on the front of the building, which was hanging from C-hooks. He leaped over the wall onto the scaffold and plugged in the electric cable. He pressed the button on one motor, but there was no power.

He looked down and saw Santa Claus' sleigh ready to turn down 34th Street. He scanned the crowd of cheering spectators and saw Omar, pushing his way through the crowd and across 35th Street, moving slowly toward the TV cameras on 34th Street.

Mohammed threw the safety rope over and grabbed it while climbing over the scaffold. He climbed down the rope six floors, his palms sizzled.

At the bottom, Mohammed ducked down on the bridge.

Cops from all directions were moving in toward him. He knew he could never reach Omar in time. Searching for a stack of bricks, Mohammed pulled a blue tarp up off a mound and found stacks of cement bags underneath.

He sprinted to the next bulge, pulled off the blue tarp, and found sand bags. There were at least a dozen more tarp-covered mounds on the bridge. He had to find the bricks quickly. It was the only thing he could think of to stop Omar.

As the cops yelled at him from below, he pulled up tarp after tarp until finding a stack of bricks, hundreds of them.

Mohammed grabbed two bricks, one in each hand. He raced to the front of the bridge and saw a few cops trying unsuccessfully to climb up. He knew it would be impossible for anyone to make it over the extended plywood. He still had a little time.

Most of the crowd still didn't know what was happening, still cheering for the parade. The people in the immediate area tried to get away, but they couldn't get far.

Mohammed threw a brick into the middle of the crowd, aiming at Omar. He missed. The brick hit a woman's shoulder. She dropped to the ground. Mohammed couldn't hear her screams above the Christmas music, but he saw her mouth moving and knew he hurt her. He was sorry and he was scared of hitting anyone else, but it was a chance he had to take.

The police chopper circled overhead as more cops tried to make their way through the crowd toward Mohammed.

Omar turned and glared at Mohammed on the bridge. He took the backpack off his back and unzipped it. Omar stood halfway between 34th Street and 35th Street. There were plenty of TV cameras around, and plenty of people to lose their lives.

Just as Omar reached into his backpack, Mohammed hurled another brick. It hit a man in the back. The man bumped into Omar, temporarily making him lose his balance.

Mohammed threw another brick. It hit Omar square in the face. Blood sprayed on everyone around as Omar fell to the ground. The crowd began to scream and push each other while attempting to scatter.

Mohammed heard a gunshot. He dropped to the wood platform and slid backward toward the building as the police began to open fire.

Bullets ripped through the planks and plywood as he crawled around the corner on his belly to the side of the building.

Just when Mohammed thought he had a chance of getting away, two cops rounded the corner with their guns out. They told him to stay down.

Mohammed did what they said.

CHAPTER 77—THURSDAY 3:00PM

Diane advanced along the white tiled floor, through the sterile white hallway with a bouquet of mixed flowers in one hand and a small white cardboard box tied with a string in the other hand. Glancing at the signs on the wall, she continued forward until finding Garcia's hospital room.

She smiled when she saw Detective Garcia's wife and fifteen-year-old son. The entire family was dangerously obese, but they always seemed to be full of joy and laughter.

Mrs. Garcia said, "Hi, Diane."

Diane kissed her on the cheek and said, "I'm so sorry."

Mrs. Garcia said, "There's nothing to be sorry about. We heard what happened. You know my husband can be as stubborn as an ox sometimes."

Diane smiled and turned to their son, who was now almost a foot taller than she was. "Hi, Ricky. I can't believe how tall you're getting."

Ricky proudly said, "I'm almost six feet. What's in the box?"

Mrs. Garcia said, "Ricky, that's rude."

Diane laughed and turned to Detective Garcia, who was lying quietly in bed. "A dozen Cannoli for your father, from that bakery he likes in my neighborhood. Regular and chocolate."

Ricky said, "Oh, I love cannoli."

Diane said, "Jack sends his apologies."

Garcia responded, "He did the right thing. That bomb would have killed us all. I'm just thankful he didn't aim higher, I like being a baritone."

Ricky chuckled.

Detective Garcia said, "I'm the one who should be saying sorry. Especially to you. I'm sorry I didn't believe you. I should have known better. It's just that after that agent questioned you at the precinct, and then he played that recording of you and your brother on the phone talking about helping Mohammed. I had had no idea the recording was altered. Then he reminded me about my brother. He knew just what buttons to push." His eyes filled with liquid. "I'm so sorry, Diane."

Diane kissed him on the cheek.

Mrs. Garcia wiped tears from her own eyes as Ricky watched in silence.

CHAPTER 78—THURSDAY 6:00PM

Mohammed stood at the front door of Mr. and Mrs. Lasalvo's house in Brooklyn wearing a pair of black slacks, a brown button down shirt, and a brown jacket. Stubble covered his head. Although he had shaved his face, he left the thin moustache and goatee, which he had learned to like. He held a bouquet of mixed flowers. With one hand and rang the doorbell with the other hand.

After a few seconds, Tony opened the door wearing an over-sized pair of slacks and a tight cotton Polo shirt. "Hey, Mo. Lookin' sharp. Those flowers for me?"

"I am sorry, but they're for your mother."

"I know. I'm just joking with you. Come on in."

Mohammed followed Tony into the house.

Jack and Diane were sitting on the sofa. Mohammed noticed how happy they looked together and that Diane had her hand on Jack's knee. Diane wore a long burgundy dress that showed off her slim, tight body. Jack wore a pair of slacks and an open-collar dress shirt. Mohammed thought they could both be on television.

Tony's wife, Angela, sat on the loveseat. All three of them got up and greeted Mohammed as he entered and admired the beautiful polished furniture and immaculate house.

Tony's wife said, "It's nice to meet you, Mohammed. I'm Tony's wife, Angela."

"Hello, Angela. It is nice to meet you, too."

Jack and Diane shook Mohammed's hand.

Diane said, "I'm glad you came."

Mohammed smiled. "Thank you for inviting me. It was very kind." He glanced at Diane, then at Jack, and said, "The two of you will have beautiful children together."

Diane said, "Let's just take things one step at a time."

Everyone laughed.

Tony asked, "So, how you feelin', Mo?"

"Much better. The doctor gave me some antibiotics."

"And what about your kitten?" asked Diane.

"She is good. My landlord took very good care of her." Mohammed looked at Jack and asked, "Did they catch Hesam?"

Jack shook his head. "I'm afraid not. Hesam disappeared and The Pentagon ordered all agencies to stop their investigations into Agent Grant."

Mohammed asked, "Why would anyone help Agent Grant? He's as guilty as the terrorists."

Jack said, "The only evidence we had was a blurry picture of a man that resembled Hesam getting into a black sedan. Not much to build a case on."

"That is not fair."

Diane said, "It's not a perfect system, Mohammed. But it's all we have."

Mohammed said, "I could testify against Agent Grant. I was there. I saw everything."

"You could do that," said Jack. "But you've seen what this man can do. I never thought I'd say something like this, but I think you should just let it go."

Mohammed asked, "And what about that young agent they killed at the warehouse?"

Jack answered, "Agent Andrew Miller. They shipped his body to San Diego for a military funeral. His wife and two children are moving back to San Diego to the wife's parents' house."

"That is so sad." Mohammed still couldn't get the image out of his head of Hesam pushing that sword into Agent Miller's neck. Every time he closed his eyes, his mind visualized the convulsing body and all that blood. Mohammed's eyes began to fill with moisture.

Tony slapped Mohammed on the shoulder and said, "Come on, Mo. My mother's in the kitchen."

Mohammed wiped his eyes with a handkerchief while following Tony into the kitchen where Mrs. Lasalvo was wearing an apron and stirring mashed potatoes in a pot. A freshly baked lasagna sat on the stovetop, the melted cheese still bubbling.

She wiped her hands and said, "You must be Mohammed."

"Yes. These are for you." He handed her the flowers.

She smelled them. "Thank you, they're beautiful." She kissed Mohammed on the cheek.

Mohammed was embarrassed and Tony must have known it because he laughed.

Two teenage girls with long brown hair scampered into the kitchen and each grabbed a fried meatball from a bowl on the counter.

Tony said, "Bianca, Maria, this is Mo, my friend from work that stopped the terrorists today."

At the same time, Tony's daughters both said, "Hi." Then without another word, they scampered out of the room.

Tony's mother took a fork from the drawer and stuck it in a meatball. She handed the fork to Mohammed and said, "Try it. Don't worry, I know about the whole pork thing. There's only chopped beef in there."

Mohammed took a bite. "It is delicious."

Just before taking another bite, Tony's father came into the kitchen. He looked at Mohammed then at Tony.

Tony said, "Dad, this is Mo."

Mohammed and Tony's father shook hands.

Tony's father said, "It's nice to meet you, Mo. You're a true hero."

Mohammed became fluttered. "Thank you, sir. But I'm not really . . ."

A buzzer rang.

Mrs. Lasalvo opened the oven and said, "Turkey's ready."

Mr. Lasalvo said, "I got it." With a pair of potholders, he heaved the gigantic turkey out of the oven and carried it into the adjoining dining room.

Tony grabbed a can of Coors light from the refrigerator. He showed the can to Mohammed and said, "Beer?"

Mohammed said, "No, thank you."

Tony showed him a can of Coke and said, "Soda?"

"Yes, please."

Tony's mother said, "He's so polite. Why can't you be more like your friend, Tony?"

Tony gave Mohammed the soda and chugged down half his beer in one gulp. "I'm polite." He let out a loud burp.

Mrs. Lasalvo shook her head.

Tony slapped Mohammed on the shoulder and said, "Come on, Mo. Let's go to the dining room and get stuffed like that turkey."

Books by Phil Nova:

FOUR KILOS
A novel
Internal Affairs and the mob both suspect pill-popping homicide detective, Victor Cohen, of theft and murder. Can Victor solve the murders and find four missing kilos of cocaine before it's too late?

JIHAD ON 34TH STREET
A novel
A Pakistani-American construction worker suspected of being a terrorist eludes a federal agent and tries to find the real terrorists before the feds find him.

BLACK & WHITE AND RED ALL OVER
A novella
A racist white prisoner and racist black prisoner must work together to escape after being transferred to a secret government facility for human experimentation.

THE VAMPIRE OF NEW ORLEANS
A novelette
Police in New Orleans investigate a murder that fits a pattern going back over one hundred years.

DUELING DUETS
A novelette
In this obscene, off-color parody, a fighter and a singer cross paths on their way up the ladder of success.

MAMA'S PLACE
A short story
A group of wannabe gangsters break into a building but only one of them comes out alive.

LAPTOP LOVE
A short story
After Alan and Tina break up, it's up to their laptops to get
them back together.

JACKED
A short story
A small time mafia crew from Las Vegas hijacks a
military truck coming from Roswell, New Mexico.

FREE short stories by Phil Nova:

A NEW START
A group of criminals in the future flees Earth with a fortune
in diamonds and brings bad luck a new world.

ALLU
While on their way to stand trial for war crimes, a group of
American soldiers in Iraq unleashes an ancient evil.

BEWARE OF GEEKS BEARING GIFTS
Government agencies investigate an outbreak of mass
murders in small town America.

HOT DOG MAN
In this vulgar and offensive parody, an aged superhero comes
out of retirement for one last mission.

THE DEATH OF ONE LIFE
A corrupt corporate executive makes his peace with God
while dying of cancer.

Website: www.philnova.com
Email: philnova@philnova.com

Made in the USA
Charleston, SC
06 March 2015